THIS BOOK BELONGS TO:

CONTEMPORARY FAIRY TALES,

FABLES & FOLKLORE

MONA AWAD
CATEE BAUGH
TIM BELDEN
DANIELLE BELLONE
AMANDA BLOCK
ANGELA BUCK
SIMON P. CLARK
MICHAEL HARRIS COHEN
PAUL CRENSHAW
KIMBERLY DUEDE
STEVEN EHRET
DANIELLE FONTAINE
J. M. R. HARRISON
JOYCE WINTERS HENDERSON
JOHN KISTE
DAVID KOLINSKI-SCHULTZ
MAUDE LARKE
CLAYTON LISTER
CARLOS F. MASON WEHBY
COLLEEN MICHAELS
ERIN T. MULLIGAN
JASON DANIEL MYERS
JOANN OH
ELODIE OLSON-COONS
JULIA PATT
MANDY ALTIMUS POND
ARIANA QUIÑÓNEZ
TAY SANCHEZ
SARAH ELIZABETH SCHANTZ
ALEX STEIN
MICHAEL WASTENEYS STEPHENS
CHERYL STILES
SAMUEL VALENTINO
ERIN VIRGIL
JENNIFER WHITAKER
SARAH WILSON

MODERN GRIMMOIRE

A CONTEMPORARY ANTHOLOGY OF

FAIRY TALES, FABLES & FOLKLORE

FROM 36 AUTHORS & ARTISTS

indigo ink PRESS

MODERN GRIMMOIRE
Contemporary Fairy Tales, Fables & Folklore

Characters and/or events depicted in this work are fictitious. Any resemblance to
real events or persons, living or dead, is purely coincidental, but any resemblance
to *actual* fairy tale realms and magic is an exciting development for us all!

Book and jacket design by Jessica Bennett.
Cover photograph, "Not Even the Woodsmen Could Save Her,"
by anthology prizewinner Mandy Altimus Pond.

ISBN: 978-0-9828330-2-5 (HARDCOVER)

LIBRARY OF CONGRESS CONTROL NUMBER: 2013932629

Printed and bound in the United States of America by
Bang Printing, Brainerd, Minnesota.

10 9 8 7 6 5 4 3 2 1

INDIGO INK PRESS, INC.
150 35TH STREET NW
CANTON, OHIO 44709
INDIGOINKPRESS.ORG

This book is dedicated to all of the wolves who swallow us whole, so that we can be brought back to this world with the slice of a blade, ready for the next adventure.

NOT EVEN THE WOODSMEN COULD SAVE HER
Mandy Altimus Pond

CONTENTS

A BODY OF KNOWLEDGE

THE DESIRE FOR WHAT WAS AND WHAT COULD BE

THE LANDS BEYOND
THE LANDS WE KNOW

IN HOMAGE TO THOSE
WHO CAME BEFORE

TROUBLE BOUGHT
AND BORROWED

FOREWORD

On behalf of Indigo Ink Press, I am pleased and proud to present this anthology, *Modern Grimmoire: Contemporary Fairy Tales, Fables & Folklore.* For those of you who love fairy tales, and who know or think you know what you are getting into in picking up this anthology, please proceed to the crux of the book, which begins aptly with the imaginative work of anthology prize recipient Michael Harris Cohen. His haunting, beautiful tale will stay with you long after this foreword will.

For those readers who are still with me and not speeding ahead, please allow me be frank as we set out together: I don't have any business writing a foreword to a collection of fairy tales, fables and folklore. I'm not versed in the history or the scholarship of the Grimms' tales, or any others, for that matter. In fact, I tried to find someone who *is*—an expert or academic on the subject—if only to lend some credibility to this collection and the talented authors and artists who contributed. Luckily, you will quickly find that our contributors stand on their own merit, and alas, you're stuck with me.

So, I know as much about fairy tales as you do. And I have come to believe that therein lies the beauty. I know as much about fairy tales as you do, which means I know this: fairy tales contributed to who I am. They are still hard at work in that regard. And I think you will discover shortly that we share that common bond, you and I.

Modern Grimmoire is an anthology for adults, who, as children, were smart enough to look under the bed before lights out with a combined sense of fear and anticipation; and now grown, still do so on occasion (guilty as charged).

These stories, told through short fiction, poetry and art, are for those of us who could transform our parents' basements into magical kingdoms using nothing but our own imaginations and the lingering memory of bedtime stories. But these tales are *especially* for those of us who kept up the charade in secret, even when the cool kids at school became important fixtures in our lives.

There's a reason why there are thousands of tales throughout the ages, with the meter still running. It is because, as this humble reader believes, they give us hope; hope of finding miracles and experiencing magic, wherever and however we can.

In 1953, during his National Book Award acceptance speech for *Invisible Man,* author Ralph Ellison said, "Despite my personal failures, there must be possible a fiction which, leaving sociology and case histories to the scientists, can arrive at the truth about the human condition, here and now, with all the bright magic of the fairy tale."

Seeking truth about the human condition in writing is something that many authors have attempted, Ellison included, but it is his wisdom in seeking to deliver that truth with his so called "bright magic" that resonates greatest with this reader.

I find myself constantly seeking out the sweet tang of Ellison's bright magic in contemporary literature. I find that, regardless of genre or intent, fiction that captures that magic wins my heart.

And it is the pursuit of that bright magic that led us to create *Modern Grimmoire*—to wonder what the Grimms' tales and others of their ilk would look like if they were created and collected today. Two hundred years ago, the Brothers Grimm began their tenure as great caretakers of our tales. We are excited, in our own very small way, to join their ranks.

In the pages that follow, you will find metamorphoses great and small, overwhelming desire and longing, lands too good to be true, characters not quite human, and those so human they will break your heart. You will see the evolution of long-loved characters, bouts of love lost, found, fumbled, foisted and forfeit, and of course, trials and triumph aplenty for our heroes.

Some of the tales set out along well-worn paths, others find footing despite the tangled undergrowth. And like the long line of tale-tellers before them, these authors and artists won't pull any punches as they deliver their magic brightly.

There are stories about the way things are; then there stories about the way we wish they were. This is a book for wishing.

If you are a lover of fairy tales, or if you simply seek some bright magic, look no further; turn the page.

JESSICA BENNETT
PUBLISHER

THE EX-COURT PAINTER, GOYA, AND THE PRINCESS

Michael Harris Cohen

The king summoned the ex-court painter at dawn: Come to the palace straight away with clothes for a fortnight. Leave brushes, paints and easel. Everything will be arranged later. A coachman dispatched the message then froze like a statue at Angelo's door. Behind him stamped the coach horse; she snorted out mist phantoms and clacked an impatient hoof on the cobblestones.

Angelo Rios Soto was a short man, and horses usually made him uneasy, especially nervous horses, but he was too dazed to be afraid. He yawned widely. He stepped back from his threshold and rubbed his sixty-year-old eyes. The knocking of the coachman had entered his dream. It had, in fact, woken him. In the dream he *drifted a river in an oarless boat. Ahead was sunset, behind him was* . . . with the knocking, *what had been boat turned coffin.* A sound like nails hammering fresh pine had roused him—the handle of the coachman's whip at the door.

Angelo blinked in the Madrid sunrise. He'd feared a debt collector catching him off guard by the hour. Instead this: the polished mahogany of the coach, the snorting horse in blinders, the inert and silent coachman at his threshold—the ever-waiting man, half his Reales earned in motionless repose, anticipating Angelo's obligatory consent.

A dream?

Angelo had been let go as court painter years ago, replaced by Francisco Jose de Goya y Lucientes, a friend of the king's and a moody and arrogant pain in the ass to most who knew him. Why would the king summon him when Goya was court painter?

Am I still dreaming?

The reek of fresh horse dung and the flatness of the coachman's eyes assured him he was not. Angelo's dreams were more vivid. The eye color of the coachman, yes, especially the eyes, would be bolder. In the first breath of sun the coachman's eyes swirled murky as wash water. His dream would have cheated the light, let shadows in. It would detail the horse's twitchy flanks, the flare of its nostrils.

Angelo nodded sternly to the coachman and noticed the flat line of the man's mouth, a mouth long deserted by its smile. The ex-court painter retreated inside to gather his things. Yes, not a dream, the room was undeniably his. His few clothes, all in need of mending, scattered about. A pall of mildew, boiled potatoes, a bed soaked with night sweats, all of it gathering into a musty scent that could be dubbed "the loneliness of old men."

His most recent canvas sat lonely and dormant on the easel, too, a well-gnawed chicken bone in the brush tray. When the painting went poorly his dreams turned vibrant. Of late, his dreams had been particularly spectacular. *Ahead was sunset, behind him was . . .* but it was no use. In the way of dreams, the dream's heart had vanished like smoke in a night sky.

The painter gathered clothes into a satchel, blew out the lone candle, and abandoned his room without a backward glance.

The coachman bounded to life. He opened the coach door for Angelo, raised the step after him, and shut the door before nimbly ascending his driver's perch. A single whip-crack, the horse veered and strained at the harness, its nose toward the palace.

Once there, a silent guard escorted Angelo through the servant's entrance to a part of the palace he'd never seen, somewhere near the kitchen. As the guard led on through the dim corridor, roasting meat smells crowded the tunnel, rabbit or perhaps pheasant. The painter's stomach mumbled a watery sigh and the guard raised his head, listening, but all the while leading onward through the snaking passages. The guard owned the bland face of a farm boy planted on the body of a circus giant, and Angelo jogged to keep up, the guard taking one step to his three.

At the end of the corridor, the guard flung open a door, and morning sun stabbed Angelo's eyes. He squinted, making out the windows high in the walls and a lone figure at the far end of the room. At last, when his eyes adjusted, he recognized the king.

Charles IV stood with his back to the painter. Though Angelo understood little of why people do what they do, he was an expert at reading what a person was in the moment. At a glance, he smelled trouble. The slump of the king spoke loudest; the royal frame seemed to implode as though his own skin was too weighty—this from a king who, if nothing else, stood up straight for portraits.

The door shut behind Angelo, and a new smell entered his head, the sharp tang of unfamiliar chemicals. He sniffed for the source, observing the single bed, the ceramic chamber pot and a freshly-built easel, furnished with a canvas and new and excellent paints. The sight of the paints pushed the smell from his thoughts and gave him a speck of courage; fresh paints always did, and he announced himself.

"Sire, I am at your service, as I was and forever will be."

The king remained frozen, but the painter heard the word "forever" echo under the royal's breath. A sturdy wooden table stood before the king, its legs parallel to the ruler's thick, ivory-stockinged calves. Charles offered a weak nod of the head, and the painter approached.

Only when Angelo stood next to Charles IV did the king's eyes shift from the table to the painter. On the table sat a decorated wooden box, like a crate for a China vase. The king held Angelo's gaze before his eyes, as if by gravity's will, revisited the box.

Though Angelo had painted dozens of the king's portraits— wild-eyed as a prince, solemn in royal regalia, the wisp of a smile in his favorite hunting costume—the painter had never seen *this* face. Even in profile, the king's eyes appeared dull, and his skin hung puffy and ashen. He waited on the king's words, but the royal lips remained thin and fixed. As Goya paints them now, Angelo thought, remembering the last portrait of the king he'd seen.

Much as he'd tried to detest Goya's portraits or toss them from his mind, his genius was inescapable. Goya's gaze missed nothing. His unerring brush forgave nothing. A confused wrinkle etched in the brow, a rabid look in the eyes, Goya caught it all. His stare perceived every flaw in royal flesh and spirit and recorded it with certain and brutal exactness.

The ex-court painter had been different. This had been the lone area of his life where his god-given shortness had been a plus. His low vantage made him naturally deferential; Angelo effortlessly cheated the weak chin, shortened the nose, and emboldened the frightened, and vaguely stupid, eyes of the monarch. He made Charles IV great. But it was no mere trick of perspective. He loved the king, even after he'd been sacked and replaced. It was no secret that the king had never felt sure in his kingliness. Charles's older brother had been passed over for the throne due to epilepsy, and there were those who said the same demons nested in Charles's head. He'd once overheard a palace servant say of the royal line, "They can't keep it in their pants, but at least they keep it in the family."

But Angelo had always veered generous with his brush out of devotion to the king and the reverent flourishes of classicism.

Without wanting to, the painter imagined the horror show Goya would make of the king's current face. Even Angelo, with all his skills of embellishment, dreaded the thought of how far he'd have to stretch if commissioned to paint the king's portrait. Angelo could hardly bear to look at Charles another moment, his mind already painting the corrections, and he bowed his attention, alongside the king's, to the box on the table.

At last he discovered the source of the odd, chemical smell. It came from the box. It stood no longer than a loaf of bread and roughly two hands wide. Layered lacquer shone on the wood, and the lid's border curled with engraved flowers. A mother-of-pearl handle was the only other ornamentation. The painter's eyes ran the flowery, labyrinthine boundary until the king at last spoke.

"I have a commission for you," said the king, his voice faraway and hardly king-like, as though, through some trick of ventriloquism, it emerged from within the box. "The princess Maria Luisa must be painted. She is the namesake of the queen . . . A portrait . . ."

"Yes," Angelo said, an inner sigh that he'd not be painting Charles.

"A portrait must be completed."

"Naturally," the ex-court painter said.

"Naturally . . ." the king echoed.

After a full minute of silence, the king, as if roused from sleep, jerked up his head, joined his hands behind his back and heel-turned from the table. His swift strides took him to the door before the painter had even turned.

"Sire?" The court painter said. "The princess?"

Hand on the door, the king nodded toward the box. "I cannot lift the lid. It is . . . heavy. If you do well, you will be paid well, and you will have another commission in a year and others to follow." With that the king exited and shut the door, leaving the ex-court painter alone in the bright room with the box.

The wood felt smooth as skin, and the grain was gorgeously marbled. Angelo traced the flowers on the lid. Quality work, he thought. He knew the woodworker, a man close to him in age and pious about carving. Every flower was unique, as it should be, and the leaves of each flower were engraved with detailed veins.

At last, the ex-court painter's fingers arrived at the polished knob. He grasped it lightly and pulled back the lid. Inside lay the princess.

* * *

IN LESS THAN A week the painting was done. The ex-court painter had left the room only to bathe or empty his chamber pot. Otherwise he painted, slept, and ate only in the room. The meals were revelatory: platters congested with fruit, spiced meats and rare cheeses; soft bread, still warm; a flagon of wine perpetually full at the door. Yes, for the first time in ages he no longer felt his ribs and his sleep had been untroubled by dreams. The painting had gone smoothly. An occupied belly helps, Angelo thought. Yes, it had been difficult at first—he had never attempted such a portrait . . .

had anyone?—but Angelo was finally satisfied and the king summoned.

The king arrived almost at once. He studied the portrait. For a moment, his dull eyes flickered. His taut lips softened and opened, as if a word lay just behind them, ready to leap into the room. Angelo leaned in, hoping to catch the word from the king's mouth, but the king was silent. Only his eyes moved.

Princess Maria lies in a hand-carved crib. The woodcarver has worked a simple motif of foxes chasing rabbits along the crib rails. A red velvet blanket splits her chest, her pudgy hands just above it. One mouse-sized fist clutches a golden rattle, a miniature of the queen's scepter, which the ex-court painter remembered perfectly. Her thumbprint lips open slightly, as if mid-coo. The detail is faultless. The fingernails glow with a milky sheen, and the princess's eyes stare at the king with the naked curiosity of infants.

The king considered the painting at length. The eyes of the princess, in particular, detained his attention. As it should be, Angelo thought, his fingers lacing and unlacing as he observed the king. The eyes had been especially difficult. He'd guessed at color and shape and fashioned them somewhere between the king's and queen's and what he could remember of the elder princess, Charlotte Joaquina.

Finally, the king nodded. He glanced at the box on the table, then left the room without a word. The silent guard entered and nodded to the ex-court painter. On the walk back the guard mumbled to himself, his pike tapping the stone floor. The painter caught only the name, "Goya."

"Sorry?" the painter said. Softly, as one might speak near a sleeping lion.

The guard grunted ambiguously. "Goya's upstairs. He's finishing a family portrait. All thirteen ugly royals gathered in a row. All but one."

Before the painter could understand this sudden alliance between him and the palace guard, they had reached the coach in the courtyard. The guard dropped a coin purse in Angelo's hands.

"By the way," the guard said, for the first time staring the painter square in the face. He had dead eyes, unreadable eyes—the eyes of an executioner's apprentice. "This work is, naturally, a secret. It's a secret of the very large variety that kings and kings' guards bear. The queen doesn't bear it, nor does the coachman. If you feel the secret is too big for you to carry, I am certainly able and willing to unburden you of this weight."

In the carriage home Angelo's thoughts twisted with worry. Goya upstairs while he was in the cellar painting . . . What did it mean? And not a word from the king about the portrait? Neither sigh nor smile? What the king had commissioned him to do was an abomination, yes, but then what exactly *had* he asked him to do?

He had pushed these latter questions out of his mind while painting, but now they spun into a knot his mind could not untie. They were tricky questions, questions that could be answered in the dungeons of the Inquisition. These days no children knew the smell of roasting heretics anymore, but Angelo was old enough to remember that distinct smoke. Anyway, the Inquisitors were not much interested in dialectics. They dealt with troublesome knots as Alexander the Great did.

Though Goya, forever smug Goya, thumbed his nose at the monsters. When they called him in for *The Naked Maja*, rumor was that he had claimed it a mere "study" that had, unfortunately and indiscreetly, escaped his hands, and reminded them that he had also painted *The Draped Maja,* which was the more tasteful, finished work. And after all that they'd delivered a mere finger-wagging and a palace-bound coach. This from a painter who, so another story went, had once kidnapped a nun from a nunnery.

Angelo had heard the *Maja* story from another painter who claimed to have heard it straight from the bull's mouth. Goya had been buying drinks and, according to the painter, the loco sono-fabitch had laughed when he told the story about the Inquisition and their discussion of inappropriately rendered pubic hair. "Next time I'll ask the Duchess of Alba to shave her chocha," Goya had supposedly said.

Outside in the Madrid night, rain pattered and female laughter ricocheted in the street. The coachman and the horse argued in their singular language, the whip-crack and the neigh, whip-crack and neigh. Angelo slumped into the cushions. Worry was a frequent dervish in his head. His mother, god rest her soul, had died from worrying her life to a well-rubbed bone. Thinking of bone brought him to the princess in the box and the portrait still drying in the cellar of the palace.

He shook the thought loose, untied the purse and glanced inside. There clinked ten thousand reales, as much as his annual salary as court painter had once been and enough to live decently on for a year. If he had failed the king, it was, anyway, an exceptionally well-paid failure. Weighing the coins in his palm he noticed a speck of rosy paint on his hands. He had mixed it to bring a flush to the princess's cheeks. Yes, he thought, the painting, abomination or not, is perhaps my best in years. It was a secret Angelo could bear.

* * *

A YEAR OF TROUBLED dreams later to the very day, the whip-knock sounded at Angelo's door. Again the coachman stood stiffly at the threshold, repeating the king's summons. Again, the nervous horse with blinders, the muted dawn light, the feeling of a dream and a knock that had entered the dream. Again, the giant guard wordlessly escorted him to the sun-lit room in the belly of the palace. Again the bed and the table, the paints, easel and canvas, and the box.

Only the king was absent from these echoing events. The ex-court painter and the princess in the box waited in the silent room. After an hour of pacing, Angelo began to prepare. One portrait, many paintings, he thought. As he mixed paints he felt a surge through him, a kind of electric pulse in his arm, as though his hand fused to brush, then brush to canvas.

Angelo had felt inspiration like this only once before. Decades ago, in his twenties, a young model had guided his brush. There had been no second guessing of color or stroke; his eye, hand, and heart had fused into one. Only when the model snubbed his proposal of marriage—with a dry laugh and a toss of her head that haunted his dreams for years—only then did the fire of inspiration grow cool, as his heart retreated to a place he could not reach. He had not touched a woman, outside of the brothels, since.

But the princess was different. After a cursory glance in the box, she opened herself to his eye without embarrassment or pose. She encouraged Angelo to push past what he knew, to abandon tricks and timeworn shortcuts. She was a tireless model and spurred Angelo to work with an energy he'd thought long lost.

He completed the second portrait in a week, and though he'd hardly slept, he felt years younger.

The princess stands now and is nearly able to walk. An adult hand, which enters the border from above, envelops the tinier hand of the princess, steadying her as her foot lifts vaguely toward the front, mid-step. In her other hand the princess clutches a petite bouquet of lilies. Bold, yes, bold, to paint a truncated arm, but Angelo had pushed further. He'd felt a defiance in the princess. He discovered it in her eyes and extended it to her mouth and chin, which is babyish but proud. She is strong-willed, if a touch spoiled. Behind the princess are the toys of a toddler's room: a hobby horse, a doll with real hair, a brightly painted ball, and beyond these an open window where, past the royal gardens, stretches Madrid. Trees bloom on the spiraling streets and far-off carriages, painted with the attention of a miniaturist, rattle on uneven roads. In the upper corner of the canvas Angelo painted his own street and house. A tiny dot in the window, one touch from the tip of the brush, is Angelo's face. He did not understand why he had painted himself into the work. But there he is.

His age-spotted hands wrestling each other, the ex-court painter watched the king study the princess, the flowers and toys, the distant city. Finally, Charles's gaze paused at the place where large hand wrapped little. The king's stare circled the painted hands again and again, and his lips softened for a moment. He raised his hand to the spot and nearly touched the wet paint. He hovered above it, turning his hand fingers down, matching the king's hand in the painting.

The king froze there. His arm cocked in front of him, his elbow unnaturally pointed toward the ceiling—as though defending his face from a sword's strike, before he finally recovered himself and again left the room without a word.

Again, too, the giant guard with the blank eyes abandoned his silence, picking up their conversation as though a year's time hadn't passed in between. "I know what you're thinking," he said. "You're thinking why you? Why not Goya, eh?"

The painter had not been thinking that, not this time, but he nodded.

"Goya's mad, that's what the king says. No more royal portraits for him. He paints only nightmares now. Witches and devils."

The guard ignored Angelo's nod and went on.

"He's got cojones spitting in the church's eye, though, and he's too good to be let go, even if he is crazy as a dungeon cat."

Of course Angelo had heard the rumors. The painters of Madrid spoke of almost nothing else, and there existed half a dozen conflicting stories. Some said Goya's madness was a ruse, adopted to paint what pleased him, and what seemed to please him of late was cannibalism, demons, and sacrifices. The more devout artists claimed Goya was possessed. Angelo struggled for an opinion then decided, perhaps wisely, that when a generally silent person speaks the best course of action for oneself is to stay quiet and, indeed, the guard continued even as they reached the sun splashed courtyard and the waiting coach.

"Of course there's another reason why you, not Goya." The guard spun the handle of his pike, the sharp metal atop glinting in the sun, a weathervane foretelling storms on a perfect day. "Goya can't bear secrets like us. He sees death; he paints death, and no one paints death better than Franciso Goya. He paints it best of all."

* * *

ALL WAS THE SAME for many years. Only the money made Angelo's life new. The steady pulse of reales transformed his clothes, his room, and his status in the eyes of the other painters. Of course, even to his few friends the source of his altered fortunes remained a mystery. Angelo, a loyal subject with a healthy respect for the chopping block, bore his king-sized secret at the pubs and occasional parties without a slip.

Though, in truth, the heaviness of the secret work had lightened with the years. It was the waiting, and not the secret, that became the hardest to bear. Angelo felt his entire year—the gatherings of artists, his health trips to the countryside, the fumbling brothel visits—could be painted in grey but for those precious moments of color at the palace.

He counted the days to the dawn knock, the palace visits, and the guard's Goya reports—darkening news that tickled Angelo with a minute sense of victory: "Goya lost another child. That makes six of his seven whelps. That's also why you, not Goya . . . they say his hearing is going, too, not that the bull ever listened anyway . . ."

But most of all he looked forward to the painting. He anticipated the princess, continually sketching her in his head. In the months between he faltered arthritically with other commissions, his eyes and thoughts squinting for focus. But always, always, the next portrait of the princess was sharp in his mind's eye, charting her growth and filling his thoughts with a new and curious taste.

One night, only days before the sunrise knock, Angelo twisted in bed with a dream: *He stands in the palace. It is night. There is no king, no canvas, no paints. There is only the box. The moon paints the walls unearthly white. The handle of the box glows in the moonlight. His reach for the handle takes forever. When his hand finally grasps the knob he discovers the box is locked. He strains at the lid. But it is impossible to open. From the box a faint sound begins to emanate. At first it sounds like crying, the whimpering of an abandoned child. But the sound changes. It is singing. A gentle melody issues from the box but also from far beyond the box, the room, the palace. Then Angelo knows, without hearing or seeing anyone, that he is no longer alone in the room.*

Angelo startled awake with an epiphany.

He lay in bed and traced this sudden insight to the moment he first sensed it, without understanding it. He had been painting the princess in her twelfth year: an adolescent's scorn crept into her face; her body angled slightly, hinting rebellion, the whole of her on the cusp of womanhood.

Though he never hurried a painting, when adding the new and slight curve to her breast he had rushed, botching the line and skipping on to detail the folds of her dress. At the time he'd been baffled by his haste—he'd painted a hundred breasts before—and troubled by how he'd let the flaw stand. He'd chalked it up to embarrassment but chastised himself. You are a painter, Angelo, he'd reminded himself in the homebound coach. A classicist. The body is a form. A breast is a form. You must steel yourself for the years ahead.

His eyes open now in the dark of his room, staring into layered black, Angelo reran this moment. He remembered something else that had begun to appear in the princess's face, alongside the sneer and the haughty angle of her chin. The princess's eyes had lost their innocence. They gazed at Angelo with the power women hold over men. She understood the effect of her face and body. Still, she did not lower her gaze.

Alone in his room, clammy from his dream, Angelo understood the color of this moment was not the red of embarrassment but that of love.

He tried his epiphany on the empty room: "I have fallen in love."

It was madness, of course, the foolish and dangerous crush of an old man on a young beauty, a royal beauty. A dead royal beauty. Yet, he knew the princess best, better than the king even. He'd watched her grow, made her grow, and she in turn had revealed herself year by year, pushing his work to greater heights than his so-so talent should have allowed him to reach. She guided. He followed, bringing life into her. If this was not love, Angelo wondered, the slow revealing of oneself to another, the other seeing, mirroring, nurturing, and hungry for more, what was?

* * *

ON THE SIXTEENTH ANNIVERSARY of the princess's death, Angelo placed himself, unhidden, into her portrait.

He'd crept in over the years. From the simple dot in the window to pieces of him: his hands—which he knew better than any part of his body, for they were an extension of his eyes—he painted on a servant in the princess's tenth year. Later, his coat drapes a bedpost ,and his eyes stare from a cat rounded in the fourteen-year-old princess's lap. He was careful at first. Even before he realized he was in love, he knew this was a perilous intimacy. Yet, as the king's visits became perfunctory, Angelo grew nervier.

The living weary of the dead. The king still descended to the bare room, but now it was more out of obligatory ritual, like a yearly tossing of flowers on an overgrown and otherwise ignored grave. The king had other children and other duties. Things were not going well with the French and, anyway, he favored hunting over everything, especially affairs of state. Charles IV would glance at the princess, a fleeting peek at her eyes, and leave the room for the year. If he had noticed the painter in the painting, the king said not a word.

The painter stands behind the princess. He has taken the liberty of peeling a few years off his age but is otherwise honest, resisting even the temptation to make himself taller. His wig rests neat but crooked, as it often does, and he does not embellish the mole that graces a nose too large for his narrow face, nor the chevrons of wrinkles at his eyes' edges. The smile is his, too, an ambiguous one directed toward the back of the princess. It speaks of thoughts pure and impure, of veneration and lust. His hands tuck behind his back, though hints of gifts peek from the edges of his coat: a bottle of wine; a rose he'd smelled as he'd painted it, having blended Bulgarian rose oil into the crimson paint. The princess he woos stands in the foreground. The hint of a smile exists on her lips. Her tightly bound hair piles on her head like a dark bouquet. She senses him behind and observes him in front, painting her, and her eyes send an invitation. Her pose is naturally open, her palms up and cradled above her womb. Her breasts swell at the dress, and there is the faintest sheen of sweat on her forehead. He has painted her dreams into the cornice that tops the walls—scenes of dancing, mirth, and love. Love between Angelo and her. Above, the sun descends in the window, and the hint of the rising moon hangs above it. The sky is cloudless and with the hint of roses in the dusk air. Night and all its promise lurk beyond the scene of the painting. Madrid spread out, hushed and ready. Street musicians, arm-linked couples, criminals, whores, all the city awaits the final bit of heat to depart and night, which is like day in Madrid, to at last release its curtains.

This time the king did not descend to inspect the work. Angelo stood between the painting and the box. He had not opened the box in years, its contents indelible in his mind. He had grown accustomed to the smell, too, which had gathered strength with time.

For Angelo the mix of chemicals, and the rising odor beneath, had become like perfume.

Soon the guard arrived. He waited by the door as Angelo gathered his things, then hurried them back through the corridors of the palace.

The painter cursed his old bones and the stiffness that came now from holding a brush for hours on end, the rest of the body a mere scaffold for the brush. He struggled to keep pace and waited for news.

"Goya resigned as court painter. He's off to France for the cure. He's at the end, they say. Deaf as a stone," the guard said. "And there are other problems, dizziness and blind spells. None of the doctors have a clue. I'd wager syphilis, but then I'm a guard, not a doctor. Perhaps it's the paints themselves. His colors, sickly greens and browns, all look like they came from an infected sore. Maybe they made him sick."

The guard rapped his own forehead with a mutton-sized fist and added again, as if there might be some confusion, "No idea. I'm just a guard, not a doctor."

As Angelo rode home in the coach, the thought that he might again someday be court painter gave him no joy. Rather, another year's banishment from his love stretched like a vast desert within him.

* * *

IN THE PRINCESS'S TWENTIETH year, Angelo began the last of his palace paintings, a work he would never complete. His hands trembled and ached with each stroke. He requested lamps to better light the canvas, as he seemed now to view the world through a fine sheet of muslin.

The last hint of the girl in the princess has vanished. There is no shyness or uncertainty in her as she faces center. She stands with the practiced rigidity of a future queen. Her posture and silent eyes are her armor. Two children stand at her sides. Both bear Angelo's features. A small boy holds his worried look; the same grey eyes glare beyond the viewer, anticipating an unpleasant and inevitable future. His daughter's expression is vaguer. Her eyes hold some dark judgment, yet she seems to smile, too, as he teases out the edge of her lips with the brush.

He was at the whites of her teeth, painting an escaping giggle, when the guard fully entered the room.

"Time to wrap it up. Job's done. Arriba. The king is dead. Long live the king and all that."

The guard stopped before the unfinished painting, glanced at the emerging princess and children and cupped his boyish chin in a huge hand.

"Hmm, the royal brood expands. Very imaginative."

Then, with a brusque movement, the guard shrouded the unfinished painting with a rough cloth, snuffed out the lamps, and closed the long curtains at the windows. He roughly gathered the box under his arm and waited for Angelo by the door.

"You were on to something, even Goya thought so."

The painter clutched the loose skin at his throat. His voice came hoarse from lack of use, "What did he say?"

"Not much. He was actually a man of few words in private. Good sense of humor, though. Always a joke on his tongue, a treasure chest of filthy ones. He mumbled something about pedophilia meets necrophilia. I laughed. He laughed. Then he left. That was about it."

The guard was already on the move, and the elderly painter lagged behind, his ears straining for words. Angelo had shrunk even further with age, and he felt he was following a titan, his eyes level with the box under the guard's arm.

"He bit the dust in a sanitarium in Bordeaux," the guard said.

"Goya?" Angelo said.

The guard was silent, and the painter thought he'd lost the mood for talking once and for all. But just as they exited the palace, for what the painter knew would be the last time, the guard spoke again.

"I've been thinking a lot about what the king said, about Goya being only able to paint nightmares. I don't think it's fair."

Angelo ventured a reply. "No?" he said.

"It wasn't his fault our country has itself become a nightmare. We Spaniards have a thirst for blood, and Goya couldn't paint

Spain without a considerable amount of red in his palette."

At the coach Angelo couldn't help himself. "Did Goya say anything else about my paintings? Anything at all?"

The guard smiled, executioner eyes twinkling. "He did say one other thing. The last words he spoke to me, in typical Goya drama: 'to be a real artist, one must go mad.' I'd say Goya succeeded wonderfully."

And with that the guard closed the coach door, handed in the bag of coins through the window, and waved a final farewell to the ex-ex-court painter, Angelo Rios Soto, before disappearing with the box from the painter's sight.

Back home, Angelo stumbled about his room. Around him were the things the palace portraits had bought: fine furniture and clothing, a crystal decanter half-filled with excellent wine, the finest paints and brushes in Madrid. Twenty years of painting a dead princess had made him comfortable; the blessings of a baby embalmed in a box, tiny and never to grow except on canvas, now underground forever.

Angelo's head throbbed. Goya's aphorism hung there unchewed. And something else, an odd hollowness at the death of Franciso Goya; Angelo felt like rather than winning the battle, he had lost an unknown brother. He remembered a Goya print: a man sleeps while owls and bats swirl about him. The caption read: "The sleep of reason brings monsters." Angelo was old with little art or reason left. Yet he understood that he, too, had given his best to those who know nothing of painting, who desire only magic mirrors to freeze time.

The shadow of a bird passed at the corner of his eye. Reflexively, he prepared a canvas to stop this flood of thoughts. The simplest movements of the medium brought only pain now. His hands shook as he stretched the canvas over the frame. Jolts of pain ran from finger to shoulder as he tacked the canvas. Wing shapes danced at the edge of Angelo's fading vision.

He had outlived another king; surely he has one painting left in him. With night closing in, he lights every candle and lamp and, shadows dancing, begins.

He starts with her skeleton. It's been six decades since his anatomy studies, but his memory serves him perfectly and he does not miss a bone.

He paints the princess's lungs, two gossamer sacs that shake and then sigh with breath. Later, a purplish heart softly knocks in the cage of her ribs. When the paint is dry enough, he layers veins and flowing blood, then muscle and skin. Her skin, which he'd boldly showed more and more of in each of his previous paintings, glows as though tiny suns burn under every inch. As the layers of paint build up, the princess seems to step off the canvas.

He at last frees her hair from its elaborate bondage. It spills like black ink down her naked skin. He shapes her breasts, unhidden by cloth or hair, the rouge circles of her nipples, her pubic triangle, too. His naked Maja.

For a moment the shadow of the Inquisition falls across his thoughts—the stake, the rack, the slow agony of the Judas chair—the meaning of what he is doing, the heresy of creating life. But the princess's gaze and the driving force of the work push him on, and Angelo forgets the world.

The princess's eyes blaze as she watches her face come into being. Her skin flushes. Her lips part slightly. Her face holds not only erotic suggestion but adoration. Unveiled love. It is a glance Spanish women dare only above a fluttering fan.

He paints her words now, too. Her voice, soft and throaty. Her smell: vanilla, sweat and sun. And the heat of her, he paints that too, and the pulse in her arching neck, the faint beating of her heart beneath the skin, the rise of her chest as she breathes. A cat twines between her naked legs. A sparrow alights on her arm.

He feels the heat of sunlight on his hand as he paints it upon her. He paints music drifting from the streets beyond and from the sky the singing of angels, for she is an angel, too. Even the cloud in her window, a tiny one that can scarcely hide the sun, has a sound and a smell: It is spring in Madrid and the last weight of the secret, the work Angelo has borne for twenty years, vanishes with his closing strokes.

Last, he finishes her hands. One sits flat on the smooth plain of her belly. The other extends. Her fingers curl and beckon.

Without a trace of guile or conceit she says, *Come.*

In his final stroke he remembers his dream from the first visit: *What had been boat turned coffin.*

He understands it was not the coachman's whip but the brush that became the hammer and the paint the nails.

Naked now, Angelo stands before her and drops the brush that is no longer a hammer. He holds the princess Maria Luisa's gaze, mirrors her smile and grasps her hand. It is warm and alive, and with her touch the pain in his aged body vanishes. He stands straight before her, his stoop forever gone, his stature tall.

Behind her the sun sets. Ahead of him is sunset, behind him is Angelo Rios Soto's room. His life. Without a backwards glance, he steps in.

SLEEPING BEAUTY'S MOTHER-IN-LAW
Samuel Valentino

A BODY OF KNOWLEDGE

SHELTER FOR THE MOON
J.M.R. Harrison

FOR ANDRÉANA LEFTON

I was small, but not asleep.

I overheard Grandmother
instructing my mother:
Promptly at midnight
they will come—
with gleaming black boots
and synchronized steps—
they will come
asking for the moon.
Her shining self
you will have safely hidden
in your shadowed hair.
Remember: smile, curtsey,
and fetch them a teaspoon,
the battered tin one.
They will judge you witless
and search elsewhere.

Just so the moon was saved.

The next morning
Mother brushed her hair,
scattering the moon's waterlily scent.
I touched one unruly strand.
She smiled,
before braiding the darkness,
preparing for the day.

NIGHT PEOPLE, IN SUMMER
Julia Patt

A family moved during the summer—a mother, father, and their daughter, whom they had given a name, but who preferred to be called Alice. They chose to move during the summer, the mother said, because it was easier than moving during the school year. Summer, the father said, because his wife started her new job in July. But really they moved in the summer because that's when the money ran out and they lost the house and had to go. So they moved in with the father's mother on the other side of the city with a few boxes and suitcases and the furniture they couldn't bear to leave behind. It would be the hottest summer on record.

Alice's grandmother kept a tall, skinny row house near the city's harbor. It had two bedrooms, a little yellow kitchen, a stuffy, old-fashioned parlor, a basement—where Alice was forbidden to go—and an attic where she would sleep. There was a small window at either end of that room, but her grandmother kept each of them shuttered and latched like a pair of hard-closed eyes.

"Can we open them?" Alice asked her mother that first night. She would sleep under the street-side window on a cot, although her feet dangled off the end. At their other house, they had central air, and she slept in a four-poster bed.

Her mother paused. She was unpacking Alice's clothes and putting them in a wooden dresser. "Your grandmother doesn't like to have the windows open. She says the neighborhood isn't very safe." Her grandmother was a shrill, shriveled woman, ten years a widow, and always complaining about the decline of the city.

Earlier, as they had carried their things from the car, a pair of elderly men talked on a porch two houses down. Several children played jump rope, shrieking and taunting each other. Broken glass littered the gutter. More than one house wore yellow foreclosure papers, the windows and doors boarded up. Nothing like the quiet suburban street where they had lived before. "So?" Alice said. "It's *hot*." It was. Already, the sheets stuck to her legs; her mother's face was flushed. The heat seemed stoppered in the attic room. Outside, cool air rode in from the water, and Alice imagined the breezes pressing against the side of the shut-up house like waves against the docks. "And it smells funny in here," she added. *Like cough syrup and cedar.*

There were new lines on her mother's face, just from that moving day. "It's very kind of your grandmother to let us stay. We should respect her rules," she said. She smoothed Alice's hair back from her face. "You'll get used to it," she added. "We all will. It'll be better than you think, you'll see. An adventure."

Afterward, Alice lay on the little cot with her hand against the window glass and listened to the sounds from the street. A car backfired; some people walked by, loud and laughing. Around her, the house settled—groaned. Something rustled in the walls. Downstairs, the adults went to bed, one door and then another closing. Once, she thought she heard footsteps, and, just before she fell asleep, the tinny sound of music playing very far away.

The next morning, Alice went looking for the few treasures she'd kept during the move: gold hoop earrings from her mother, her favorite teddy bear who was thin and raggedy and missing one button-eye, the small nothings she'd collected at camp the previous year—smooth stones from the lake, friendship bracelets woven out of string, an iridescent turkey feather—and the most recent postcard from her best friend Charlotte, who was summering in Colorado. She wanted to put them on the little dresser in the attic, so it might seem more like hers. But she couldn't find them.

"Stuff gets misplaced in a move," her father explained. "Are you sure you didn't put them in the storage unit?"

"Maybe," she said, although she knew she hadn't. Everything had been in her suitcase.

Other things began to go missing. "Have you been using my perfume again?" Alice's mother asked her. Her face was very stern, her mouth puckered, as if drawn shut with a string.

Then, it was her grandmother's brandy. And her father's reading glasses, although they would reappear from time to time—inside the freezer or the record player and once in her grandmother's hatbox. Nothing really valuable disappeared, never money or the silver or her mother's jewelry. But the books no one finished. One of Alice's gloves. Her grandmother's medication. The adults told her it was unimportant, but they grew snappish and short with each other. They asked Alice if she hadn't moved something, said it would be alright, that they wouldn't be angry.

At night, she lay awake and listened. The same sounds of footsteps on the stair, the same hallway creaks. Sometimes she would turn her head, just missing a flash of movement. But there wasn't ever anyone there. Once she tried to tell her father about it, but he said, "It's just an old house, honey. Don't worry."

Two weeks after the move, her mother began her job. She worked the night shift as a nurse at a hospital downtown, 9:00 p.m. to 5:00 a.m., six days a week. She'd get home just as the sun was coming up. The front door whined, and her sneakers made dull noises in the foyer. She started the coffee pot. Alice's father got up. Most mornings, Alice crept to the second floor to watch them before they parted—her mother off to bed and her father to look for work at the harbor. They stopped at the foot of the stairs, her mother still in her scrubs. "Five words about your night," her father said, his face the same blue-gray color as the pre-dawn glow coming through the windows, full of shadows and streetlights.

She told him—how busy it was at the hospital, a patient who'd gotten better, another who hadn't, the overbearing supervisor, the friend she made on her shift—and he kissed her. They parted as the sun rose. Alice scurried back to the attic. Sometimes she fell asleep, but more often she lay listening to the city come awake:

dogs barking and cars grumbling to life and people closing their doors and the bus yawning to a stop at the corner. Even though the water was blocks away, she imagined she could hear the crews out on the boats, cranes lowering cargo or fishermen loading gear, men jumping from dock to deck and back, never missing.

Then, her grandmother would come wake her for breakfast. They sat on the plastic-covered sofa and watched the old woman's morning game shows. Then they ate lunch and watched the afternoon soaps. Sometimes they played Scrabble, although after the first week Alice didn't like to because her grandmother always beat her. There was little else to do—no internet, no video games, not even good television. The second day Alice asked if she could go outside for a walk. "Outside? Are you crazy? You'll get snatched up in a minute."

"What about the basement then?" Alice asked. "Can I go exploring?"

"I told you, that's no place for a little girl," her grandmother said. "What if you fell and hurt yourself? Just sit quietly here with me, won't you?"

I'm not a little girl. Alice sat, fuming.

That night, she called her friend Kimberly. "I'm having the most wonderful summer!" She didn't wait for Alice to respond. "Darcy Miller and I were at the pool today, and *Chris Watkins* came by and talked to us. He said his older brother is having a big party when their parents are out of town and that we should come! Then Darcy and I went behind the shed and *smoked a cigarette*," she whispered this last part and Alice could picture her cupping one hand around the phone, "Darcy says she'll teach me to smoke the French way. Isn't she so sophisticated?" Sophisticated had been Kimberly's favorite word for the entirety of sixth grade. Alice gritted her teeth as her friend talked about vacations and trips to the mall and everything she had assumed would be hers, too, this summer but wasn't.

"We miss you *so* much," Kimberly said when they were about to hang up. "I can't believe you live in the ghetto now. You should come visit ASAP!" Alice agreed, but they said goodbye without making plans. She knew she wouldn't be calling Kimberly again, and there would be no visits. That night she dreamed of climbing through the attic window and escaping into the city.

Three weeks after the move, while Alice and her mother and grandmother were making sandwiches and iced tea for dinner, the old woman asked pointedly if Alice's mother wouldn't mind cleaning up after she cooked in the morning. The last several days, the kitchen had been a mess: dirty skillets on the stove, batter splattered on the countertops, coffee mugs pressing wet rings into the kitchen table. Once, they had found the shards of a plate in the trash. Another time, the whole place reeked of burnt bacon.

"But I *don't* cook anything," Alice's mother said. "I only eat cereal." She pursed her lips, and the old woman folded her arms, so Alice went into the living room to watch television. It seemed like every angry word they said, the hotter the house got, like the air just before a storm, except it never did storm, not really. Her mother and grandmother didn't speak the rest of the night, even when her father tried to make jokes at the kitchen table.

The real blow-up happened nearly a week later. Alice woke up early one morning, even before her mother got home. Because, she realized, she was cold. The attic windows were open. She remembered, then, somewhere from sleep, the sense of someone being in the room with her and leaning over the cot. A cool hand on her cheek. She had thought, still downy with dreams, that it had been her mother. But now she heard the door opening, her mother's soft tread in the hall. Alice ran her fingers over the windowsill and looked out onto the street—the houses across from theirs, the water beyond, pink with sun. And there, on the corner of the sill, was one of her gold hoop earrings. It caught the light. Glimmered. She curled her fingers around it and fell asleep, listening to the traffic below, with the harbor breeze on her face.

Later, when her grandmother came in to wake her, she scowled when she saw the open window. Without a word, she stomped down to the guest room. Alice crept to the attic stairs. Her mother was shouting. "I didn't open them, although I should have. It's a wonder she doesn't suffocate in there, the way you shut this place up." And then her grandmother— "This is my home. And I don't ask much, but you can't just do whatever you want." The fight ended with her mother leaving the house, slamming the front door behind her. Alice stayed crouched on the stairs, her legs drawn against her chest, her earring still clutched in one hand. If she was a little older, she could go too, she thought. And she wouldn't come back.

That evening, when her father returned, she heard them talking, their voices low, snagged. "Your mother" and "have to be patient" and "I can't do this" and "Please don't say that."

No one came to check on Alice before bed. No one even said goodnight. She dozed, fitfully, until she couldn't anymore. There were voices downstairs. The faraway sound of someone singing low and throaty. She unfolded from her cot. Moonlight came through the shutters and threw her shadow strangely, like a bird's. Down-stairs—laughter. Real laughter, not something on television, not something small and trapped in the speakers. She went down the stairs, so concerned with being quiet that she almost tripped over the girl.

She was only a shade or two lighter than the darkest corners of the attic; she sprawled across the landing with a book in her lap. Older than Alice, but by how much it was difficult to tell. Her face was indistinct, like seeing yourself reflected in a dark window. She wore hand-me-down clothing, nothing that fit her; her shoes were unlaced, their tongues flapping. She looked up with big, pale eyes, the eyes of something that was born underwater. She smelled like the harbor, a damp, chemical smell, and when she reached out to steady Alice, her hand was cold and moist, like water condensed on a glass.

"And they all lived in the land of Night forever and ever. The end," the girl read from the book, although there was no text on the page. She had a voice like attic air, slow and still and stale.

"What are you doing?" Alice asked.

"Reading," the girl said and rolled her eyes. "Did I scare you?"

"No."

"What's your name?"

"Alice," she said. "What's yours?"

"Don't remember," the girl said. "Or I never had one. Come on." She stood, the length of her oozing up from the stair. Alice followed her down into her grandmother's house, which had gone dark and chilly like the inside of a cave. Every window in the place was open, letting in the city—the smell of wet exhaust and the sound of cars.

"Nicer this way, isn't it?" the girl said. They passed the guest room where Alice's father slept alone, the door cracked open in case she called him during the night. He was curled up like a kid, only occupying half the bed, leaving the other half for her mother. The night girl reached around Alice and tugged the door shut. "He won't wake up," she said. "They never do. But best not to risk it." They passed her grandmother's room, already closed up tight. Flowered wallpaper covered the hallway—dark, bloody roses crept up greedy green vines.

Downstairs, a dozen people like the girl lounged around the parlor. They were all the same shade of blue-gray, their faces vague, their clothing loose and threadbare. Welfare people, her grandmother would have said. They'd stripped the plastic covers from the couches, rearranged the furniture so they could put their feet on the coffee table. They smoked, tapped their ashes onto chipped saucers, drank coffee from her grandmother's mugs. A drowsy blues song wound around the room from her father's old turntable. Album jackets splayed on the carpet like fallen leaves, the people on the covers staring up, sad-eyed and fading. A few of those gathered in the parlor sang along with the music, their voices rough from smoking, drinking, whispering. When the girl and Alice passed, they waved and grinned at them. Their teeth were very white—very sharp.

The dark kitchen stank of burnt batter. Two people, a man and a woman, were making breakfast together, the way Alice's parents had before the move. Alice reached to flip the light switch, but the girl put a hand over hers and shook her head. A stack of pancakes teetered on a plate, some of them shaped like crooked stars, others like claws reaching out. The percolator burbled and murmured. The girl offered Alice a pancake and a cup of coffee, and they sat at the kitchen table, which was already sticky with maple syrup. Alice wasn't allowed to drink coffee, but she tipped the mug back, then gagged on the thick, bitter sludge. The people—night people, she decided—sang in the other room, a lonely, lovely song she didn't recognize.

The next day, she woke up, panicked, and ran downstairs to close the windows, to put the furniture back, to soak the blackened pans in the sink. But the windows were closed, the sofa neatly covered in plastic, the plates washed and stacked. She stood in the kitchen in her pajamas until her grandmother came down. The old woman ghosted her hand over Alice's hair. "You're up early," she said. She went about getting breakfast ready. "The heat wave is supposed to break today. You can feel it already, can't you?"

For a moment, Alice considered telling her all of it, about the strange people in her house, the ones who made the messes in the kitchen and stole drinks from her brandy and opened the windows at night. But she liked the lingering taste of syrup, the faint smell of cigarette smoke, the echoes of guitars and saxophones, the phantom feel of the night girl's hand in hers. So instead, she sat at the kitchen table with her grandmother and thought about the sound of laughter in the next room. That afternoon, she napped on the sofa. Her mother sat at the kitchen table with the Classifieds and there was no fighting—they were too tired to fight.

A week later, the night girl came and sat on the edge of the cot. Her eyes snatched the light like a cat's and glowed green. "Want to see something?" she asked.

They went down to the street, Alice in her pajamas. There were people everywhere, ten times as many as the night before, all blue and tattered and not quite solid. They crowded the sidewalk, leaned against the garbage cans, perched on front steps. A group of boys kicked around cans and tossed empty beer bottles down the street where they shattered. Someone brought over a radio and stretched out the long silver antenna. Music filled the street. The night girl took Alice's hands and spun her around. Everyone laughed and danced. The streetlights threw their shadows under them, and the shadows danced too, shadows of the night people tossing their arms up and twirling each other until they fell over dizzy. Two men grabbed Alice by the hands and swung her; her legs kicked high in the air, and she shrieked. She waited for the moment when someone would come to the window, would tell them to be quiet, but no one did. They danced until the clouds went violet overhead and the few city stars faded into the sky. She went to bed humming and snapping her fingers. When she finally fell asleep, she dreamed of the rough pavement under her bare feet.

The next morning, she couldn't see a radio or any trace of the people, only the brown splintered shards of bottle glass in the street.

Another night, Alice and the girl snuck out into the streets, went down one narrow alley and then another until finally they were at the marina, all the bright, artificial city lights reflected in the water, the boats lined up and tethered to the docks, sleek and white and shining. Night people bathed in the moonlight, stretched out on beach towels with stripes of pale lotion on their noses, big floppy summer hats, sunglasses. Some of them in borrowed bikinis and trunks, others naked, their bodies strange and colorless, as if they were made of ashes. Alice watched them as they shifted and tanned; their skins lit up by the night lights. And then, for no reason she could guess, they all got up from the docks at the same time and jumped into the bay, made the water frothy with splashing, and vanished into the cold, inky dark.

Some days later, her father came home early and said, "I thought we might go down to the harbor before it gets dark, kiddo. What do you say?" She shrugged, listless, and said she was too tired. She was tired most days now. Her grandmother didn't seem to care—she preferred Alice quiet, low energy. "It's just hot," she explained to her mother when she worried about it. But Alice didn't mind the heat anymore. She spent the sticky afternoons dreaming of the night—glass breaking in the alley and the streetlights' yellow glow and the black bitter coffee smell and the way a turntable needle scratches on a vinyl record. The night people taught her to make pancakes, to flip them high and catch them in a hot pan. They played her the same songs over and over, sad songs and dancing songs, all of them sung low and raspy, and even the lively songs were full of broken hearts. They taught her how to blow smoke rings from stolen cigarettes. Gave her beer to drink. Sometimes they curled their blue-gray fingers in her hair, sang her lullabies. She liked that, too.

She stopped seeing the bags under her mother's eyes and the way her father's skin had gone pale. Stopped hearing the sharpness in her grandmother's voice when she bemoaned the state of the neighborhood or accused Alice's mother of breaking a ceramic figurine. The false brightness of the television no longer bothered her and neither did the fact that her friends across the city didn't call. She had stopped hoping her parents would move, stopped dreaming about the big, clean, cool house where they had lived. Now she had the breeze off the bay and the feeling of dancing in a crowd and the night girl, holding her hand, guiding her through the darkened city streets.

One morning, instead of sending her back to bed as usual, the night people pulled her with them into the spaces between the walls, the place where they hid from her parents and grandmother during the day. It smelled like rotting wood. She was wedged under the night girl's arm. "Try and sleep," the girl whispered. But she couldn't.

She heard, once, her grandmother call out for her. "Alice? Don't you want to get up?"

The girl nudged her. "I'm not feeling very well, Grandmother," Alice responded. "I'd just like to sleep if that's alright."

"Okay, dear," the old woman said. "Let me know if you're hungry later."

"She'll go fall asleep in her chair," the night girl giggled. "She's always doing that."

"How long have you been here?" Alice asked then.

"Oh, none of us remember anymore," the girl said. She waved a hand. "Go to sleep now."

"Tell me a story first?" Alice whined. "Please?"

The night girl rolled her eyes. "Fine, if you're going to be a baby about it." And she told her a bedtime story, the kind Alice's parents had read to her when she was little—an adventure story about a brave girl who hunted buried treasure and found a magic ring and battled a dragon. Except she wasn't a normal little girl from a story, with blonde ringlets or lips as red as roses. She was a night person, and she crept past evil queens and sinister magicians easily, hiding in the shadows the way night people did. She only came out after sunset, spent her days behind closet doors and under beds and inside kitchen cabinets. She had no name, and she didn't live happily ever after. Alice asked what happened to her, and the night girl shrugged. "Went to live in some old house, I guess."

When Alice woke, it was to the sounds of her parents' voices. She was back in her bed, as if she hadn't spent her day stuffed up with the insulation and mice. There was a note pinned to her pillow. *Come to the basement tonight.* She started down the stairs to say hello to her parents. Then she noticed her skin—it was slightly gray. Not true gray like the night people's skin, but tinted, as if behind smoke. Then she heard her father: "Okay. Okay. You're right. Soon."

That night when her mother came up to say goodbye, she told Alice, "You know, I'm so proud of you. This hasn't been easy. But you've done so well. And we're almost out of it. You'll see. Another couple weeks and we'll be able to get a place of our own. I promise."

She lay in bed until midnight, waiting for her father and grandmother to go to bed. It seemed to take ages—the two of them sat awake, talking about the old neighborhood and her dead grandfather—but finally both doors closed on the second floor. Alice went down the stairs as quietly as she could, as quiet as the night people were. On the bottom attic step, something gleamed. It was an old-fashioned marble, dusty but otherwise fine. She put it in the pocket of her pajama bottoms. Farther down the hall, she found a lace glove. A child's Mary Janes. Then the tie she'd gotten her father for his last birthday. Her one-eyed teddy bear. A scattered rainbow of her grandmother's medication. Scrabble letters. She followed the trail to the parlor, her pockets swollen with lost things.

Downstairs, the night people were dancing to one of the blues songs they loved. She loved it, too, although tonight it made her shiver. It was difficult to pass through the crowd—they clung together, a bundle of shadows, and swayed to the music. Orange embers flickered at their lips. Alice pushed into the middle of the knot. There, she found a friendship bracelet from camp. She put it on. The night people looked down at her, smiled their sharp smiles. Then they tucked their faces into the crooks of each other's necks, as if they were dreaming. They smelled like the harbor, like green water, diesel, and garbage, and she covered her nose as she walked past them.

Postcards littered the kitchen. And by the basement door: the mate to the earring she had found on her windowsill weeks ago.

The basement was a vast, dusty room, with a boiler like a squat fat man and rows of metal shelves filled with keepsakes—a whole rack of ratty fur coats, her grandfather's service pistol, tins of cast iron soldiers, and a taxidermied sugar glider. Cobwebs hung from the beams like rotting lace. Off in the dark, water dripped, slow and steady as a metronome. And voices. Alice followed them down the rows to a cluster of night people who had gathered around the boiler, the girl in the very middle of the group.

"What's going on?" Alice asked.

They all murmured and shifted and looked at the night girl, even though in that moment, she seemed very young. She said, "We want you to stay with us."

"With you?"

"It isn't hard," she said. "You did so well today hiding in the walls. We could do that every day. Your parents and the old woman would forget about you soon enough. You could be one of us. We heard them talking earlier. We heard them say they're leaving soon. But you. You don't have to go with them, Alice, go back to all that. Stay."

There could be no end to it. No end to breakfast at midnight and moonlight swims and running in the house and all the other things she wasn't allowed to do. No more arguing, no more rules about windows or basements full of treasures or going outside. And she could drink beer and smoke cigarettes and learn every word to every sad song. Briefly, she dreamed it, dreamed her skin going blue and gray, her eyes getting pale. Dreamed she was a faded, tucked away thing hidden in the walls. Of being Alice forever. She squeezed her fists together, dreaming, and for a moment, it seemed it would be true. Then she felt the cool metal in her palm, the gold earring her mother had given her only a year ago and said, "Well, you're almost a woman now, aren't you?" And there were other memories—her pockets were stuffed with them, the things they'd lost, the things the night people had stolen during the summer, not anything she needed to live in walls and run the streets at night. Just memories: the lake at camp, water splashing, her friends shrieking, the sun bright above them. Her father putting her on his shoulders at the harbor, showing her the boats. Playing Scrabble with her grandmother.

She thought of a world without sunshine, without her mother's steps on the stairs in the morning, without her father's deep, soft voice. Without, even, her grandmother calling the answers to Jeopardy. She could go away into the night without them, could abandon the chance to move back across the city, give up stories with happy endings and meals after breakfast and growing up, really growing up—and the dream ended. She looked at the night people and saw that their faces were sad, empty except for shadows, full of nothing but the quiet creaks of a house at night, nothing but the dust in the places no one bothers to clean, nothing but the sense of someone lingering in a dark room before you turn on the lights. She put the earring in the night girl's hand. "That's not my name," she told them.

The night people parted around her. When she looked back, their eyes glowed in the dark, but they were growing paler, fainter, until there was nothing there, just the impression of shadows in the basement, just the memory of blue-gray light. She climbed the basement stairs, slow, one by one, and went into her grandmother's little yellow kitchen. She turned off the stove and the coffee maker, put the dishes in the sink and filled it with hot water and soap. Then, she went into the living room, which was empty, the furniture out of order, the windows open, the record player spinning the same song, over and over, a song she would remember for years to come. They had taught her the words over that summer, and she sang along, her voice low and rough: "I mean I'll see you, after I cross the deep blue sea."

THE BLACK WIDOW
Clayton Lister

'm not an attractive woman. On this point, I am not, and never have been, under any illusions. I didn't bloom in youth as much as distend. Arms, legs, fingers . . . (Predictably, 'stick insect' was a favourite zoomorphic jibe of my school chums; 'praying mantis' another—rarer, but in retrospect rather pleasingly ironic, I should say. For I misapplied that modifier's homonym. If monstrously elongated, I was a timid creature: the suggestion that I might prey upon anybody . . . well, really!) My hips, breasts, those should-be outward signifiers of womanhood, never did swell. The only filling-out there has been down the years was to my belly. My taut pot mockingly pregnant-in-appearance-only belly. My shoulders, narrow anyway, hunched; my neck lengthened. My face, please, just let's not go there.

But, as unlikely as it sounds, I have known love. Good love, too. The best. Given by and returned to the most brilliant of men. We met as postgrads, me directly from the provincial redbrick that I was as fearful of leaving as I had been of enrolling—which is not to say that I wasn't as miserable for all my four years there as I would have been in a nineteenth-century workhouse. However, the standard platitudes I offered on my MA in Vic. Lit. were sufficiently dressed to deceive, evidently. I myself hadn't seriously entertained the possibility of a doctorate at all. I was appalled that any City of

Dreaming Spires college should have so warmly received such a turgid proposal. *Hysteria & Bereavement: Herstory*, if you will. Hackneyed perhaps, though since Fate dealt its cruel hand, a subject that has held me in no bad stead, referentially. Steve, when we met, was two years racing into his doctorate. Some called him foolhardy. *European Transformations in Narrative Subject, Form & Structure*—*Ovid* 'all the way through to bloody' *Kafka*! he'd boast—and made his doubters eat their words.

At first, I was horrified to find myself the object of this self-confessed literary fanatic's, this self-proclaimed genius's, attentions. Steve defended the College title for perverseness proudly. I could not easily be disabused of the suspicion that he was toying with me. Though even once convinced that his intentions were honourable, I resisted. Not out of coyness: vanity, if you can believe. The idea of being one half of the College's most unprepossessing couple sat very uneasily with me. Steve was my podgy squat antithesis. Together we'd be twice the laughing stock we were as persons in our own right. He was comically myopic to boot. His hair and eyebrows were those of a serial electrical socket-poker. So we were the butt of jokes. Steve just didn't care. If anything, Steve revelled in our conspicuousness. Of course, it took the realisation that he honestly did not feel compromised by me for me properly to fall for him. All these years that have passed, and I haven't stopped falling. How many more years separated prematurely—severed—as we were, than we were together?

That couples should wed was a personal tenet of Steve's. Although willfully unconventional in many respects, he held the institution of the family sacrosanct. From the moment he was sure, therefore, that his feelings were reciprocated, he asked for my hand. Yes, that formally: on one knee, from the top step of a flight of three—to be sure, he said, of reaching my hand. Such was his sense of humour that for that reason alone I'd have had to be a fool to decline. Who else could have made me laugh with an allusion to our difference in height? Proudly curious, I did once ask what he'd have done had I turned him down. He would, he said, have waited for me to change my mind—till death came between us if necessary. A good job then that I didn't make him wait.

I haven't remarried. Coward that he was at heart, Roger never asked. Roger was a man so blusteringly socially inept that on the occasion of our first meeting, having the decency at least first to have asked after any significant other, he presumed familiarity enough to quip at my beloved's expense ("At least, it was a *swift* death"). Steve, you see, was flattened by an open-top double-decker tour bus whilst hurrying to deliver a lecture on *Gulliver's Travels.*

Oh, I suppose Roger was not a bad man really. Though you try convincing Ces of that. That is, the eminent Professor Cecil Wriggly. It's thanks to Ces—confirmed bachelor and bastion of the old boy network—that the demise of my own career, if I may be so bold, drew on and on. This isn't false modesty: it was solely my attachment to Steve that won me that Research Fellow's post in the first place. For the first few months after Steve's death, Ces mourned his protégé almost to the same debilitating degree that I did. But he is too kind by half: my depression only deepened; nobody else would have honoured that contract, I'm sure. Then when it did expire finally, Ces insisted on throwing me a farewell party. "My dear but you must start socialising. Shed this mantle of grief! It's what Steve would want." It was at that gathering that Roger and I met.

Ces was mortified. He hadn't a clue who Roger was. "From the Mathematical and Physical *Sciences* Division?" Honestly, a greater, more lovable snob than Ces you'll never meet. You'd have thought Roger had stepped in unwashed from a leper colony. "On the *technical* staff team? Of the *Zoological* Department?" You'd have thought he'd left the tip of his little finger in a vol au vent. "And he came with *who* did you say? Oh, my dear! And he *cornered* you. I saw him, the ghastly little oink."

Following an acquaintance of an acquaintance, perhaps of an acquaintance, is how Roger had found his way to Ces's that evening, emboldened by an afternoon in The King's Arms. I don't think Roger knew who he'd come with, whose party he'd crashed or, for that matter, whose phone number he left with. I waited. He didn't call. I called him.

I said: I'm not an attractive woman. But I was aware that if I am not to wither into old and lonely widowhood ("Shed this mantle . . .." a curious choice of words, premonitory even), I would need to return any interest shown me. And Ces was right, I should get out of the house more. Here was my opportunity, the first that wasn't born of another's pity. Poor soul, I don't think Roger could believe his luck when I made that call. He'd as little experience with women as, prior to Steve, I'd had with men—and that with good reason. He was as ugly as a gargoyle—though weren't Steve and I living proof that looks needn't be an obstacle to love?

A truer reason, perhaps, for Roger's lack of success prior to me: as drunk as he was when we met, he had in fact maintained admirable professional discretion. For, yes, he worked with animals, just not in the Department of Zoology. He worked in the university's new animal testing lab, that one in need of safeguarding by an injunction. Campaigners, activists, protest daily. Crazies all, in Roger's considered opinion, who, feeling that strongly about animal testing, ought to volunteer themselves as subjects and certainly be denied treatment for their own cancers, Parkinson's et al. Though that's really not the half of it. For as well as his salaried feeding and mucking out of caged monkeys with their brains half hanging out, there was Roger's own 'research' conducted at home on his . . . pets?

Oh, don't get me wrong. I despised Roger at least as much as he seemed, not unreasonably, to expect women would. But my contempt was mine and mine alone. I'll confess I did warm to his perverseness. After all, although it pains me to identify even one similarity between them, Steve was not devoid of that quality. The difference between their particular brands? Steve's was for the delight of impressive intellectual debate. For all his boyish energy and playfulness, he was never childish. Life was a serious business to be enjoyed. Roger's bosses were undoubtedly appreciative of his dedication. No less sure am I of Roger's blithe obliviousness to their condescension. Roger was destined forever to be a child amongst adults.

And of my own perverseness, my acceptance of his 'research' on his . . . *pets*? Well! I am quite without shame. I delighted in the crazy-paving effect that caffeine will produce on the web of an orb spider. High on marijuana, it will lose interest in the web it's spinning only forgetfully to begin another and another. Slipped a dose of chloral hydrate, a hungry wolf spider nodding off mid-chase? Come now. It's funny. Or a Colombian giant red-leg, say, drunkenly wrestling a Chilean rose. I defy anyone to resist the spectacle. With a measured dose of MDMA they can be reconciled.

And no, moving in with Roger, I did not mind sharing our tiny one-bedroom flat—bedroom itself, needs be—with how many pairs of palps silently padding the thin division of glass between us? I've no idea. How many multi-pairs of eyes peering; fangs gnawing at the air vents of their tanks? In the quiet of the night you could sometimes hear the tinny rattle, but they were secure. Roger had learned long before I came along that tarantulas will eat their way through plastic grills. And, anyway, they are such shy, timid creatures at heart. Even those that do present a hazard don't do so willfully. Our goliath bird-eating spider now, although as large as a dinner plate, would never have tried to overpower us when we fed her—live frogs on occasion; once, a baby blackbird Roger found in the street almost dead anyway. But she would flick urticating hairs whenever we lifted the lid of her tank. I once got some in my eye. Bitch.

Oh, I don't blame Roger for not wanting to marry me. I wasn't a loving girlfriend. Not even respectful. I'd soon disabused him of the delusion that his experiments were of any scientific value. (But you see how his perverseness was a child's? So innocent.) Once he had lost interest, I myself assumed responsibility for the spiders. My days with Ces no more, I'd leave the flat only to restock essential supplies: flies and crickets. Roger on the other hand began to stay out after work more often and for longer. You know, beneath his gratitude for my tolerance of him, I think Roger was always a little wary of me. For the sole purpose of prettifying tangle webs, I would share my acid that he after all had procured for me. What sort of woman, he wondered, could happily while away hours and days so engaged? When he'd return, he reeked of beer and smoke. He'd fall directly into bed and sleep.

But that didn't change the fact that I did—I still do—so badly want a baby. Through youth I never imagined the opportunity would be mine. Steve planted the metaphorical seed; in his absence Roger's would do. In the beginning it seemed an impossibility that his seed wouldn't serve. Truthfully? I enjoyed sex with Roger more than I ever did with Steve. Because he was so grateful, I could do just whatever I wanted with him. It took time to reach the point where, without guilt or fear of retribution, I might take him in my hands, say, or mouth and squeeze or bite so hard that the neighbours above and below would hear him cry out, sobbing. But reach that point we did and step well beyond. The flat might have been his before I moved in; it felt to both of us like my territory now.

The irony is that, for all the degradation, I do believe that what came to disconcert Roger about me more was the very feature that in the beginning most fascinated him. It's a mark that, as it were, has always been upon me just above my navel. I always presumed it was a birthmark randomly hourglass-shaped. Did I *really* not know what creature carried such a sign, also right there on its belly? To see it for the first time, Roger was incredulous in his enchantment. I let him have his moment. It was actually Steve who first told me about the black widow spider. Roger's discomfort grew as it gradually enlarged, then began to change colour. It used to be common or garden tan; now it's wine-stain red. But my skin began to tauten all over, split in places to reveal a darker, harder layer beneath ("Shed this mantle . . .."). Stretched out naked in the strip-light glow of those serried towers of tanks banked up against each wall, I quite began to cherish the sheen on my belly.

What really did for Roger, though? What so revolted him beyond all tolerance of me? He might have grown to dread and fear my attentions but could not resist them. When, for what proved, yes, sadly to be the last time, I raised myself from his flushed and crumpled little fizog, he came up spluttering not my usual juices but some other substance. I laughed dismissively at his tentative suggestion that I see a doctor, then slapped him hard. My standards of personal hygiene have always been impeccable. But I had grown a little anxious of late, I will confess. It seems absurd to me now that I should have been at all concerned—that I had not guessed the meaning and purpose of those protuberances newly formed on either side of my vagina. But I guessed now all right! when, still squatting over Roger, to his really comical horror, I found that not only could I produce that sticky stuff at will, I had a taste for it. It is edible, you know. Alarm a spider while it's spinning: it appears to climb its web back up to the ceiling, yes? No. It's eating it.

By now I was used to Roger sometimes not coming home from work at all but sleeping on the couch of whichever of his acquaintances might have him. He was gone for the best part of a week this time. Not that I minded. He would have to return eventually. And, of course, his absence allowed for my further transformation. It isn't complete even yet. While my existing limbs' new joints creak and crack slowly into place, my middle pairs of legs are but half-formed. His absence also meant I'd time enough to weave my web. Forgive the pun. It's awful. But Roger would appreciate it.

The sensitivity of a web is a marvellous thing, you know. Deep inside my own dense tangle, I feel every movement in this block of flats. On whatever floor a door clicks shut, a cupboard, even the soft suck of a fridge opening; all vibrations carry. I am all-feeling. I know everything. I'll know that in the dead of night a mother paces to and fro, her child upon her shoulder, and in my swollen womb-less belly I feel envy—worse than the hunger.

So, in the dark early hours of this very morning, the opening of the entrance hall door alerted me before it had clicked heavily to. I recognised instantly the slow creeping footfalls up the stair. Who else would it be, treading so hesitantly into his own home? I needn't stir, only wait. Our bedroom door, facing our front door, I had left open purposely. Roger would be suspicious, light from the tanks obfuscated now by the coarse silk of my nest. But I was prepared. Over the hallway carpet I'd woven an ankle-thick deep gummy rug. Poor Roger. He knew what I was up to, of course. He knew spiders.

So, it wasn't wholly without pity for him that I emerged from the funnel I'd made of our bedroom doorway. For once I was not rough with him. I wanted his sperm, after all. Back in our nest, my eggs waited in their snug little sac I had so lovingly spun especially. Precisely because Roger had been failing to perform for so long, all sex had been of the forced cunnilingus variety. His impotence now would be nothing less than disastrous. I did have to embrace him tightly to keep him from thrashing, but whispered seductively, offered all the reassurances I could that I would release him once he'd yielded up to me. Alas, all to no avail.

I didn't *mean* to bite him. I was just so frustrated. But once I had nipped him? Well. He soon gave up the fight. And the old digestive enzymes would break a body down anyway. Don't get me wrong. It broke my heart to drag Roger into my nest and lay him down lifeless alongside my poor unborn, unfertilised spiderlets. But as well as broody I was hungry.

And there is hope yet: as old as he is, bachelor boy Ces. If only out of love for Steve, I am by no means forgotten to Professor Wriggly. He writes, as is his old boy's wont, and calls occasionally. It's only mistrust of Roger that has kept him from visiting all this while. Ces has even ventured to hint that he worries for me, living with such a man. So, since I will not be responding to his letters or his calls, it will, I'm sure be a matter of time only before he calls in person.

Perhaps Ces will be understanding of my predicament, accommodating of my needs. As Steve's supervisor, he was, after all, hardly less convinced than I by his arguments for redemption in transformation. And Steve, long before Roger came along, would joke about my most likely mutation. The writing, so to speak, was on my belly.

ISLE IN MAN
Sarah Wilson

The double shot of tequila moved gently inside its tumbler as she touched the glass to her lips. Snapping back her head in one smooth motion, the liquor slid down her throat in a familiar, pleasant fire. Setting the glass down, she bit down on the wedge of lime before swallowing the tart fruit, rind and all.

The bartender gave her an odd look, but she just grinned and waved his concern away. He raised an eyebrow and turned without comment, lazily spot-cleaning the bar with an old rag. With the liquor warming her belly, she spun around on her bar stool and looked out over the dance floor. Unidentifiable music with a rapid-fire vocalist was pouring out of the wall speakers, creating a bass pulse that she could feel in her bones. The wooden floor had all but disappeared under the shoes of the dancers who gyrated in time to the throbbing in their blood.

The club was hot and close, chaotic with flashing lights and threaded through with cigarette smoke. It was one of the few places left that allowed such things, which was why she drove out of her way a few times a year to indulge. A bit of decadence was good for the soul.

The little fan behind the bar oscillated in her direction, blowing a few strands of curly black hair into her face. She tucked them behind one ear in an absent gesture and smiled at the man on the neighboring barstool, who raked his eyes over her before turning away.

Rolling her own eyes in amusement, she pulled a cigarette pack from the pocket of her jeans and lit up a menthol. Her zippo lighter snapped shut, the snick of metal on metal easily drowned by the music. Setting the pack and lighter down on the counter, she leaned her back against the cheap wood, the cigarette dangling from her long fingers. All that was left was to wait for an opportunity.

It wasn't long before one came in the form of a tipsy college kid who tripped on a crack in the flooring. He tottered on uncertain legs, but was abruptly saved when she grabbed his forearm with her free hand and steadied him.

He blinked at her with cornflower blue eyes, his sharp cheekbones flushed with drink, before grinning sheepishly. "Thanks, er . . ." Trailing off helplessly, he tried to pull his arm away.

She held on for a moment longer, soaking in the essence of him, his soul pouring into her skin and pooling in her chest. It was a sweet warmth that told her all about the character of the man, and it was with affection that she released him with a pat on his wrist.

"Call me Mare, love," she said, her voice raised to be heard over the music. "You might want to sit down for a bit. You're looking peaky."

He smiled a bit unsteadily and left with another murmured 'thanks.' Mare watched him as he weaved over to a nearby table and was pulled into a circle of his peers. Such a lovely one. She'd have to taste him again one day.

Feeling refreshed, she took a drag from her cigarette, ashes trailing from the cherry to decorate the scuffed floor with dots of gray. The man next to her scowled in disapproval and pushed a battered ashtray across the counter. She took it from him and let the blade of her finger brush his knuckle. She tasted him in one quick pull and then drew her hand away before he could do more than shiver.

Tapping her cigarette against the tray, she paused for a moment as her neighbor's tired, muddy essence flowed through her. Huffing in fond exasperation, she touched his hand again, ignoring the way he stiffened under her fingers.

"Go home," she said, carefully sending a flicker of reassurance across the contact of skin on skin. Almost immediately, he relaxed and turned his head towards her, his eyes glazed from drink. "Things will be better after a long sleep."

"Yeah." He cleared his throat and then nodded. "Yeah. 'M tired."

The man stood without another word, passed the bartender some money and left. She watched him go until he was lost in the crowd and then smiled. He would fall into bed tonight, she knew, and after a recuperative sleep, would have only a hazy recollection of the strange little woman at the club. Strong drink was an ally for someone like her.

With the sense of a job well done, Mare stubbed out her cigarette and spent the next while simply looking out over the dance floor. They were beautiful, each and every one, from the lithe young man with the predatory sway to the wide-hipped older woman with her comely blush. She wished she could go up to each one and pour the knowledge of beauty into their skins to show them just how tragic and funny and foolish and wise they were, each in their own ways.

She wondered how they would react knowing that a stranger loved them so.

Probably not well, she acknowledged. Mare had been alive so long she could no longer remember how she began, but she could vividly recall previous attempts that had all ended in disaster, back in the raw times when humans huddled around fires for warmth and lived in fear of the night. They weren't ready then to know of her and what she could do.

Things have changed, though, a desperate part of her protested. Humans no longer were focused inward with such manic intensity. They had removed their heads from the sand and were now tentatively seeking out things beyond themselves, accepting life for what it is without cloaking their fears in the arcane and calling themselves the center of all things.

They will be ready soon, she told that lonely bit of herself. *Soon.*

A touch of old melancholy threaded through her, souring the already fading tastes of the college kid and the drunken man. She considered leaving but quickly dismissed the idea. It had been too long since she had been here, in a place where she could touch with little fear of retribution. She deserved it, needed it like a plant needed water.

She decisively shoved her cigarettes and lighter back into her pocket and hopped off the bar stool. With a flick of her wild hair, Mare waded out onto the dance floor. She lifted her hands slightly as she walked, her fingers spread, and brushed against everyone she passed. Touching, tasting. Reveling in the feel of each bright, fluttering soul.

A light stroke of a back offered up the sweet spice of lust, while the touch of another's hand set her teeth on edge with the bitter taste of envy. Love flowed from the skin of a tall, raw-boned woman, and Mare circled her once as the music changed to a slower tempo, before being brought up short by a tap on her shoulder.

She looked up into the gray eyes of a man in his mid-thirties, clad in black and sporting a pleasing grin. He held out his hand and jerked his head towards the other dancers who had begun to pair off in obedience to the new beat. His invitation was obvious, and her blood sang with jubilation and gratitude.

Attempting to rein in her enthusiasm, Mare's smile still spoke of happiness as she took his hand. The nameless man smiled in return and placed his free hand gently on her hip, drawing her into a loose, swaying dance.

Moments like this were somewhat rare in Mare's long, strange life, and she felt nearly drunk with it as she tasted her fill of him. He was a good soul, she quickly discovered, with a surprising spice of humor, like smooth chili chocolate on her tongue. Unable to help herself, she closed her eyes in bliss, and her heart jumped as she felt the rumble of his laughter.

There was the danger, the temptation that was nearly impossible to resist. He was beautiful and open, offering up a great gift completely without his knowledge. As easily as breathing, she could pour herself into him, wrap the flames of his soul around her like a blanket, and use it to burn away the loneliness that made up the core of her being.

It would be so easy—

Her hand had tightened unconsciously around his own, she suddenly realized. She loosened her fingers in dismay, her eyes snapping open, and attempted to draw away from him. *Not ready*, a dwindling, rational part of her warned. *Not ready*.

The music had slid gently into a violin solo, and his expression was as sweet as the instrument when he smiled reassuringly and drew her closer, touching her cheek with two fingers. It was a simple gesture of affection, and it broke her will completely.

She reached up to press his hand more firmly against her skin, and those fingers that had touched her so kindly stiffened as she silently flooded into him. Mare had collected many names over the eons, the man quickly learned. She was Mara, Lilin, Succubus, Hone-onna. She was alone, inimitable, and she loved him with a depth and completeness that drowned.

Faced with such an affectionate invasion, his bright essence hesitated, allowing her to draw more of his warmth and light around herself. For one moment, all she felt was joy, followed by a swelling hope that he would not turn away. That she could love him simply for what he was—young and innocent and heartbreakingly human—and that, incredibly, he would love her back.

But then, as his heart sped up to beat in tandem with her own, she tasted a sudden sour spike of horror. Whirling away and folding in on itself, his soul left a widening circle of cold in its wake, with Mare at its center. Physically, he staggered backward and wrenched his hand from her grip, narrowly missing another dancing couple. Even in the dim light, she could clearly see him mouth the word 'monster.'

The warmth of him fled from her skin, chased away by a numbing sense of déjà vu. Mare could think of nothing at all to do as he pushed his way through the crowd and out of her life forever. Curious human eyes watched him go, leaving her alone, unregarded, and sick with loss. An island in a sea of man.

SOMETHING GOLD
Tay Sanchez

ina grows her hair long because once, between cuts, I told her I liked how it softened her face. She's got a sharp jaw, but it looks kind of nice with the hair hanging just there. We took the bus to Silver City one day to walk along the dusty rows of folding tables at the flea market, and I got her a gold bracelet that looked good when she held it against her skin. Neither of us had given anything to the other before.

She said, "You get that money from your dad?" and I said, "What if I did?" But I didn't say he wouldn't have given it to me if he'd known I was spending it on her.

"Next time tell him to get you car." She knew my dad would buy me a car if I asked, and she knew that I was too old to be taking money from him at all, and I knew she liked to test me, so I almost told her to get fucked.

But then she laughed, and she had one of those laughs that made her shoulders hunch up and her chin tuck in, and, when she did that, her hair fell forward along the lines of her cheek and mouth, and that bracelet caught in the sunlight and sprayed gold bits everywhere, on every part of her. There wasn't a cloud in the sky that day.

So instead I said, "You'd look pretty with your hair long." She brushed it back with her fingers, and we walked on. She linked her arm through mine and pressed her head against my shoulder, and all day long I felt the weight of the metal against my wrist.

It turned green a week later, and, when she left it on her bedroom dresser, I threw it in the trash. I don't think she ever looked for it.

* * *

FINA GROWS HER HAIR long so she can tent my face, the waves and ripples smelling like coconut as she lies on top of me, every soft piece of her body in contact with mine, her face inches from mine, her black hair hiding us from the world outside. I think sometimes that if she could create this dark little world for me every night, all night long, then maybe I could sleep more.

One day when she did this as we lay on the old mattress sitting on the floor of her bedroom, she leaned close to my ear and whispered, "I love you," and I didn't say anything back. I don't know why because I guess I did love her, but saying it would have made things different. She tensed, and every cell of her body moved away from every cell of mine. She rolled off of me and onto her side, tucked her waves behind her ear and propped herself up on one elbow, her jaw resting against her hand. She took my palm and placed it against her belly, which was harder and rounder than it had once been.

"It's been months," she said, and then, "You know what's going on, right?" She smiled just a little.

"Yeah," I said, "I know." I'd known for a while. But we had never talked about it.

She lay on her back and sighed. I didn't want her pushing me, and I didn't know how I felt or what I was going to do until I did it. I sat up and leaned over her and placed my head against her stomach, ear to navel, and waited there. She put her hand on my neck, and something darted about inside of her. I heard it move, felt a quiver beneath my cheek.

"Can you feel it?" she asked.

"Yeah," I said. "It's like a little fish, swimming around in the sea."

She said she'd never seen the sea.

FINA GROWS HER HAIR long so she can pull it tightly into a bun, the thick coarse strands stretched tightly across her small round skull. She carries the weight low in her stomach now, and she sighs when she reaches up to tighten the yellow rubber band that holds her hair at the base of her neck. Her body is swollen, but her face is sunken, and mostly her black eyes don't say anything about anything any more.

Fina gets up when her mother does so she can help her make the breakfast that she and her father will eat together before they leave for work, he at the mines and she at Saucedo's Motel. I don't like the thought of her there, bending over and shaking her ass in those men's faces as she makes their beds, but she says one of us has to work. I work, get jobs here and there, and she knows it. It's just hard to keep up with things. Her dad tried to get me a job in the mines a few weeks ago, but I didn't last one full day in that hole, with all those things moving around in the darkness. When I got home that day she just stared at me.

One day Fina got up out of bed with a bruise on her face.

"What happened to you?" I asked.

She opened the door to the hallway to let in the light. She looked in the mirror and ran her fingers over her cheek, a large patch of skin darker than the shadows around us. I rolled over to face the wall.

"You punched me in bed," she said. "In your sleep, I guess."

"You guess?" I rolled back around and looked at her.

"If you hadn't been drunk, I would know," she said, moving her hand from cheek to hair, patting and poking it into place, pieces slipping back out as soon as her fingers moved on. A lot of days she didn't even bother to brush it anymore, just straightened it a little with her hands.

"You have a man's face when you pull your hair back all tight like that," I said because there wasn't anything else to say.

"One of us has to be the man, right?" she said and closed the door behind her.

* * *

FINA GROWS HER HAIR long so she can dust the lampshades with it. She won't keep her hair in a bun anymore because it does what it wants to do and she lets it. But she can't have it in her face, so she pulls it back at the nape of her neck. She can't work anymore because of the heaviness inside her, so she helps her mom with the cooking and cleaning. I haven't worked much lately. Her parents don't speak to me; they look away if I come into the room. Fina and her mom, they whisper to each other sometimes, like I'm not sitting right there in front of them. I can't hear what they say, but I think I know.

Fina says I'm crazy, that she doesn't dust lampshades with her hair, and what the hell is wrong with me anyway? Take your medicine, she says. Maybe, she says, I don't know she uses the blue-dyed feather duster her mom keeps in a kitchen drawer to do that shit because I've never thought to get off my ass and look for it. Maybe if I got out of the house and got a job I'd have better things to worry about than what she and her hair are doing.

But here's the thing: I can hear her when she does it, sometimes in the day when I'm not in the room and the TV's on loud to hide it, and sometimes at night when she thinks I'm asleep. But I don't sleep much, and I can hear her walking around out there in the house, her and the whisking sound of her hair against fabric, and sometimes she sings to it as she walks along. She says she doesn't do that, but in the morning the ends are coated in grey and the top is streaked through with it.

"What I don't get," I said one night, when her parents were in bed and the television was on but no one was watching, "is why someone would try to hide something if they didn't think it was wrong."

Her fingers, which had been twisting the ends of her hair, froze guiltily. Her hands dropped to her lap. She closed her eyes and sat for a moment, completely still, a statue waiting for a prayer.

She opened her eyes and looked at me, and I looked at her. Her eyes were small, but her gaze was clear and steady. Steadiness that moved beyond the flicker of the TV. She didn't answer, and I didn't say anything else. There wasn't anything else to say.

* * *

FINA GROWS HER HAIR long to give the piojos and spiders a home. She acts like she doesn't see them, when they crawl out of their hiding places deep within her dark roots, when they crawl around her face, in and out of her mouth and nose when she looks at me, when she tells me I'm worthless, that her parents would have kicked me out a long time ago if they didn't still hope I would marry her so she wouldn't be the town whore. In and out and around they crawl, because there are worse things in her mouth than them.

She wears her hair loose now, but it's too long to soften her face anymore, and instead she uses it to shield against her breast the little bird that she found in the woods. The heaviness is gone from her and she has this creature, wrapped up in her hair at her chest, and she feeds him treats from her hair to pass the time, to make him grow. Her body is thin again, but there is a flatness to her that wasn't there before, and lumps of damp yellow skin and grayish hair hang around her in the air, below her eyes and at her stomach. She sits in a chair and she rocks and she moans, with the little bird attached to her, and now I think there is more of the hair, probably, than there is of her.

Sometimes she sings to the hair, and the little bird chirps, its bright eyes watching the movements of her mouth, and I wish that she would sing to me. Sometimes she lets me see it up close, lets it sit upon my lap and peck at my pants and shirt buttons, but she always carries it away before I'm done with it.

"You're drunk," she says, as though that's all there is to say.

One day, while Fina hung laundry on the line, the little bird sat on my lap and looked into my face, so close I could see tiny flecks of gold in the darkness of its eyes, and it tilted its head sideways and chirped, and I chirped back. It looked around the room and, assured that it was empty, chirped again. Then it began to whisper in words that I did and didn't understand, and I whispered back, quickly, telling it that it belonged to Fina, yes, but after all it was mine as well. Someday, I said, we could maybe go somewhere, just the two of us, and then, when it needed to fly away, I would let it. I explained that, unlike some people, I had no interest in owning a little bird, that I only wanted its willing company, to have it perch upon my shoulder and sing and chirp to me as it pleased.

Just as we began to come to some sort of understanding, Fina came up from behind us and whisked the little bird away. She placed it at the top of the tallest tree and stayed with it there for the rest of the day, singing to erase in it the memory of all I had said. I know this is what she did.

She brought it home with her later that night, and none of us spoke.

* * *

FINA GROWS HER HAIR long so she can sweep the floor with it. It doesn't quite reach the ground so she hunches as she walks, trailing the tangles and cobwebs behind her. The bird follows her, hopping and singing at her feet, and both seem happy. Although it sometimes still comes to perch on my lap, there is something wary in its eyes, and it hops away without regret when called.

Fina. I think maybe she doesn't know that the hair is jealous, that it hates the little creature as much as it hates me. That it is only waiting for the right time to strike.

One day, the bird played on the floor behind her as she stood washing dinner dishes in the kitchen, and I sat at the table and watched as the inky darkness crept down her back, pulsing with red and fluctuating in the last strong rays of the evening. It moved towards the bird slowly and then, when it was close enough to be heard, it began to whisper. The bird turned its head and listened, and I wondered what it said.

But when it began to wind itself around the little creature's neck I jumped from the table, knocking over the wooden chair, and yanked the bird up by its frail little wing. In the second before Fina turned, the hair hissed and recoiled, and I knew then that it would come for me next.

When she turned to face me, I still held the little creature in midair by its wing, safe for now, but it chirped softly and swung its frail body pitifully. She grabbed it from me, too hard, and it chirped louder, panicked, as she pinned it against her hip.

I tried to explain it to her, make her understand what had happened, but she shook her head and backed away.

"You don't touch him," she said.

FINA GROWS HER HAIR long so it will strangle me in my sleep. When she lies there breathing deep, I can hear it growing. It pulses and whispers as it strings itself around her legs and coils itself around the bedposts, under the mattress. I worry about the small bird who sleeps in a wicker nest placed next to her side of the bed, and so I don't sleep. I sit up and listen, and wait.

One night I fell asleep and woke to find one slick, cold coil wrapped tightly around my neck. We fought silently through the night, the coil and me, one gaining over the other until finally, close to morning, I tore the piece from her head and watched it disintegrate in the gray morning light. Fina did not wake up, and the bird cheeped happily in its corner of the room.

She grows her hair to strangle me, and all of us know it and know that it is only a matter of time. One day I will tire of fighting the darkness, and I will let it.

***

AND WHEN IT HAS done its job, Fina will spin a web of hair and drag my body behind her to the sea. The little bird will perch on her shoulder and make small cooing sounds as she casts out her net and waits until the tide pulls it far from the shore. And when it is far, far away, far enough so the fishermen cannot see it from their boats, so the sun and moon cannot spy it in its dark depths, so the small blind white fish are startled by its presence, then she will reach behind her neck and cut the hair with her long yellow nails, and she will shed those too in the process.

But the bird will fly from her then, startled by this act, and ever after it will spend its life roaming the ocean, circling its path over and over again, peering into the depths in search of a glimmer of something green, something that used to be gold.

GOURMAUNDETH
Cheryl Stiles

Woe unto you, for whan bothe these corporalmeates and drynke wherewith ye so delicately and voluptuously fede yourselves, yea and the bealie too whiche gourmaundeth, shall be consumed, then shall ye bee houngrie and fynde no relief.

> Erasmus, 1548
> Paraphrase of the Gospel of Luke
> ch. 6 v. 25

Trawling   trawling
        my net of   dark space and   ether
                my vial of   tranquilizers
                        my flask of   schnapps and
                                cough syrup   elixir—
Night Nurse   Mother

Mother   I wear your clothes   I hear
        your voice in mine
                and I made   of   your room
                        a shrine
                where   no light comes through

                Ich bin das schlechte Kind

                your hair brushes   your mirrors

By day I dated   women
            By night   I baked marzipan
        in the shape of men
                anatomically correct   They were sweet   so sweet
        and I ate
                but was   never   filled   quite

Several men came
        to this Hessean   town

        to my half-timbered   home of forty-three rooms
            rooms Mother named   Sunlight
             and   Morning Dew

        and then to one   certain   room
            I   call
            der Schlachtraum

They were   yes   so well hung—
        from a   harness
            and   meat hook

then I wrapped   them in   clingwrap

        used   sticky notes   and dressmaker's pins
to mark   all the best
        and   most flavorful   parts
            steak   filet   bacon   ham

But there was   one   a special one
            my Hansel

Time for a   chat   a few words
        at   the   AnthroCafe
        from   me   to   handsome Hansel

        I'm sorry   so sorry   in this story
            there is no   Gretel
            no   wicked   witch

        Only me   *dein Doppelgänger*

He finally said   I'm tired   Cut the thing   off   Bitte
     And so I did
         held it in my hand
             Take   eat   this is my body
             and tasted

Is it good?   he asked

It is bitter   I replied   bitter
         but I like it
         because   it is bitter

             Thou preparest a table before me

I kissed him   again   I prayed

         for   forgiveness   for me and   him

I stored   the cuts in   butcher's wrap
         labeled   and   frozen
     Prepared a   new dish   every day
         biceps   in Marsala

         schnitzels of   loin

     ahh   yes   thigh steak   with
         a   South African   cabernet

         Like taking communion
Later   in   the   garden
     over his   buried teeth   bones
         organs
     I recited   the 23rd Psalm

He maketh me to lie down

Mutter   ich bin   ein   Menschenfresser
         und   ich   habe   Hunger

and there are   others   waiting
                                        many others
and Mother   I hunger

                        I still

                                    hunger

Reader's Notes for Gourmaundeth

Based on newspaper and magazine reports (including the extremely graphic cover story in *Der Speigel*), court testimony, forensics, etc. this poem chronicles the recent exploits of a German cannibal who surfed the net to find his victims. The perpetrator was initially convicted of manslaughter as Germany at the time had no laws relating to cannibalism, but he was later retried for murder and sentenced to life imprisonment.

- **gourmand** (*use as a verb is obsolete*): to devour greedily or gluttonously
- **Night Nurse**: commonly available European cough remedy widely known for its sedative effects
- *Ich bin das schlechte Kind*: I am your evil child.
- *der Schlachtraum*: literally "the strike room" or butchering room
- *Mutter ich bin ein Menschenfresser und ich habe Hunger*: Mother I am a maneater and I still hunger.

NOT ONE BUT MANY
Michael Wasteneys Stephens

THE DESIRE FOR WHAT WAS
AND WHAT COULD BE

THE WISHED-FOR
Catee Baugh

There is something uncurable in your body.

In the old stories, the body
is always changeable in some way—
if you sing the right song the bones become a body.
And if you make the shirts just right,
your brothers are no longer swans, even though you didn't finish
in time, and the youngest has a wing for an arm.
A patch of feathers unable to grab, or fly.

Your womb inside you useless as a lone wing.

And in the old stories all you do
is wish for the child—just look at blood
on the ground and one is planted in you.

O friend, o sister, I am no story—
I wish I could give you the womb
in me that need only say "please,"
and it would receive, but I cannot change a body.

I only have one power—what I can give—
that is, what I can give away.
Body inside and outside mine.

And here is the child,
here is the babe
leaving my arms.

Child I carry and
child I bleed and bleed into this world for you.

THE MIRROR CHILD
Amanda Block

"Once upon a time in midwinter, when the snowflakes were falling like feathers from heaven, a queen sat sewing at her window, which had a frame of black ebony wood. As she sewed she looked up at the snow and pricked her finger with her needle. Three drops of blood fell into the snow. The red on the white looked so beautiful that she thought to herself, 'If only I had a child as white as snow, as red as blood, and as black as the wood in this frame.'"

—From 'Little Snow-White' by the Brothers Grimm*

Once there lived a young Queen who wished for a child above anything else in the land. Her husband, the King, also desired an heir, but his want was nothing to the Queen's longing. As the years passed, and no child was granted to the royal couple, the Queen grew desperately unhappy. Finally, when she could endure her empty womb no longer, she decided to enlist the help of a fairy.

Now fairies are tricky creatures: some are good, some are bad; and most are somewhere in between. The fairy that appeared to the young Queen was a mischievous thing with a wicked streak in her soul. When the poor lady spoke of her wish for a child, it was all the fairy could do to keep the smirk from her pretty face.

"I want a child who I may look upon as my own," said the

Queen. "Who will look upon me as a mother, who will be the very reflection of me."

The fairy pondered this. "I can grant your wish," she said, "though you might not thank me."

"Oh, I will! I will!" cried the Queen.

"Very well," said the fairy. Then she waved her wand and vanished.

The Queen waited and waited, but it seemed no magic had been done. Assuming the fairy had lied to her, she sat alone on her bed and lamented that she was still childless.

The Queen's bedchamber was a grand and ornate room, dominated by a great free-standing mirror. The lady was not a vain sort, but each morning she would look into the mirror and spend a few moments with her reflection, pinning up her dark hair and powdering her white face.

It was a few weeks after the fairy's visit that the Queen noticed the swollen belly of her reflection. She ran her hand over her real belly and, while that felt normal and flat, her mirror image traced a small bump. As the weeks passed and the belly of her reflection continued to grow, becoming round and ripe while she remained her same slim self, the Queen was finally forced to concede that her reflection—and only her reflection—was pregnant.

She summoned the fairy again, who could barely contain her mirth.

"What have you done?" the Queen asked of her.

"*I want a child who I may look upon as my own,*" the fairy cackled. "*Who will look upon me as a mother. Who will be the very reflection of me.*"

"A *real* child!" cried the Queen.

"Too late!" said the fairy. "You shall have a Mirror Child."

The Queen looked at her pregnant reflection in horror.

"But how will I reach it?" she asked.

"You cannot!" The fairy tapped the glass of the mirror and sang. "You cannot touch, you cannot talk, or else the mirror realm will crack."

And before the Queen could call her guards, the creature had vanished again.

Nine months after the fairy's first visit, the young Queen had a strange dream: she was looking into her mirror when a tiny piece of glass fell out of it and into her outstretched palm. The fragment had seven sharp edges, and she lifted it to her mouth and swallowed it whole. It scraped against her throat and the Queen began to bleed. But the blood was not in her mouth; it was between her legs, and mixed into it was sparkling mirror dust . . .

The Queen awoke, dry and whole. Trembling, she hurried to her mirror and peered through the glass. Her reflection, no longer pregnant, peered back, and, on the bed behind her there lay a newborn child. The Queen turned and looked into her real chamber: no baby was there.

A low moan escaped her, and she pressed her palms against the mirror. Her fingers scratched its smooth surface again and again, but she could not get through. Eventually the Queen sank to the floor, tears streaming down her cheeks as she stared into the mirror at the child she could not have.

At first, she thought it might die, for there was nobody to care for it. But then, struck by an idea, she approached in her room where the child should be. Tentatively, she stretched out her arms, curved them against the bedclothes and brought them slowly to her chest. Her reflection picked up the baby. The Queen hugged the air. Her reflection hugged the baby.

So, like this, the Queen cared for the Mirror Child. She sat in front of the glass with her gown unbuttoned, while it fed from the breasts of her reflection. She waved rattles at empty spaces and wrapped blankets around thin air. Then she left piles of toys and towels and clothes for the maids to remove, saying they were used or soiled or outgrown, though in reality they were clean and untouched.

The King was deeply troubled. He believed his wife spent her days playing imaginary games and feared she was losing her mind. One day he came across her staring into her mirror, rocking her arms from side to side.

"What are you doing now?" he demanded.

"Helping my Mirror Child sleep," she replied.

The King craned his neck and strained his eyes but could see no one in the mirror other than himself and his wife.

After she had continued to act in this way for many months, shunning the court for the company of her mirror and some creature he could not see, the King called for the best doctors in the land.

"Can you not see her?" the Queen asked those learned men, pointing at the mirror. "My little girl is crawling now."

The doctors quickly declared the Queen to be mad and advised that she be locked up for the good of the kingdom. Her husband saw no alternative but to agree and ordered the guards to take her to the tallest tower. As they prepared to drag the Queen from the mirror, she let out an anguished scream and threw herself at her husband's feet.

"You may lock me up as and where you like," she cried, "but do not separate me from my child. I beg you – grant me my mirror!"

Moved by her desperation, the King took pity on his wretched wife and gave his permission that she keep her mirror.

The days turned to weeks, the weeks to months, until the young Queen had been imprisoned in front of her mirror for a year. She had watched the Mirror Child take her first unsteady steps around the tower room. She had watched the Mirror Child grow more like her, with dark hair and a pale complexion. And as the Queen sat on the floor watching her, the Mirror Child would scramble into the lap of her reflection and watch back. Then the Queen would place her hands upon the mirror and the girl would place her palms against the glass, so she was like the Queen's second little reflection. Both would stare and stare with their hands so close, as though if they pressed hard enough they might fall through the glass and into each other's arms.

On the anniversary of her imprisonment, the King visited his wife in the tower. He was shocked by her altered appearance, for her days in front of the mirror had rendered her thin and worn. His heart, which had loved her once, was distressed, and so he asked if he might bring her anything.

The Queen and her reflection considered this.

"I would like another mirror," she said.

The King nodded and ordered a mirror be brought to the tower.

So the Queen had two mirrors through which to watch her Mirror Child.

One day, when the Queen, her reflection, and her Mirror Child were sitting in their usual way, the Queen realised that the little girl was trying to speak. She could not hear anything beyond the mirror, but she leaned forward so she might lip-read what the child was saying:

Mama.

That one word—that *first* word—darted soundlessly from the mouth of the Mirror Child and directly into the breast of the Queen. Like a shard of the glass itself, it pierced her heart and she leant against the mirror frame for support. She was not a real mother.

Another year passed. The King returned to the tower, where he found his wife thinner and more worn. Once more, he asked whether he might bring her anything.

"I would like another mirror," she told him again.

So the Queen had three mirrors through which to watch her Mirror Child.

Four more years passed; four more mirrors were brought to the Queen. She hung them about the tower, so the seven surfaces reflected her hundreds of times. And although the mirrors only ever showed one Mirror Child, the girl flitted from mirror to mirror, following the Queen wherever she looked. She, like the Queen, looked a lot older now. But while the Queen had grown haggard and gaunt, the Mirror Child had blossomed, and it was only the expression of great sadness that diminished her lovely features.

On the seventh anniversary of the fairy's first visit, the Queen had another curious dream: as she sat in front of one of her mirrors, she was peeling off her skin. She picked it from her fingertips, from up over her wrists; stripping off all the skin of her arm. It was raw and red underneath—exposed muscle and bone—but it did not hurt, so she laughed and wrenched a great band of flesh from her chest. Then, when she looked at the reflection in the mirror of her naked organs, she saw that her heart was made of mirror. *This is wrong*, she thought as she prodded through her ribs . . .

She touched the mirror heart and it shattered.

The Queen awoke. She ran shaking fingers over her unbroken skin and hugged her chest. Then she stumbled to her first mirror from which the Mirror Child watched her. The Queen waved the girl away: *go back, go back*, until, hesitantly, the child walked backwards from the glass.

The Queen was crying; she could bear it no longer. Her heart was breaking; her whole self had been breaking for seven years. And so she took the empty goblet that had accompanied her meagre evening meal and smashed it against the mirror.

Crash.

The first mirror shattered. The Mirror Child screamed a silent scream before—

Crash.

The second mirror shattered.

Mama! the Mirror Child mouthed, and then—

Crash. Crash. Crash. Crash.

The Queen approached the seventh mirror. The Mirror Child cowered at the end of the reflected tower room.

Crash.

The Queen wailed. She looked around at the seven ruined mirrors and wanted to destroy them completely. To grind them to dust. She hurled the goblet against each one, lashing out again and again, until hundreds of tiny mirror pieces whirled in a blizzard around her head. All she could see was shimmering mirror fragments, suspended in the air before they fell—

—Only they didn't fall. They stayed, hanging about her head, while everything else was falling away.

Crack.

The real world—her dingy prison—had gone. And it was the quietness, thicker than silence, and not the bright silver place of reflection she saw, that told the Queen she had entered the mirror realm.

She saw herself, hundreds and thousands of times, all the reflections she had ever been: a bride adjusting her veil, a Queen preparing for a ball, a child putting rouge on her lips. Her younger self looked so much like the Mirror Child, the Queen almost reached out for her. But then she remembered the fairy's words: *you cannot*

touch, you cannot talk, or else the mirror realm will crack.

She began to walk through her reflections: before her coronation, wearing a new dress, on her birthday. Some of the mirror Queens were feeding or dressing or changing empty space, while many more were just sitting and staring, gazing at a little girl only they could see. Then the Queen understood: the Mirror Child was not like these reflections, frozen in moments of the past. She was as real as the Queen herself, but trapped on the wrong side of the glass.

Something new and unfamiliar flickered inside the Queen's heart: hope. If the Mirror Child was real here, in the mirror realm, then the Queen would be able to find her.

She began to search through her reflections, careful not to brush against them, careful not to utter a sound, terrified the mirror realm would crack. She searched and searched, though for how long she did not know. Until finally, there she was: a little girl huddled in a ball with no reflected mother. Without thinking, the Queen reached out for her and spoke:

"My child."

As she talked, as she touched, there was an almighty crash and the mirror realm began to splinter.

Tiny mirror pieces fell through the air like hail stones. The Queen squeezed shut her eyes and fell to the ground. There she crouched, holding the child in her arms, protecting her while the sparkling splinters scattered.

When the ringing stopped and all was silent once more, the Queen did not open her eyes. She wanted to pretend, for just a little longer, that she had fetched her child from the mirror realm. She wanted to pretend that the girl was there in her arms, and she was not just hugging her knees.

"Mama," said a voice. A real voice.

The Queen looked up: the seven frames hung quite empty and the floor was littered with silver puddles of dust. Secure in her arms was her child.

The Queen stared; the girl stared. The Queen blinked and shook her head: this could not be real—the child could not be real. Shaking, she raised her hands, and the girl mimicked her. Their palms met, but instead of feeling cold flat glass the Queen felt warm soft skin. Their fingers entwined, clasping and keeping one another. Then the girl threw her arms around the Queen's neck, and the Queen held her tightly, sobbing into her dark hair, "my child, my child, *my child . . .*"

They left the tower that very day. The King had no choice but to free his wife, considering her mysterious child had materialised at last. He begged her to return to the throne, but she and her daughter decided they would travel around the land—for neither was fond of confined spaces. Thus they began a new and fairly ordinary life, and the former Queen's daughter grew up normal in all ways but one: she possessed no reflection.

* * *

As FOR THAT WICKED fairy? She tried to trick another desperate soul—a young lover—yet when she attempted to trap the pretty maiden he desired in the mirror, her spell backfired and she trapped herself instead. Perhaps one day someone will take pity on her, but until then she remains stuck in the mirror realm. You might have seen her: she is that shape behind your reflection, the thing that darts out of sight when you try to look closer, because she is hiding her face in shame.

*Jacob and Wilhelm Grimm, Sneewittchen, Kinder- und Hausmärchen, (Children's and Household Tales—Grimms' Fairy Tales), final edition (Berlin, 1857), no. 53. Translated by D. L. Ashliman.

THE MUSIC BOX
David Kolinski-Schultz

I t was an odd little shop, tucked away on a side street in the old section of Boston on Beacon Hill, not too far from the Park Street subway station. How had he not noticed it before? Surely he had been down this street many times. This quirky little establishment with the multi-paned windows and gaslights looked as though it had been transported out of a story by Charles Dickens. Still, he thought, it might be a pleasant distraction for a while. And Shawn needed some distraction. Despite all of the people here, Boston could be a lonely place at times.

As he entered the shop, the chime on the door played a little melody that seemed vaguely familiar, but he couldn't quite place it. The shop was filled with a myriad of trinkets, all shimmering on the shelves and in cubbyholes. Like so many gift shops, there were pendants, wind chimes, candles, and many other bits of tchotchke. He noticed he was the only customer in the shop at the moment.

"Welcome, please come in," said the shopkeeper.

"Thank you," said Shawn. "Has your shop been here long? I thought I knew this neighborhood, but I don't remember seeing it before."

"Oh, yes. Quite a long time," said the shopkeeper. "Quite a long time."

The shopkeeper looked to be an older gentleman, but Shawn

had no idea how old exactly. He had a mop of white hair and side-burns, but his eyes were of a remarkable shade of bright blue—almost crystalline in intensity.

"Is there anything in particular I can help you find, young man?" the shopkeeper asked after Shawn had been perusing the shop for a few minutes. "A gift for a young lady perhaps? I have some lovely items over this way."

Shawn smiled ironically. "No, I wish there was a young lady for me to buy a gift, but there isn't one right now."

"Oh, you *wish*, do you? Well, that's a different department. Come this way." And the shopkeeper motioned Shawn to follow him through a beaded curtain into an anteroom.

This room too was lit by gaslights, but the room was enormous; much larger than Shawn expected considering how small the shop had looked from the outside. When he looked up he couldn't even see the ceiling; it seemed to fade away into the darkness. Once he got over the shock of the room, the shopkeeper led Shawn to a set of shelves and picked up a music box. It was made of glass but with an intricate filigree of what looked like gold wrapped around the glass. Shawn's first thought was about how expensive this music box must be. He was only a poor grad student. He would never be able to afford this, even if he had someone to buy it for in the first place.

The shopkeeper opened the music box, and it began to play. It sounded like he expected a music box to sound, a tinkling melody like classical music. He'd never had a great ear for music, but the more he listened to it, the more unusual it became. The song didn't sound classical; it sounded somehow older, perhaps even ancient. Shawn found himself almost lost in the music. He became aware that the shopkeeper was saying something and forced himself back to the room as the shopkeeper closed the music box.

"A very special music box indeed," said the shopkeeper. "I see you have already felt its effect. And that is only a small sample. If you truly wish for something you desire, this music box can help you to realize that wish."

Now Shawn became skeptical. He had to admit, he had felt something, and the shopkeeper had a good sales pitch, but, after all, this was the twenty-first century, and magic music boxes and granting wishes were the stuff of children's books and the movies.

"I don't think so," Shawn said cautiously. "That's not how things work in the real world," he said, emphasizing "real" maybe a bit too much.

The shopkeeper smiled. "Oh, it's not that easy! You think you just wish for something and it appears? Oh, no my worldly friend. This will require some time and effort on your part, as all worthwhile things do."

Caught off guard by this apparent change of sales tactics, Shawn muttered "Well, I'm sure I don't have the money for the music box anyway."

"You haven't even learned what you must do and already you're ready to give up. I thought this wish was close to your heart," said the old man.

"Yes, of course it is," Shawn protested. He'd had his fill of meeting women in bars and online dating. It was depressing and could really do a number on your self-esteem. Why not hope for a little magic?

"What do I have to do?"

"Only what you have been doing, but the music box will help. When you meet a young lady, at some point allow her to open the music box. If she hears no music, then she is not the one for you. However, if she hears the music, you have found someone special!"

Deciding he had nothing to lose, Shawn bought the music box. He just wouldn't mention it to anyone so he wouldn't feel too foolish. Magic music boxes! Was he really that desperate?

Two weeks later, Shawn had a date to meet a young lady for lunch at one of the sidewalk cafes on Newbury. She was attractive, and they had a pleasant—if somewhat uninspired—conversation over lunch, as he had come to expect from such meetings. He had brought the music box along in his backpack. Maybe, if nothing else, it might be a conversation starter.

"Are you interested in antiques at all? I found this in a little shop on Beacon Hill a few weeks ago," Shawn said as he produced the music box.

The young lady smiled and picked up the music box to examine it. "It's very pretty," she said, carefully opening the top. "It's too bad it doesn't work anymore," she said, handing it back to him.

"Yes, too bad," Shawn said, trying to hide his amazement. He had heard the music playing, but apparently she did not. He hadn't really believed the old shopkeeper's story at the time. Could it be true?

The following week Shawn agreed to meet another young lady for a drink. During a lull in their conversation, he produced the music box, which, while playing clearly to Shawn's ears, was again silent to this young lady as well.

Shawn went back to his apartment after this latest encounter. Now he was worried. Was he imagining this? Things like this just didn't happen! He placed the music box on the coffee table and was pouring himself a glass of wine when the doorbell rang. When he opened the door a very pretty young lady was standing there.

"Hi, I'm sorry to bother you. I'm Megan, and I just moved in down the hall. My cell battery is dead, and I need to make a call. Could I possibly use your phone?" she asked.

"Sure! And I'm Shawn, by the way. My phone's there on the coffee table. Can I get you glass of wine?"

"Thanks, that would be great," Megan said as she walked over to the coffee table. "What a lovely music box, and such a beautiful, haunting melody!"

Shawn leaned out from the kitchen holding the wine bottle. "Yes, I've always thought so," he said cautiously. Could she really hear it? he thought. So it seemed.

Megan and Shawn enjoyed their glass of wine together and talked for hours that evening. They began dating, and it was as though they had always known each other.

The next few months flew by, and Megan and Shawn fell deeply in love. As the holidays approached, it occurred to Shawn to show Megan the shop where he had found the music box that had brought them together, even though he hadn't yet told her about its magic. After all, he wasn't even sure he believed it. As they were walking toward Beacon Hill, a gentle snow began falling, giving the old section of the city a magical look all its own. They turned down the street toward the old shop, but it wasn't there! He was sure this was the right street, but there was no sign of the shop. Nothing else seemed to have changed. There was no new construction, nothing new at all on this old street, but the shop was gone.

"Well, I was sure the shop was right here," Shawn told her.

"It doesn't matter," Megan said, kissing him on the cheek.

And although Shawn couldn't see the shop, standing just inside the multi-paned windows, the shopkeeper could see the pair perfectly. "There's still room for some magic in the world," he said, as he smiled and brushed his white hair away from his pointed elfin ears.

As the couple walked down the street holding hands, Megan looked back over her shoulder smiling and, looking in through the shop window, winked at her uncle, who had helped her find love in the big city.

FISH
Elodie Olson-Coons

You are still not used to it. Every afternoon, you slip into the lukewarm turquoise of the swimming pool, marvel some days at the slippery softness of naked flesh. Other days it makes you feel sick. You kick your legs, feel them beating their separate pulses. You move slowly. So much more slowly than you want to move. Watery sounds echo and glimmer around you as you drift in the luminous shift of this tiled and captive tide. The pool is small and smells poisonous, warm and mineral. You slip underwater. Rocked by the soughing and humming of strange currents, little pumps, you watch the electric gold glow of the underwater lamps. You often stay until closing time, holding your breath full of chlorine, watching them glimmer through the water. Imagining moonlight, you try not to feel the black stretch and tightening of fabric that bites red marks into your hips.

You hate to look at them. Squirming around in the water, you make yourself glance down. He tells you he loves them you remind yourself; trying to smile at the thought. Half-sinking in the warm water, you try to think about the way he slips his warm, dry hands between them, but your stomach clenches. You do not think about it anymore. You hold the gold ring up to your face, wish your mother could see it. A band of gold that binds me true, you sing in your head, half-remembering her voice in song. The flux of ripples laps across the surface of the water, warping the light into fluid fragments that curve and rearrange incessantly. You remember that you should breathe.

Eventually you climb out, awkwardly, hating the feel of metal rungs on your feet (although it is not as bad as the tight, hot lacing-up of shoes). You feel like everyone is staring. The great windows are dark now, and the neons inside glare down on your drying skin. You want to slip back underwater, crouch in a corner of the pool until they turn all the lights off and go home. Instead, you walk slowly and carefully away from the water, remembering to balance. In the showers, everyone looks like you. You feel like a fake. You don't want to dry your hair.

The California night air is warm and muggy, and it clings around you as you walk out. From the top of the steps you see him waiting. You descend gingerly, stiff-kneed, clutching the handrail. When you climb into the car, he holds your face in both his hands and kisses you, and you try to feel a tightening in your chest. He smiles. You are still surprised by how dry his cheek feels against yours, the strange friction of stubble. His face is still the same as the first time you saw him, peering down over the side of the boat, blurring dark above his orange slicker through the pucker of pouring rain. Bright eyes, big smile, sharp cheekbones.

"Long day at the office?" You try to smile. This is something you heard someone say on television. He laughs. "The sea was pretty rough today, but it wasn't a bad catch."

You are still not used to the speed of the wheels on asphalt. Your hands clutch, white-knuckled at the sides of the seat. Wet hair drips down onto your shoulders.

"Some of the guys are going out for dinner tomorrow, that all right?"

Your shoulders slump a little. "Yes. Yeah," you say. You have been practising sounding like the others, standing in the empty carpeted lounge, echoing the televised voices. "Sure." You glance over, but his eyes are on the road.

"So what's for dinner?" You are sure your voice sounds cheerful.

"Fish," he says, and he turns on the radio.

* * *

DINNER IS HOT, AGAIN. Once when you were first married you went out for sushi, you balanced on sharp high heels, him squeezed into a black tie. You loved the delicate rolls of cold rice and seaweed, the smooth slickness of fish under your teeth. You ate the whole plate, and when you looked up, wanting to thank him, you saw something like fear in his eyes. He never took you out for sushi again. At least you eat fish often, but its texture is so soft, its taste bland, and you cannot get used to the heat that numbs your tongue. But you never say so. He already resents having to cook you realised early on from the mumblings and patterns of microwave door-slamming. He expected you to be different. To know more. You poke at the slime of white sauce and eat all the hot vegetables and have seconds of salad. You don't mind salad, especially when you add salt to the dressing. Only when he isn't looking do you permit yourself this. He is supposed to feel at ease. He is supposed to trust you.

"Baby," you try on your sweetest voice, but it sounds wrong. You do not speak very often anymore.

"Yeah?" His voice is not unkind.

"I was just . . . You know, the swimming pool. I like it there, but it's so busy and warm, it's like . . . swimming in other people's sweat." You look up, hoping for a laugh, but he is frowning a little. "I just . . ." You pause, press your lips together, breathe out. "Do you think I could come with you someday? Out to sea, I mean? Only for a little while, just one swim—" You hear the whine in your own voice and stop short.

There is a sadness in his eyes, bare and lonely, but it is a hard look too.

"You know I can't do that. Honey." A caress like an afterthought.

"Can't you just trust me?" You reach for his hand, and he does not pull it away. "I promise I won't swim off. I can't even . . . I can't swim like that anymore—"

You choke up and look down at the tabletop. He sighs.

"I'm sorry. It's not that—just . . . not yet."

He picks up his fork again; eats fast, noisily. You stare at your plate.

* * *

AFTERWARDS, YOU DO THE dishes in cold water, a few drips of salt falling unchecked into the soapsuds. You wipe your face and sit next to him as he watches television, the blue-green light flickering strangely across his face. On the screen, little bodies run around on grass. Someone is shouting in the background. Your two bodies do not touch. Your mind wanders, and the nasal voice and the glow of the screen blur.

You try to remember the whales, their huge calm movement through the water as you swam along their flanks. Their great barnacle-rimmed eyes. The fluctuating skin of the sky above, the scatter of shining fish, pebbles soft and slimy as jewels in your hand, great waving forests of kelp to wind around. Already you aren't sure what you really remember and what you've made up. Months seemed to slip through your fingers when you changed, as if time moved faster in air than water. You try to remember yourself, the powerful surge of muscles, the lithe glitter of scales.

He laughs loud and hard at something, and you start. Your cheeks are hot and wet. He is looking at the television.

* * *

"Is IT OKAY IF I just go up and take a bath?"

He sighs, rubs his hand across his eyes. "Sure."

"I'll see you upstairs."

You bend down and kiss his cheek, your lips damp on his warm dry skin. He does not move. You leave him sitting alone in the bare living room, the light from the television falling in a glowing rectangle across the floor. Padding up the carpeted stairs past the bought, framed postcards of fishing boats, you notice the paint is flaking into white scales.

You turn the shuddering right tap on full and sit by the side of the tub, listening to the splashing, staring at the rust spots. You unclothe gingerly and stretch your legs out in front of you, make yourself look at them. You hate the hair most, the poke of black like feelers. Climbing into the bath, you sit in the few inches of cold and wait for the water to rise. Already you feel a little lighter. You slide your slippery weight around, still so awkward, reach down a razor. Shivering, you slide the blade slowly along the length of your leg, bracing yourself not to look away. The pink flesh quivers vulnerably, tiny hairs rising up in the cold. The sharp metal slips accidentally once or twice, leaving fine lines of blood, and the pain is the same pain you would have felt before the change. Momentarily, the wet slickness after the blade has gone by is almost as smooth as scales. The water is high now, and you sink down under it. The cold is delicious; it washes away the slime of chlorine and the blood on your legs.

You listen to the cars going by. A band of gold that binds me true.

* * *

THERE IS A QUIET knock at the door, and you sit up suddenly, the porcelain squeaking under you.

"Can I come in?"

You smooth your hair, adjust your legs. Awkward. "Yes. Of course."

He comes in, gentle, rough, and stands looking down at you. You feel the water lapping up and down your body; it feels the same all over. It is not entirely unpleasant.

"You're so beautiful," he says a little hoarsely. He looks tired.

"Do you want to come in?" You smile shyly up at your husband.

He runs a hand through his hair, then unbuttons his shirt slowly, revealing the tangle of hair underneath. "You sure?" You nod. You suddenly remember pulling him underwater the first time, the cold salty struggle of your two forms deep under the sea. Him clasping you tight in his arms. The thump of bones and wet rope as he hauled you up onto the rough deck. The rising excitement and panic as he claimed you; the strange slipping, dissolving feeling as your tail started to melt away. How you lay on the rough plastic, heart pounding, waiting to fall in love.

He kneels down at the side of the bathtub, strokes your face. His large, hairy hand smells a little of fish. You bite the heel of his palm, and he flinches a little but leaves his salty warm skin in your mouth. Your heart aches. You reach out to pull him in, but when his arms slide around you he jumps back, splashing. "Christ! That water's freezing. Are you crazy?"

You stare back at him, hollow-eyed. He backs away from the tub, shaking his head, rubs his hand around the back of his neck. His hairy back turns towards you, and then the door slams. You hear him muttering as he paces the room. Then you think you hear him crying.

* * *

You sit for a long time, unmoving. This is not your fault, you think, and you wrap your arms around yourself. How are you supposed to remember everything, all the time? After a long time you see the light go off in the room. You grasp the sides of the bath and pull yourself out. You wrap a terrycloth bathrobe around your clammy skin and stare at the mirror. A pale, drawn face with fierce blue eyes stares out. She looks tired and sad. You hear him start to snore. The TV is still on downstairs; you can hear tinny voices buzzing. You tiptoe into the room, look down at the rumpled, warm sheets, his damp mouth open, his stubble-darkened cheek. The limp, pendulous hang of him. The hair. You look away.

* * *

You tiptoe down the stairs. The moon is shining in through the window, smooth and clouded. You cross the living room, lit for a moment by the blue glow of the television and the cold white light filtering through the curtains. At a touch from your finger, the screen goes dark with a short crackle of static. You stand staring at the empty screen. Water drips off you onto the floor. You walk across the carpet to the door, slowly lower the handle.

Until the cold night air hits you in the face, you don't know why you opened the door. In the dark, you see the bus stop glowing neon across the road. You could go anywhere. You could get to the sea. Even just for a moment.

You stop. With a smile, you pull your bathrobe tight around you. The moon glows on.

BURY ME IN FAERIE
Joann Oh

We never buried Grandma. We cremated her, even put her ashes in the designer urn she requested—that was Gran for you, glamorous to the end—but never interred her remains. *Bury me in Faerie*, her will said. *Grandma, Faerie doesn't exist*, we wanted to reply, but by that time, she was already dead.

So we took her home, put her urn in her favorite rocking chair and draped her unfinished knitting over the armrest. Jack cracked jokes at her whenever he was in the room. "So, Roxie," he'd say. "Whatcha doing later? Nothing? Maybe we could go get drinks."

"Rox-in-a-box," he liked to call her. "Good ol' Grandma Roxie."

Ma would tell him to shut up or she'd put him in a box herself, one about six inches shorter than he was tall. She would take Grandma from the chair and put her back on the mantle where she would sit until Ma's back was turned, and then the jokes started all over again. Whenever Ma worked the late shift, Jack set an extra place at the dinner table, and we ate with Grandma's urn resting next to the peas. "Pass the butter, would you, Roxie?" Jack would ask and laugh into Ma's famous macaroni casserole.

We didn't think it was wrong or disrespectful even. Gran would have liked it. She was always a prankster, a trickster. As a kid, I watched her palm caramels and shiny red apples at the grocery store countless times. She always charmed her way past the clerks and baggers, tossing her dyed, *oh-Roxie-you-don't-look-a-day-over-thirty* curls over her shoulder as she chattered about their smart-looking uniforms, the price of eggs, or any other nonsense that came to mind. Later, when the two of us shared her spoils on a park bench beneath our favorite willow tree, I'd ask her how she did it, how she could get away with anything.

"Oh you know," she said coyly, tapping the side of her nose with a perfectly manicured nail. "A flick of the fingers, a wink of the eye, and people will see whatever you want them to." She polished an apple on her new mink coat and passed it to me. "You'll catch on one day, Genny dear."

I didn't know what it was I'd catch onto until the night she was teaching herself how to cable-knit. Those who knew Gran were always surprised to learn that she knit. *Really? Roxanne? She never struck me as the domestic type.* Evenings were Gran's knitting time, when the dramas of the day had dimmed with the sun. Hair immaculately coiffed, she would settle into her rocking chair beside the yellow reading lamp and pull needles and yarn from her patent leather handbag. Her newest accessory—be it stole, scarf, or shawl—was draped over the back of her chair as she cast on and rocked. I always sat on the rug by her feet, sometimes with a book, most times without. I played cat's cradle with her yarn, tried on her lipsticks, and waited for the stories to begin. The night she learned to cable-knit, she was working with fine sable stuff that felt like dandelion fuzz in my fingers.

"Where'd you get this yarn?" I asked her, holding the dark ball against my cheek. It was softer than a summer midnight.

"From a singing tree," she replied in the same tone she might use to comment on pocket lint.

I told her she was a liar. The great thing about Gran was she always understood what I meant, even when I said the opposite. The creak-creak of her rocking chair slowed as the click-click of her needles picked up. A scarf grew like black moss from her fingers. "It's made of caterpillars' dreams," she said. Her voice was low and gravelly and sent shivers down my back—her Faerie story voice. "The trees sing the caterpillars into their cocoons where they spin in their sleep. For years and years they spin until they've dreamt their last dream. Then they wake up as butterflies." Gran bent down to take the ball of yarn from me. "This took a hundred years to make."

"A hundred years?"

"Yes, darling. I got it from a grove of soprano elders on my last visit to Faerie. Divas, the lot of them. They sang me the lament from *Dido and Aeneas*."

"Trees don't sing," Jack butted in from across the room. He was sitting in Da's old chair, the toes of his socks brushing the carpet. Ever since the funeral, he'd been acting all grown-up and tough, but I knew deep down he was just as sad and scared as I was.

"Here they don't," Gran said, "because they're sad, dumb shits. But they do in Faerie."

That shut Jack up. We were both young enough to be shocked when grown-ups cussed. Gran went back to her stockinette stitch.

"Grandma Roxie," I asked, "how do you get to Faerie?"

Gran set her knitting down and gave me her best Cheshire smile. "Simple, darling. A trip of the toes, a blink of an eye, and you'll find your way before you half know what you're doing." She got up after that and went to Jack. He was sulking with his chin on his chest. She said something to him I couldn't hear. He nodded, and they left the room "to oil up these old knees of mine beneath that beautiful full moon," Gran said, wrapping herself in her foxfur stole. "It's a fine night for a walk."

I didn't follow them, but later that night I asked Jack where they went and if Gran had taken him to Faerie.

"Faerie doesn't exist, Genevieve," he said and slammed his bedroom door in my face.

I thought I heard him crying inside, until I rubbed my eyes and my knuckles came away wet. Then I realized it was me.

* * *

GRAN NEVER DID FINISH that cable-knit scarf from the caterpillar yarn. She hardly finished anything she started knitting. There were about a hundred sets of needles and balls of yarn tucked in odd crannies around the house. Garter-stitched scarves, stockinette mittens, tricot socks, seed-stitched blankets, all in various stages of completion. When we lost the TV remote and had to hunt for it in the couch, we always found one of Gran's knitting projects jammed between the cushions. It's a wonder no one ever got stabbed by a stray needle. One year, I found a half-knitted doggie sweater snarled in the Christmas decorations. We never even had a dog.

The knitting was the hardest part for Ma after Gran died, even worse than "Rox-in-a-box." Cast-on needles and tangled yarn cropped up everywhere in the months after the funeral—buried beneath old magazines in the bathroom reading basket, wrapped around Jack's recital programs inside the piano bench, nestled behind Ma's wedding china in the hutch. When Jack and I found a bit of knitting, we'd put it on Gran's rocking chair. When Ma found anything, she'd cry.

Eventually, I put Gran's projects away in a duffel bag in my closet. I meant to finish them someday. The one completed piece I had from Gran was a Technicolor polyblend poncho. I wore it whenever I was home. Somehow, beneath the smells of me, laundry detergent, and whatever I might have spilt on it, Gran's scent still clung to the yarn. If I stuck my nose in it and inhaled really hard, I could get the faintest whiff of Chanel No. 5 with a hint of caramel and willow leaves.

* * *

GRAN STARTED DROPPING STITCHES about a year before she died. I had to help her count rows because her eyes were weakening and she was too vain to wear glasses. I bought her bigger needles and thicker yarn, but she went right along using her number two gauges, her fingers knitting away as nimble as can be. It wasn't her body that went first.

Gran also talked about Faerie a lot more in her last few months. "Did I tell you about the time a whistling spider taught me how to knit?" She had, but I told her to go on anyway. "I beat him in a whistling contest in front of the whole Faerie Court. The Queen of Faerie herself was the judge. She was wearing this gorgeous silk gown that looked just like a Valentino. Her hair spoiled it, though. Looked like a vampire had drooled all over her. Anyway, I did the *1812 Overture*. The spider tried to whistle *Ride of the Valkyries* but couldn't quite get his mandibles around it. I learned everything I know about knitting from that spider." She frowned at the red sweater sleeve in her lap, as if surprised to see that her hands had kept purling. She patted her hair and squinted at the clock. "When is your father coming home? I didn't sign up to watch you two forever, you know." Jack and I looked at each other from across the room. For once, he didn't crack a wiseass joke.

* * *

THE CABLE-KNIT SCARF OF caterpillar yarn turned up again three months after Gran's funeral. Ma found it in the pantry, crumpled behind a dusty bag of jasmine rice. She was sniffling on the kitchen floor when I came home, the fine, soft yarn snarled in her hands.

"She never stopped talking about it," Ma said between gulping sobs.

"About what?" I asked her, gently untangling the scarf from her fingers.

"About Faerie and how wonderful it was and how she always wanted to go back. And then she had to put it in her will . . ." Ma dropped her head onto my shoulder and dissolved into tears.

I wanted to comfort her, like Gran had comforted me, but that always involved Faerie stories, so I knew it was a bad idea. Instead, I held her and said, "There, there," in my best soothing voice, feeling sad and stupid and more helpless than a flipped beetle.

"I don't know what I'm going to do, Genevieve," Ma mumbled into my collar bone. "I don't know what to do."

That night, I pulled on my Technicolor poncho and wrapped the cable-knit scarf around my neck. The ends barely crossed in the front, so I pinned them together with knitting needles and stuck the extra yarn in my pocket. I waited till I was sure Ma was asleep, then snuck downstairs and pulled Grandma Roxie down from the mantle.

"What the hell are you doing?" Jack's hiss from the stairs nearly made me crap my pants. He looked silly in his too short flannel pajamas, his ginger hair sticking up in the back like a hedgehog's pins, but he was madder than I'd ever seen him.

"You scared me!" I hissed back. "I almost dropped her!" I

wrapped my arms tighter around the sleek urn.

"What are you doing with her at this time of night anyway?"

"Just something I gotta do!"

"It better not have to do with Faerie."

"So what if it does?"

"Genevieve!"

"What are you going to do, wake Ma?"

He had nothing to say to that. Just as well, because our whispered argument was getting heavy on the decibels. Under Jack's suspicious glare, I stepped into Ma's rain boots and left, the kitchen door swinging behind me.

* * *

I ASKED GRAN ONCE how come she hadn't gone back to Faerie for so long. It was the night Ma got the phone call from Da's work, telling her that her husband was dead. Gran and I were sitting on my bed, and she had her arms around me like I was a baby. I had snotted all over her silk lapel. Her cold pearls pressed into my face. "Because the trees stopped singing," she said, then shushed me and stroked my hair.

* * *

I DIDN'T KNOW WHAT I was doing, blundering around the woods that night with my grandma's ashes clutched to my chest. It was cold and quiet. My breaths sounded ragged, but they looked like beautiful white spirits in the moonlight. I followed them, hoping they would lead me to Faerie. The moon was full, too, which had to be a good sign. My hand was sweaty around the caterpillar yarn as I thought of a story from school. It was about a Greek guy named Theseus. A spool of golden thread had led him through a labyrinth. I hoped the caterpillar yarn would do the same for me. It was from Faerie, after all.

Ma's boots were too big and my poncho too thin. I felt more like a frozen rainbow popsicle than a human being, but I wasn't turning back. Not with the moon so big and beautiful in the velvet night sky. Around me, leafless trees raised naked black branches in a fey-like dance. The air was thick with magic and caterpillar dreams.

I racked my brains for every Faerie story Gran had ever told me. "How did she say she'd get there?" I muttered aloud. "A chink in your eye? A flick on your nose?"

I stumbled over Ma's boots and the woods whirled around me, as if I were in a snowglobe being shaken upside down. I hit the ground with a *crack!*, my eyes shut tight. As I lay there for a few heartbeats, pinpricks of light bloomed against the dark insides of my eyelids like fake snow swirling around a toy forest.

The woods were the same when I opened my eyes again, gnarly, leafless, and flooded with moonlight. Beneath me, Grandma Roxie was broken, her ashes scattered on the cold ground. The wind picked up, cutting through my poncho. A wisp of ash rose into the trees and, for the briefest moment, I thought I heard singing.

ONCE, I WAS AVEDON
Tim Belden

1. Vision War

I was born willow boned, a legacy of Russian Jews
who survived winter by feeding sinew with poetry.
My mother told stories of huts dancing on chicken legs
where the witches lived. Baba Yaga and Vasilisa coexisted
with bread lines that cast black shadows on winter
New York streets. But Vasilisa, the Beautiful, was a ghost.

Grey faces flickered on a white screen, documentaries
of the Okie exodus, and the blossoming of war
across an ocean where fabled ancestors forgot
medieval ritual, replaced by Blitzkrieg. Panzer tanks
and concentration camps flashed across white silk
in dark, crowded rooms, forums for reality in black and white.

When I joined the Merchant Marine, we scanned
monochrome horizons for the bubble trails
of torpedoes from U-boats as invisible as sea serpents.

In dark cities with nameless streets, words failed,
but images held. The out-of-focus masses passed
and disappeared in a diaspora from one place
to somewhere less dangerous. I was witness
to this. The war ended for a short time.

Wedding gowns dropped in folds around the fractured ankles
of Aphrodite. Consumed by images, I danced with my tender
film prisoners. America and Europe built bridges of bomb
shattered brick, and celebrities paraded across ramparts.

Desire and fashion realigned in the west, among victors—so called.
I was an outsider, the secular Jew with a camera. My Rolleiflex
had two eyes, aligned vertically on a skull of aluminum,
stretched with skin. The silver film-brain glowed through sockets,

a fire I brought home to burn away my idealism on panatomic-x.

Silent streets filled with manic laughter. New York
was Babylon, city of exiles. I was the portraitist of diaspora.

2. A Lens
I imagined my Dovina in a dress by Dior as she
captivated elephants. Everyone wanted a new mask.
Marilyn was once too; she pulled curtains apart, revealing
Norma Jean transformed into Venus. She bore witness
to the furnace of the creation of human spirit, a courage
of the vulnerable, whose price was the scorn of those
who rejected a procession of a soul toward a human wisdom.

And Groucho was my wise, old, Jewish clown, my father
who cannot die before me, an observer of the riotous
dissolution of language, the comic, Yiddish, Golem,
destroyer of pretense, created from dust by his own hand.
His comedy was born in an ecstatic loneliness.

Before him, a silent knight named Charlie borrowed the horns
of Bacchus and flaunted pleasure in the face of McCarthy's
Red Scare. In the wake of his escape to Switzerland, he left fugues
of laughter, and danced as Pan in a cave that he dug with cane
and cello. He is the father of my compassion in hard times.

3. Spun Compass
Migrations measured the dispossessed, of those so failed
in community that loneliness is the last chimera. In the American West,
I leapt from the car when I saw him, a drifter among mountains
with a warrior's eyes. A Siberian prince with sinewy limbs,
I saw the eyes of my distant past. But his was an eastern star,
and mine west. We met in the middle, inheritors of two migrations.
James Benson was my transcendent mirror, an ancient self portrait.

Billy Mudd drove a truck in Texas, loaded with dynamite.
He was a giant on the edge, grinding teeth as his explosive
payload jolted over Texan potholes. He enjoyed comparison
with Pecos Bill, who ate dynamite for breakfast, but Billy
truly lamented, over a mug of rye, the loss of his
Slew Foot Sue. He was pure Irish, he said, and his hoard
huddled on the banks of the Ohio River before the gold rush
dispelled fear of Indians and memories of potato famines.
His Baba Yaga became Coyote, his mind-bending trickster.

Ronald Fischer found us in California. Chimera in the land
at quest's end, this new, imperfect Okie home, the bee-man lent
me his body, half-man, half-hive. His skull houses the colony,
his brain, a honey. He was as close as I dare come to a pure poetry.

* * *

I am here in this silver place with gratitude to those whose light
in my lens gives me life. Once, I was. Now, we are.

THE PERSISTENCE OF UALA
Erin T. Mulligan

THE LANDS BEYOND
THE LANDS WE KNOW

AUBADE
Jennifer Whitaker

This isn't how the waking goes: delicate brush of lips,
kiss of sunlight, a single red rose at the breast.
The glossy pages try to spin this lie to gold,

but it's the older story she knows is real: land dry
as a mud-caked palm, tower's bell rusted, dulled tongue,
a girl asleep on a rotting throne.
                              A single thread of flax,
and the world went dark: a cursed girl, left by a father for dead.
Roses clotted and thorned the gates; even daylight
dimmed wicked there, the pin-sharp shadows growing tall.

Then the man who smelled like a king—
boxwood and exotic citrus—peered in,
                    his hounds wailing, plaintive
                    quivering legs commanded to stay,
and the sight of her lying there—cursed sleep
an elixir paling her cheeks—brought him in.
He trembled, her beauty
                         still and silent
as a copse of willow, as a cool corpse on the field.
He cops a feel. His luck: the sleeping can't scream.
And since no one saw, it is forgotten:
the moths startling from her dress,
her trellised veins cloyed to bruise.

She wants to warn this other girl how she'll really wake:
alone again, gown a heap of shadow on the floor,
still cursed to see the coming dawn
strike axe-like through the dark.

AROWANA
Carlos F. Mason Wehby

It has been told that in the village of Paduchai lived a woman of sixteen named Diache. Her parents were poor farmhands, and Diache worked for no money as a kitchen apprentice. Each day after her sunrise meal, she reported to the town kitchen to prepare, serve, and clean up after the town workers' noon meal. Then Diache took leave of the other apprentices who went swimming or smoking at the river, and she hiked from the poorer outskirts of the village up Paduchai Hill to the wealthier town center.

There among the luxurious houses and lavish gardens was a deep, dirty old fountain. It was tiered—there were five circular steps—and at the top, floating upon the water that cascaded down around it, was an enormous stone water lily plant. The flower itself hovered triumphantly over the fountain, as if it had dragged itself and its lily pads up the stairs, against the current, to reign above tumult. Diache spent her afternoons peering at her turbulent reflection in the base of the pool. She listened to the susurrus of the fountain's waterfall and occasionally lifted her eyes up the five steps to the floating lily.

Of the fountain's history or significance, Diache knew nothing. Diache simply loved the fountain, whatsoever a relic it was. She had spied it as her parents had dragged her around town some years previous begging for work, and since she had found the fountain again a year ago, she had come every day to visit her floating lily.

Thus Diache visited the fountain every afternoon for a year without incident. But as she found herself there alone the following day, a voice spoke to her from the fountain.

"You are almost seventeen," it said.

The voice wasn't unfriendly, but there was a grating or scratchy quality which made it unpleasant. Diache turned to search for the source of the voice. Had someone sneaked up behind her?

"Don't you wish to be married?" the voice said.

It was coming from the fountain. Diache returned her gaze to the deep fountain pool and spotted—

"You are a fish!" she said. The fish was long with dark scales the color of the murky fountain water. "What are you doing in my fountain?" Diache said, and she waved her fist at the fish: "Remove yourself at once!"

"The fountain is my home, Diache," the fish said. "But there is man I want you to meet. Come back tomorrow, as usual."

Diache ran away. Somehow the fish could speak and it knew her name—and it must have been watching her for how many days now? It was also true that her parents, being so poor, had yet to arrange a husband for her. But the fish was intruding on her fountain! Could she remove it somehow?

Diache raced home. She would ask her parents for advice about the fish when they returned from the fields for the sunset meal—

Only her parents were already home when she arrived. They had both been fired that afternoon. "You work too much together, even when there is only work for one," the farmer had said, and he dismissed them. Typically they brought the makings of a sunset meal home with them from work, imperfect specimens from the farmer's gardens, but tonight there would be no food. Tonight they would all go hungry. Diache did not want to disturb her parents' grief with any ridiculous news about a talking fish.

Diache's stomach allowed her little rest. She awoke early. She circled her morsel-less home until she found herself setting the table for a bountiful sunrise meal—plates, knives, forks, and spoons. Between her parents' plates, Diache left a note in which she promised to return with food.

"Greetings, Diache," the fish said as the young woman approached the floating lily fountain.

Without word, Diache went knife first into the fountain. She slaughtered the talking fish, a feast to feed her family. She hoisted the fish up onto the lip of the fountain pool, and then she climbed out of the fountain and shivered, slimy wet.

The fish was too heavy. Diache rolled it off the lip of the fountain into her two open arms, but the weight sent her reeling backwards—

Strong hands supported her from behind. Diache looked up behind her, and into the face of the farmer's son, Rodgo. Rodgo recognized Diache as well, but he was more impressed by the fish.

"That is an arowana fish," he said. "There is nothing more delicious."

Diache had never heard of an arowana fish. She remembered the fish's words about meeting a man at the fountain—but surely the fish did not mean the farmer's son?

"I saw you catch the fish," Rodgo said. "But your home is too far and the fish too heavy for you to carry it there alone."

"My parents will help me," Diache lied, but maybe she could send someone for their help?

"If you prepare that fish for me, I will get your parents their jobs back," Rodgo said.

Diache knew it was a good bargain. Though her parents would be hungry for now, they would be pleased to have their jobs back. Reluctantly, Diache accepted Rodgo's help and followed him to his parents' mansion.

Diache had never cooked arowana before, but her apprenticeship served her well. She knew how to clean and prepare the fish, and from the arowana's texture, she guessed how to season and cook it as well. The farmer's son was impatient, though, and Diache did not have time to taste the fish before she was ushered into the dining room to serve the farmer's son.

Diache watched as the farmer's son took a bite—and another and another. He was enjoying it! Diache was proud at having won her parents' their jobs back—

But then Rodgo's throat began to swell, and his face turned black.

"What is happening?" he said. "Didn't you remove the tongue?" he choked.

But why would she do that? "Fish tongues are delicious," she said.

"Arowana tongues are poisonous, you beast!" Rodgo wheezed, grasping at his throat. "Fetch the doctor!"

Diache ran for the doctor. How could she have known the tongue was poison? Where did the doctor live? She did not know this part of town well, so she asked and was directed to a modest house close by. The doctor's house was directly opposite the floating lily fountain.

Fortunately the doctor was home and available. Diache was shown into his study where he sat alone, engrossed in a book.

Diache stood and waited for the doctor's attention, but he continued to read. With Rodgo dying, she could wait no more:

"Are you the doctor?" Diache said.

The doctor pulled the book away from his face, but his expression did not change. Diache almost forgot Rodgo altogether—this doctor was the most beautiful man Diache had ever seen. She wanted to hide, but with nothing to hide behind, she remembered why she had come.

"The farmer's son—Rodgo—he is sick with arowana poison," she said.

"Yes," the doctor said, without smiling or frowning. He waved Diache over with one hand as he set the book down on his lap and reached into his pocket with the other. From his pocket he withdrew a small glass bottle from which he withdrew a pill, and the doctor placed the pill in the center of Diache's outstretched palm. The doctor's fingers did not touch Diache's hand, but she felt a tingle as the pill passed from the doctor's hand to hers.

"Have him take this," he said. Then the doctor returned to his book.

"Is that all?" Diache said. Was it so simple?

"It will pass," the doctor said.

"Won't you come yourself?" Diache said. The doctor was so

handsome, and his house was across from the arowana's fountain. Could he have been who the arowana intended? Had she thrown his love away when she butchered the fish?

The doctor ignored her. Seconds passed, and Rodgo's emergency overtook her. She hurried to the farmer's house with the pill.

Rodgo's hands had now turned black as well. He could still breathe, but he sounded like a wounded animal.

"The doctor said to give you this," Diache said, and she gave Rodgo the pill. The farmer's son hesitated—it was not a small pill. "Here," Diache said, offering Rodgo a glass of water.

The farmer's son put the pill in his mouth, and then he drank the water, swallowing the pill—

Rodgo's mouth began to foam and his body began to shake. He fell from his chair.

"What have you done?" he said. "Are you trying to kill me?"

He meant it. The proud and arrogant young man was on the verge of tears now. He began to vomit and Diache pitied him.

Hysterical, she ran back to the doctor. She explained everything—the pill, the water, the foam, the seizures, the vomit—

The doctor flew to his feet and out the door, Diache in pursuit. They found the farmer's son still very sick on the dining room floor, surrounded by his servants who were trying to both clean the mess and somehow make Rodgo comfortable.

Again the doctor withdrew a glass bottle from his pocket and a pill from the bottle—was it the same one? Then he explained to Rodgo:

"I am going to place this pill below your tongue. Let it dissolve there." Then emphatically he said, for all to hear: "Do not swallow it."

Rodgo nodded and took the pill. The vomiting immediately stopped, and the fits subsided gradually. Color returned to the young man's face and hands. As the servants helped the farmer's son into his chair, the farmer himself returned from the fields having heard of his son's emergency.

Diache was relieved to see Rodgo healed, no matter the miscommunication that passed between the doctor and herself. She was about to thank the doctor for healing Rodgo when she heard the farmer's son speak:

"Call the police, father. Diache has tried to kill me."

Diache looked to the doctor to speak up for her, but as before in his study, the doctor only ignored her.

Diache panicked. The farmer blocked the front door, so she made for the back, out of the dining room and through the kitchens. She screamed when she saw the arowana carcass—what had moved her to slaughter the magical fish? Diache took the arowana remains with her, carrying it over both her arms, as she ran out of the kitchens into the streets.

But where should she go? Already the arowana grew heavier and heavier in her arms. Diache dashed to the floating lily fountain. She hoisted the arowana carcass into the fountain, contrite for her murder. If only returning the arowana to its home could somehow undo the day's mischief. Instead the floating lily fountain immediately began to flow with blood.

Diache ran to her home. She knew the way well. She would grab what little she could, some extra clothes at least, and run away from the village before the police arrived. She would not stay and shame her parents, adding to their burdens.

Quickly she entered her house. "The police are coming for me!" Diache said as she packed her few belongings into a bag.

Her parents had been waiting for her return at the table.

"The police?" her father said.

"But where is the food?" her mother said.

"Did you try to steal food?" her father said.

Diache tried to tell them her story and leave, but they interrupted her—

"You took the arowana to the farmer's house?" her father said.

"You took the food to our persecutor?" her mother said.

Diache tried again to explain, but her parents' confusion and interruptions ruined her escape. The police twins arrived.

Diache's parents' home was plain; it had no back door. Diache was trapped. She surrendered herself to the police.

As per the Paduchai custom, the police came bearing bread. They sat Diache and her family at the table and they broke bread with the family that was to be divided.

"Enjoy your last meal together," the police said in unison.

Diache looked to her parents—her father began to contest her crimes.

"You will eat in silence," the police demanded. "The court will decide her fate."

Diache's family chewed their bread slowly. As per the custom, the police ate with them. The bread was delicious, especially to those so hungry, but Diache could not properly enjoy it. Her parents did not understand, and Diache could not explain. When they had all finished, the police placed a burlap sack over Diache's head and escorted her out of the house to be tried.

The police twins marched Diache across town to the court by the farmer's house, but the judge was not there. This judge was the farmer's brother and Rodgo's uncle. He was away helping tend to his nephew who continued to demand care though his dangers had passed.

The twins marched Diache to the next closest court, yet this judge was also gone. She had been called away to investigate rumors that there was a corpse found in a nearby fountain.

Finally, the police twins escorted Diache to a third judge, closer to her home. Ghotai was his name, and he had only just completed his apprenticeship. He wore the bright yellow ceremonial robes of a novice judge.

The police twins sat Diache in a chair across from the judge, and she made her confession to him with the sack over her head. Ghotai was thorough, and he questioned Diache extensively.

"Where did you find this arowana?" he asked her, and, "How did you know it was in the fountain?"

Diache cried as she told the judge of the talking fish in the floating lily fountain.

"What did the fish tell you?" the judge asked.

"The fish told me to return today and it would introduce me to my future husband," Diache said.

Though she did not expect the judge or anyone to believe her, Diache felt relieved to tell someone the truth.

"Had fish or other creatures spoken to you before?" Ghotai questioned.

"No."

"Why did you kill the fish?" Ghotai asked.

"My family was hungry," Diache said.

"Why was your family hungry?" Ghotai asked.

"The farmer dismissed them from their jobs," Diache admitted.

Ghotai stopped there. He did not second guess her account of the magical fish, nor did he ask Diache if she poisoned the farmer's son on purpose.

As per the custom, Ghotai said to the police, "Has she tasted her last bread?"

"She ate with her family," the police twins responded in unison.

"Remove her mask so she can receive her sentence," Ghotai said.

The twins removed the burlap sack from Diache's face.

"Diache," the judge said, "You have two choices. You can leave Paduchai and never return. Or you can stay in Paduchai—but if you stay, you may never cook again."

"But I am a kitchen apprentice! If I am not to cook, how will I work?"

"Diache, I am a judge, not the suitor your arowana suggested. I will not ask you to join me in marriage, but I ask you to join me as a judge. I cannot easily believe that a fish spoke to you, but I do believe you, that you have spoken truthfully. If you have lied to me, I ask that you leave Paduchai. But if you spoke the truth, sit with me here today and everyday. Help me listen for the truth in people's stories and in people's hearts."

Diache considered her choices. She loved her parents, but she hated the farmer, his son, and the doctor. Another judge would have had her killed or enslaved. Perhaps it would be better to leave . . .

But perhaps she could always leave. Perhaps she could stay and learn to listen as Ghotai had listened. Though Ghotai could not believe her story, he believed in her.

"I will stay, Ghotai," Diache said. "You have taught me that people's words are perhaps like arowana tongues: they can be impossible to swallow. But indeed I have spoken the truth, and I will listen to the accused like they are arowana fish—for today I am married, if not in the way I imagined."

STARLIGHT!
Alex Stein

A king and a queen were in a carriage. The king was eating quince, if you catch my drift, when the carriage rolled to a stop. "What is it?" the king called out.

"Robbers, your highness," called back the coachman.

"Pay them no mind," said the king. "Drive on."

"I've tried ignoring them, your highness, but they have pointed their guns," said the coachman.

"That would tend to distract one," the king relented. "Have them wait a moment and I'll come out and speak with them."

"I think that is what they had in mind, your highness," said the coachman.

"I'll just be a moment," the king said to the queen, "try to remember where we were."

"Hurry," said the queen.

The queen was monumentally impatient, although since she was a queen, she was generally referred to as imperious.

She was wearing the most beautiful long gown ever worn by royalty in any court, at any time, anywhere. It was made of spun gold and silk threads from China. From China, mind you, on the whole other side of the world. You had to pass through sea monsters of every kind, just to get there. She ran her palms over the fabric. It was like perfectly cool water.

The king emerged from his carriage into the bright afternoon. A little too bright for his tastes. He had always found the summer sun in these parts impertinently harsh and he longed to invoke his royal authority over it, but he was not quite so mad, yet, that he actually believed he could.

(The time would come, though).

Three masked men on horses were waiting for him, all with their pistols pointed. It was outrageous. "Put those weapons down immediately!" commanded the king.

And then, what do you suppose happened? The queen stuck her head out of the carriage door. "The queen!" one of the masked men cried out. "We didn't know you was in the carriage, your highness," said another. All three jumped down from their horses and bowed low. Without, however, ceasing to grip their pistols.

"Drop your weapons!" the king commanded again.

"I'm afraid we cannot do that, your highness," said one of the masked men.

"You can and you will," said the King.

The queen had retired back into the carriage where she was buffing her nails. She was a little hungry, too, so she called out to the coachman, "Driver, have we any peaches?"

"I'll have a look in just a moment, your highness," the coachman called back. He was slowly uncovering the gun he always carried in a basket on the seat beside him.

"Your highness," said one of the masked men, "we are thieves. Please hand over all your jewels or I shall have to shoot your coachman."

"I don't care if you do shoot my coachman," said the king. "Go ahead. Be my guest."

The coachman decided it was time for a desperate gamble. He didn't like the direction things were headed. He pulled out the gun, cocked it, fired it, cocked it, fired it, cocked it, fired it. All three thieves fled. One died about a hundred yards distant. Another died at home a few days later when the bullet wound on his shoulder got infected after his brother tried to remove the piece of bullet still lodged in the muscle, using rye whiskey as a sanitizer and a hunting knife as a scalpel. The third had been grazed in the leg. A month later, he was back thieving.

"Good shooting, driver" said the king. "Now, try to make up for lost time, will you? We don't want to be late. Run the horses until they froth. I've got a stable full."

He stepped back into the carriage.

"The coachman has forgotten my peach," was the first thing the queen said to him.

"He has done his duty by us," replied the king, "never you mind about the peach."

"I asked him to find me a peach," said the queen.

"Driver," called the king, "did your queen ask you for a peach?"

"Your highness, I have it right here, I was just about to bring it to her."

"I don't want it," said the queen. "Fling it to the ground and get the horses moving. These delays are intolerable."

* * *

THE CLATTER OF THE carriage wheels and the clopping of horse hooves. The sound of thunder. A very agreeable silence fell upon the king and queen. All in all they were quite happy together. What she needed, he could arrange and what he needed she had. Also their ambitions ran parallel. Both wanted to be infallible. "Though it would be enough," the king, in a perhaps regrettable moment of candor, once admitted to the queen, "just to be considered infallible."

"Lovely, isn't it?" said the king.

"Don't spoil everything," said the queen. But it was too late. He had spoken, when it was really the time to let the atmosphere do the speaking. She folded her arms across her breasts. Always a bad sign. And her face went tight.

Fortunately the king suddenly remembered where he had been, before the interruption by would-be-thieves. He got down on his knees in the carriage. The only time he ever got down on his knees. The king would not even pray on his knees. But this, he did gladly.

The queen, with her head back, listened to the rain driving harder and harder upon the carriage roof.

He hadn't spoiled the atmosphere, after all, he had just impeded its reception. Now he was augmenting its reception. Life had a funny way of giving you back anything you thought you had lost, the queen thought.

She remembered suddenly being a young princess and watching lightning from her balcony. She had two ladies attending her at all times and they had joined her for the spectacle. A three pronged fork crashed into the forest just a few hundred yards away and when the thunder came immediately afterward, she had felt weak and the ladies attending her had each taken one arm and led her to her bed.

"You," she said to the younger of the two ladies, "stay. And you," she said to the older of the two, "go."

When they were alone in the room together, the remaining attendant curtsied and asked, "What would you have me do, your highness?"

In the carriage, under the ministrations of the king, the queen had gone quite over the edge.

Afterward, she slept and the king slept, too. It was deep in the night when the carriage finally bumbled to a halt. "We're here!" cried out the coachman.

In a moment, two dozen servants descended upon the carriage.

When one of them finally made bold to open the carriage door, their repeated calls and knocks having produced no response, they found the king and queen wrapped in one another's arms, sleeping like wolf cubs sated at their wolf-mama's teat.

For the servants it was a rare moment of being able to look into the faces of their lieges without the fear of being looked back at. They looked at the two faces. Just another pair of sleepers. All the same when we sleep, we are. Kings and servants, alike.

* * *

THE FOLLOWING MORNING, OTHER kings and queens began to arrive and our king and queen, Robert and Eleanor, rose to greet them.

"You are looking well, your majesty."

"Not so well as you, your majesty."

Only kings and queens, not even princes and princesses, just the upper crust of the upper tier and a few hundred necessary servants.

"Aren't we handsome."

"Haven't we the finest clothes."

"Don't we make the most glorious community."

Would that there were only castle after castle and king and queen after king and queen, just as it was in that place, on that morning.

"Shall we repair to the dining hall?"

"May I take your mantle?"

"Crown polish is deucedly difficult to purchase, don't you find?"

"Has anyone seen my jester?"

". . . so then we drank wine from the Holy Grail, which had somehow found its way into his possession along with a number of other sacred artifacts and art objects . . ."

". . . for getting the wax out of signet rings . . ."

"And then I said, 'No, my country is declaring war on you, how do you like that?' And he said, 'War? No, no, no, I said Mike Huntley is the clarion we are on to.' Frankly, that didn't even make sense, but I was quite relieved. It is costly to declare war and often other people's children are made to die by such declarations and while that is far better than one's own children dying, it is still something that ought to give one pause."

"But other people's children are what keep us free."

"Yes, let's drink to other people's children and the inevitable wars in which they all must die."

* * *

BY THE AFTERNOON, MOST of the kings and queens had gone to their rooms to rest. Many of them made love. Some, even to one another.

Our king and queen, Robert and Eleanor, wrote letters and conversed idly.

"How does this sound, Robert?" Eleanor asked her husband. "Dear Penelope [their daughter]: Your father and I miss you terribly. Your father especially. I love you so. It's a blessing for you, of course, but I will be glad when you have married. Guess what? We met a queen named Penelope. Perhaps, when you become queen, you and she can enjoy a laugh together over the coincidence. Her husband King Hubert is quite insane. He has two crowns, one that he changes into when he uses the toilet to evacuate his bowels and one for the rest of the time. Why does he need a crown at all when he sits on the toilet? Can he not just leave it with one of the attendants for the duration? Dear Penelope, do not think I did not ask him that. I did. Do you know what he replied. "My dear, what if the toilet is the place I drop dead? That is the one thing even a king cannot know. His hour." Can you imagine, Penelope? What gaucherie. And I think he believed it a drollery, if he did not in fact believe it a profundity. Never become deluded, dear Penelope. I forbid it, your loving mother, Eleanor."

"I like that forbiddance at the end," said Robert. "It is a good gesture. Really feels imperious. But I wonder, is that precisely the tone you mean to take with our daughter?"

"It is my tone, for good or for bad. I haven't another."

"Quite right, my dear. But, I may add a line or two, if you don't mind."

"How about I just write, 'Your father says,' and you tell me what you'd like to say?"

"Excellent."

"So, what do you say?"

"Hello, precious Penelope, it is your father. Have you noticed how the farther away from me you get, the younger you become?"

"That's it?" asked Eleanor.

"Too cryptic?"

"It's what that Belgian king's jester said in his routine yesterday."

"Add that I love her. Put it like this: I love you."

"Anything else?"

"We'll be home soon. The conference is very dull, but your mother and I are accomplishing a lot in the way of diplomatic relationships. Oh, and mention that several of the kings and queens brought chessboards with the pieces made in their likenesses and the likenesses of their court. Tell her it is so totally cool watching two royals compete over likenesses of themselves on a chessboard. Tell her, I'm thinking of having one made for us. No, don't tell her that. She already thinks I am the vainest, most self-centered person alive. No offense, Eleanor. It's just perception."

"None, taken."

"Should I tell her?"

"I think she'll think it's a charming idea."

"I never know how she will react to anything, anymore. It's that Prince Whatsis from the Kingdom of Hooey."

"It sounds pejorative the way you say it."

"I know, but that's just his name, isn't it? And the name of his father's kingdom."

"You're jealous."

"And isn't that a father's right?"

"It's more like a father's shame. Or should be."

"How can my own thoughts shame me? How can the thoughts of a king ever be shameful? No, it is my divine right to be jealous of that dope, Whatsis from Hooey. I hope he breaks his cock in a horse riding accident."

"Robert! Enough."

Robert laughed at his own divine faculties. What insight he possessed. "That dope, Whatsis from Hooey," he'd said. A triumph of observation. And as to the comment about him breaking his cock, just think of it. His own daughter Penelope would otherwise be receiving the brunt of the thing and that couldn't be good for family morale, now could it? Yes, he was perfectly right to hate that prince and he was perfectly right to want his daughter all for himself.

* * *

THAT EVENING WAS THE masquerade ball at which all the kings and queens dressed up like other kings and queens. It was a stitch. One king and queen even cross-dressed one year, but the next year the king had the queen committed and the cross-dressing was one of the acts he cited as evidence of her extreme imbalance. Of his own participation he simply said, "At that time I was still doing everything I could to help Brunella [for that was her name] feel that she was still participating in a shared reality."

Eleanor loved the masquerade ball. She was dressed as a French queen. The real French queen would be dressing (*quel jeste!*) as the queen of China. The real queen of China would not be in attendance.

Robert was dressing as the king of England. All the other kings dressed as the King of England. The real king of England stayed home. A messenger said that he had food poisoning.

"Last year it was an attack by crocodiles," the other kings complained.

The king of England never came. He did not have to. One by one the other kings and queens would come to him. Some looking for favors, some merely to witness the marvels of his court, about which they had heard so much.

"Are you ready?" asked Eleanor.

"I'm not," admitted Robert, "but if you give me five minutes, I can be."

* * *

"CERTAINLY I DON'T THINK beheading should be decreed gratuitously. If, for example, the man has children, and his crime was not callous, they should be able to bury his body decently. Most of the criminals I sentence are not congenitally evil, they became criminals through lack of alternative. So a beheading seems excessive. Call me sentimental, but what about death by asphyxiation? Just as simple to effect upon a bound man, and leaves the children a beautiful corpse. Temper with mercy, that is my motto. Temper with mercy."

"God made us kings and queens, but we must make ourselves wise."

"Hear, hear!"

"Whatever the cushion on your throne is, that should be the cushion in the coffin, under your head. If you wear an ermine mantle, don't get it wet. It will smell funny. That was all the advice he ever gave me. Fathers, 'eh? Not that I'm complaining. I got his kingdom. That's better than good advice."

"I hear the palace of Versailles has been overthrown."

"No, no, it's just being redecorated."

"The peasants have no bread? I said. Let them eat cake. In retrospect a bit of unnecessary incitement. But in my own defense, they were just peasants. Who knew they would rise up and destroy me?

They usually just wallowed in their own filth and genuflected. Who knew they had these other dimensions buried in them, awaiting birth. Revolution? Good grief! Who could have ever seen revolution in those idiot faces? If I had given them cake, they'd have eaten it until they exploded. I did them a favor. They were not ready for rule, whether or not they were able to take it. They were never going to be ready. Not in my time, nor in my children's children's children's time. And did I really have to be beheaded? Really? If I'd been them, I'd have kept me around and humiliated me sexually, but hell, the peasants lack real imagination and that perhaps is why a violent revolution was the only means around which they could organize. They might have tried asking first, is what I am saying. You never know. I might have said, yes, peasants, take the throne, and the palace, it was yours all along, you had only to believe that. Hell, I might have said anything. I was the queen. A queen can be as whimsical as she wishes to be. Hell, she can be a madwoman and so long as she is queen her madness can be made into law."

* * *

"Lovely night," said Robert, afterwards. After the costumes were removed and both were abed.

It had been a lovely night. Eleanor's heart was full.

* * *

First thing the next morning, Robert and Eleanor had already to be getting back. The kingdom could not run itself, you know. Besides, they looked forward to the carriage ride, the long hours of unbroken privacy.

A king and a queen are really just a husband and a wife, are they not? Just a man and a woman.

Who were once a boy and a girl.

And before that puking, mewling babes.

And before that?

(Starlight!)

DETOURS:
A SUBURBAN FAIRY TALE
Sarah Elizabeth Schantz

I: The woods line the backyard like a fence. Even during the day, they stand dark. They watch and night falls. The roots of the trees reach deep. Silhouetted against the sky, the filigree pines point upward, like arrows—their boughs and needles inky. Ephemeral, the sky is absorbent, like newsprint, and the space in between smears. This gives way to definition and looks cut-out, like something Mother clips from construction paper. Like the paper dolls she makes for Daughter, paper girls unfolding forever from each other's bodies. The eye returns to that place in between the sky and woods—where the separation occurs; that raggedness, the way skin tears. "*Rough around the edges.*" Like something Father sands smooth in his woodshop.

II: The flagstone patio opens into the yard by way of puzzle-pieced rock, flat and marked by the signatures of thyme, silver under the moon. The grass is experimenting green. Tall thistles guard in between the kept and wild. The sliver moon is upside down, and the stars blink: on off, on off. The kitchen window is a square of warmth, and dirty moths thud against the glass.

Daughter has left the flashlight in the grass.

III: Just a second ago it was playtime, and they had run in circles, bath towels tied like capes around their necks (hers was red). They were imitating super heroes. It's not often that parents pretend to fly, but parents really stop playing when they are done. "Get that flashlight!" Mother says, turning faucets and squirting dish soap. "*Now!*" she says, from another world.

IV: Her small hands wrap around the edge of the door; she fingers the textured screen. Inside Mother readjusts her weight, fitting the blue willow into, and beside the other blue willow; the plates and bowls drip dry on the metal rack. Mother is tired. The girl can see that just as she can see *them*. Their long snouts, the bristle outline of agile bodies. They dart from tree to tree, along the cusp, aware of borders, but not necessarily mindful.

V: First one foot (hard enough), then the other. Barefoot, her skin is periwinkle against the stone. The creatures chase each other and breach the perimeters of the yard, lacing: in out, in out, *scurry scuttle*. She ignores the sky, watches her feet and the earth beneath—she makes it to the grass. The blades tickle her legs. As she runs, she bends to scratch her ankles, and this makes her trip, makes her fall. Her white nightgown stains green, and she skins her knee so there is dirt and blood as well; brown and red. She crawls toward the flashlight just within her reach. The woods shift. Tree and shadow switch places. Seek hides. Sliver moon dives and stars drop. Telephone wires remain strung between worlds. Wolves bark and dogs snarl.

* * *

VI: Having bled for a year, Daughter knows how to bandage herself. Mother taught that Vaseline helps with tampons. In the bathroom, she washes her face with Noxzema; she scours the angry zits. It feels like spiders are nesting in her pubic hair, spinning webs. She cannot predict herself. She reaches—trying to fit this new body; it takes the bones forever to catch up with the growing.

VII: She must meet Boy in the woods. She knows how to run the zigzag between the trees. Yellow flashes through the branches, dust shifting: the exchange of molecules. That constant *scurry scuttle* close behind. The Boy reaches for her; he fits inside her body, which helps her fit inside herself; she lies down with him, and she unfolds. Night falls and her uterus swallows the sky. Inside the stars blink: off on, off on.

* * *

Sickness morning. "*I just don't feel well, Mother.*" She feels their footsteps inside. *Never Again the Same.* The Boy wrote this, again and again on the alley wall, and she worried the police would come; she shifted from one foot to the other, wearing the weight of his studded and spiked leather jacket. It was raining and the water made the red spray paint run.

She knows her Mother's story. Pregnant at sixteen with no turning back. Yet the Mother got the Husband with the leather brief case and the paisley neck ties. The credit cards and the two story house with the unfinished basement, in the brand new housing division, Legacy Estates, built where once there had been woods. Before a Land Protection Act stopped the sprawl and the hungry bulldozers; that stopped the houses that would have marched on— all the way to the interstate. The freeway where the signs are posted every half mile: No hitchhiking.

It was her poem, but the Boy stole it from her. He didn't just write it on walls. He submitted it to their teacher, and the teacher told him to read it out loud, and after he did all the girls wanted to be his, and he forgot all about her. She vows never to return to school. At night, in bed, the Daughter breathes in and out, and just to see—she inflates the belly as big as it will go.

* * *

VI: There is no denying anymore, the Daughter. She is full, will deliver soon. Thus Mother must. She takes to the woods after Husband falls asleep with the newspaper and the television muted. The headlines read: *Reintroducing Wolves* and *Suburbia Says, Send Them Back!* On the screen a wolf bares his teeth and the camera zooms in on the bloodstained snow; the deer carcass blooming red on the cold white. The antennas try to pick up what she's doing; they twitch and sniff the air: *What are these rituals?* Not for you to know. Husband snores as Wife opens night. Into the woods, she carries the almost grown Daughter, and like nesting dolls, she also carries the other Daughter, the one who is barely.

V: "*I've been waiting,*" the Wolf says. He is feeding furniture to the fire. Standing upright for tonight, his movements are robotic. Or perhaps the stiffness comes from his tuxedo. Black and white, and from this comes the gray; he's taken off the bow tie, and from his flesh sprout tufts of salt and pepper fur. This Wolf, who walks the line between beast and man, can only appear when summoned; he has wearied from centuries of undoing.

He feeds the fire, just as anyone on a quest because that is all there is to do.

No notion of monthly credit card statements or mortgage rates. He only cares that it will burn. They still owe on the chaise lounge and the kitchen island, but the points of light leap higher. The Mother knows that they will always owe. The Wolf has his own debts to pay. He has the same contract; to replace himself. The Mother lays the Daughter down—the white cast iron bed is there, domestic and waiting in the woods; the girl is so heavy the Mother wonders how she carried her own body. The Woman undresses; she throws her nightgown on the fire. Her breasts, belly and hips streaked silver—from stretching, again and again and again. She uses the scissors (the ones the Wolf always remembers to bring) and cuts her brown hair; she hands him the braid. The Wolf will weave it into his fur and the lice will busy themselves.

The Wolf gestures, and in the wake of his outstretched arm— the path unfolds. The trees step aside, to make the part, and the stars drop down as lanterns to light the way. One foot in front of the other, and she reminds herself: It will get easier. She walks until dawn. And then it's time to nest; body begins to heave, but she's done this before. The coughing turns her inside out. The hair balls come. She won't be able to speak for days, telling the neighbors it is only laryngitis. Her husband secretly thinks she has cancer because she sneaks cigarettes out the bathroom window; he always gets the secrets mixed up with the truth.

IV: The wolf hair and bits of cartilage glisten with bile, and she wishes just once she'd remember to bring along some water. They roll about, removing the membrane and cutting themselves open on jagged rocks; the rupture releases tissue, muscle, matter. Unfolding, the arms and legs come, and then the tail. From the paws uncurl little fingers and opposable thumbs, pink and bald they blossom cuticles and see-through nails. The hair is terse, electric with fright and living. The hirsute faces are the last to form. Lidded eyes, green and blue irises, framed by blinking baby doll lashes, but the wolf ears are pointed, twitching as they listen. They root around; once they've picked up her scent, they come to suckle— but she knows better than to make that mistake again. She lunges to frighten, to make them run away: *scurry scuttle*.

III: Steam hisses on the charred wood. She sees all the things that would not burn. Like the smoldering fire-retardant upholstery, and the blackened hooks from the kitchen island, meant for hanging oven mitts and utensils. She sees how the Wolf took precautions; he extinguished the fire with water before he left to find the cubs: to see, to see. There are bones in the fire pit like sporadically tossed runes. Impossibly small, she notes the tiny skull. And the open rib cage without the little heart. The fractured femur, and how this splinters; the disconnected vertebrae, scattered and brilliant white, fallen stars amidst the soot. The cast iron bed is still made and there is Daughter, a newborn again; on either side there are two pillows to keep her from falling. The Wolf has always been careful. She is sleeping. Her hands rolled into fists, her arms and legs moving in the air like she is swimming. This means starting over, again, from scratch—but only Mother will know as only Mother has always known. She picks the baby up and begins to nurse; the Daughter sucks: in out, in out. Like this, Mother/Daughter weave in and out of trees; there never was a path.

* * *

II: EMERGING FROM THE WOODS, a naked woman carries a naked baby; barefoot she navigates the thistle, over lawn and flagstone, and through the sliding glass door. She has to locate the room with the crib, but she finds it and puts the baby down. Yesterday, this was the home office. But the computer is gone and so are the laminate filing cabinets. She spins the mobile above the sleeping baby, and it too circles. She tiptoes past the sleeping Husband, still on the couch. In the bathroom mirror, she's relieved to see she left enough hair to pass as a soccer mom. She scrubs her face with scalding water and brushes her teeth until she spits red.

I: The paper boy hurls the new paper at the door and wakes the Husband. He stumbles toward the unfolding current events, as the newborn Daughter murmurs, then cries. And she will be screaming by the time Mother gets there. The trash truck is next, metallic clatter as hydraulics lift the aluminum cans, empty them, and set them back down. The alarm clock buzzes from the nightstand in the master bedroom where no one slept: on off, on off, it calls a new day.

CATSPAW
Jason Daniel Myers

A fairy tale is a precarious dance of fate and luck, a delicate balance between the actions of the servants of evil and the agents of good. The sorcerer, the wolves, the huntsman, the old crone, the prince, the heroine—each have their own role to play. But if even one of them fails to play his or her part, or if even one happenstance fails to occur, the tale could end badly, or, even worse, the tale could end before it begins. This is the story of Catspaw, or will be, if destiny and chance don't miss their cues.

nce upon a time, when magic still held some sway in the world, there lived a merchant whose daughter was the loveliest creature on earth. The merchant also had six sons, and each was lazier than the one before him, so that the merchant scowled to think that his blood was in their veins. Nonetheless, the merchant did not need his sons' help, because he used his daughter's beauty to his great advantage. Each day at the market, when the merchant cried his wares, his daughter would be right beside him. She helped her father out, fetched things for him, and conversed pleasantly with those who came to the merchant's store. So captivating was she that people would buy whatever the merchant was selling: cloaks, pottery, trinkets, just to have a chance to look at and speak to his daughter. Indeed, descriptions of her beauty traveled far and wide, so that commoners and traders and princes from distant lands came to the merchant's store to get a glimpse of her. In this way, the merchant began to grow quite rich.

One day in her seventeenth year, as she was crying her father's wares, a powerful sorcerer caught sight of her. When he looked upon her ruby lips and her smooth ivory skin and her long golden hair, he fell immediately in love with her. He took the merchant to a side and said, "I come from a land to the north far beyond this realm, a land which holds things more wondrous than any you could imagine, but never in all my travels have I seen anything so beautiful as your daughter. I must have her for my wife."

Now the merchant looked at the man's intricately woven cloak, and his long coal-black hair and mustache, and his right hand, which was stained a deep purple-red, and he was afraid, for he had partially guessed the true nature of this imposing stranger. Still, he told the sorcerer the same thing he had told those who had sought his daughter before.

"Sir," he said. "My daughter is both the joy of my life and the source of my prosperity. I could not bear to have her taken far from my sight."

In reply the sorcerer offered the merchant a handsome dowry: twenty sacks of gold, each the weight of the merchant's daughter.

Now, this fortune was more than any that had been offered him before, and the merchant was very afraid of what might happen to him if he refused, but the merchant gathered his courage and shook his head.

"I'm sorry," he said, "but I cannot do it. My daughter is worth more to me than any fortune you could offer." In truth, the merchant did love his daughter not a little.

When the sorcerer heard this, he looked into the merchant's heart and saw the great love the merchant had for his daughter; he knew then that his power could not touch that love, that the merchant's daughter would never be his. And so he left the merchant's town for his own realm, and the merchant and his daughter and their family were prosperous and lived happily ever after.

Or . . .

WHEN THE MERCHANT HEARD the offer of the twenty bags of gold, avarice quickened his heart. Still, he did not agree to the stranger's offer. He realized that his daughter would be the greatest sale he had ever made in his life.

"Sir," he said, "surely you do not expect me to accept such a paltry dowry. In my lifetime my daughter will make for me far more than twenty sacks of gold."

When the sorcerer heard this, he wanted nothing more than to destroy the merchant for his insolence. But the sorcerer's power was such that he could not hold the girl in his thrall unless she was given freely to him. So he brought his red right hand up to his sallow cheek, as if he was in deep thought.

"Very well," he said. "In addition to the twenty sacks of gold, you shall receive ten sacks of diamonds, each your daughter's weight."

The merchant's head pounded at the thought of such a fortune. There were kings in the realm who did not have that much treasure. But the merchant was a shrewd man. "If this man can offer me such things," he thought, "then there must be more he can give me."

"Sir," the merchant said, "your offer is tempting. Nonetheless, I am certain that my daughter is worth more than these things. Surely there is something you can give me in addition, something more valuable than gold and more wondrous than diamonds."

The sorcerer was furious. He would have to go to great trouble to satisfy this merchant's seemingly boundless greed. Still, a contract had to be made and honored, or else the girl could not be fully his. So he looked into the merchant's heart to see what type of a man he was. After a while, the sorcerer spoke.

"In my realm," he said, "there are ships that sail not on the seas, but in the air. Their great sails catch the wind and pull them through the sky more swiftly than any bird can fly. Surely such a ship would be of great use to someone such as yourself."

"Yes . . . yes it would," the merchant said. His eyes sparkled.

"Then it is settled, the sorcerer said. "I will return to my realm and build you such a ship. In three years' time, I will come back for my bride. When I do, I will bring the air ship."

"And the bags of gold and diamonds will be on the ship," the merchant quickly added.

"Yes," the sorcerer replied.

Thus, the bargain was struck and the contract was signed. The merchant introduced the sorcerer to his daughter.

"This man," the merchant said, "is a prosperous traveler from the north. In three years, my daughter, you are to be married to him. You should feel lucky," he said, "that such a man wishes to make you his bride."

The sorcerer was not an ugly man, but when the merchant's daughter saw his waxen face and his oily-black hair and his dark scarlet hand, she was repulsed and afraid. Nevertheless she spoke pleasantly to him, as was proper.

Soon the sorcerer left. And though the merchant's daughter shuddered at the thought of wedding the strange traveler, she resigned herself to her fate, because she had always obeyed her father.

At the appointed time, the sorcerer returned with the air ship and the gold and the diamonds. The merchant's wife and daughter wept and begged the merchant not to honor his bargain, but when the merchant saw the magnificent wooden ship with its towering masts and gossamer sails, he became deaf to their pleas. The merchant took the ship and the treasure, and gave his daughter over to the sorcerer, who took her to his castle, where she lived as his wife and his slave for the rest of her life.

Or . . .

SOON THE SORCERER LEFT to build the air ship he had promised. The merchant's daughter knew that she was bound to do what her father told her, but she could not stand the thought of being wedded to the stranger. Though she did not know why, she was terrified of him. Every night, she dreamt of his return and woke up crying. She told this to her father. He did not listen to her. Instead, he just kept telling her that she should be happy.

One night, after her father had become angry with her constant entreaties, and when she felt particularly hopeless, the merchant's daughter bundled up a few of her belongings and crept out of her house.

She traveled for several days in a dreamy haste, because, though she was gone from her father's house, she feared that the stranger would come for her still. One night, a few hours before dusk, the merchant's daughter entered a gloomy wood. She hurried along the path, but the forest was more vast than she had thought, and the darkness caught up with her. She pushed forward, but soon she had lost the path, and found herself wandering, lost and without direction. Weeping softly, she sat against a large rough-barked tree and began to eat the last of the bread and meat she had taken with her. She was just beginning to feel calm and more herself, when she realized that she was not alone. A hungry pack of wolves had smelled the meat and followed it to her. Pairs of moon-white eyes glowed in the darkness. The merchant's daughter was terrified. She threw the last of her food and began running through the woods, her skin and clothes ripping on the outstretched branches. The wolves fell on her, teeth gnashing. She pulled her traveling cloak over her, but it did no good. The wolves tore her apart.

Or . . .

A HUNTSMAN WHO LIVED in those woods heard the screams of the merchant's daughter. He ran into the midst of the pack, knife flashing. He killed some of the wolves, and, when the rest had fled, he bent over the bloodied form of the person he had fought so hard to save. She was alive, but badly hurt. The huntsman picked up the merchant's daughter and carried her back to his home. He spent many weeks nursing her back to health, and as her strength grew, so did her love for the man who had saved her. Before long the huntsman and the merchant's daughter were married, and the two of them lived happily ever after.

Or . . .

BEFORE LONG THE HUNTSMAN and the merchant's daughter were married. Time passed. The merchant's daughter bore a girl child. And as each season waned and gave way to the next, she thought less and less of the stranger and of her father's betrayal . . .

As the end of the three-year term came nearer, the merchant became more and more vexed. He worried at what the stranger might do when he returned to find the wife he had been promised gone. Also, the thought of the riches the stranger had offered him burned in his mind. At night the merchant lay awake in his bed, trying to decide what to do. At last, the merchant came up with a plan: he would disguise one of the servant girls as his daughter.

At the appointed time, the sorcerer returned to the merchant's town with the airship and the gold and diamonds. It had taken him nearly that long to procure such an extravagant dowry. When he thought, though, on the lovely prize he was to procure with the dowry, he counted all his labors worthwhile.

The merchant came out of his house and greeted the sorcerer with smiles and great ceremony. But when the merchant cheerily called his daughter, and a girl in a hooded cloak walked out of the house, the sorcerer knew immediately that the merchant was trying to deceive him. He ripped the cloak from the servant girl's body and then flew into a rage, pushing past the merchant and rushing into the merchant's house to look for the wife he had been promised. He encountered the merchant's wife, the merchant's sons, and the house servants, but the merchant's daughter was nowhere to be found. The sorcerer was furious. He pulled a large flask from his cloak and stalked from room to room, dousing each member of the household with the strange liquid inside it. One by one, each was transformed into a large white bird.

When the sorcerer emerged from the house, he saw the merchant trying to climb the braided ladder of the airship. He pulled the merchant to the ground and pressed the heel of his boot into the merchant's throat. When the merchant opened his mouth to gasp for air, the sorcerer took another flask from his cloak and poured it between the merchant's lips. The merchant trembled and cried out, and then he began to shrivel up. He grew smaller and smaller and became a small wood spider. The sorcerer bent down, picked up the spider, and with his red right hand he carefully plucked out each of the eight legs. Then he opened a glass jar and placed the spider inside it.

His anger soothed, the sorcerer ascended the ladder to the airship, and began to search the countryside for the merchant's beautiful daughter.

The sorcerer was obsessed with possessing the merchant's daughter and, after much searching, he did find her. One night, he came upon her and the huntsman, sleeping in bed with their two-year-old child. When he pulled her from the bed, the merchant's daughter recognized him, and began calling to her husband for help. Now, the merchant's daughter had long ago told the huntsman about the deal her father had made with the stranger, and from her cries he immediately realized that this was the man she feared would come for her. He leapt up and plunged his hunting knife into the sorcerer's heart. The sorcerer fell dead, and the huntsman and the merchant's daughter lived happily ever after.

Or . . .

THE SORCERER CREPT UP quietly on the sleeping three. He pulled the merchant's daughter from the bed and dumped a potion onto the huntsman. The huntsman awoke, and he would have gone to the aid of his wife, but the pain of transformation held him immobile. He could only scream as the sorcerer took his wife from the house. His hands and feet pushed themselves into paws, his teeth sharpened, and soft bristles of black hair rose out of his skin. In this way, the huntsman was transformed into a great cat. The cat jumped down from the bed and padded out the door. The child was touched by a few drops of the potion, and so she, too, was transformed, but only in part. She lay in bed that night, crying in terror and confusion. Then, in the morning, the small deformed creature got up and made her way into the wood. There she wandered for a few days until, overcome by fear and hunger, she lay down and died and became food for the animals.

Or . . .

AN OLD CRONE, WHO lived on the very edge of the forest, came upon the child. The ancient woman was crouching down to gather some herbs when she saw the creature curled up under the leaves of a tall bush. Because the child seemed half-human half-animal, the old woman thought that she must be an orphaned changeling. The old woman had never had a child, so she took the frail cat-creature in her arms and resolved to raise it as her own. Now, the old woman was ugly and eccentric, but she was not unkind. And so the child grew up as happy as any in her situation could, and she came to consider the hag her mother, because any memory of her life before seemed a pale, fading dream.

Life was hard for her. As she grew, she began to understand that the people in the nearby village did not like her or her mother. The villagers had long believed that the old crone who lived at the edge of the wood was a witch, and if ever they needed confirmation of their suspicions, they received it in the form of the beast-child that the old woman raised as if she were a little girl. Her eyes were like yellow topazes set in her head, and her long thick ebon hair only partially covered the velvety triangular ears that grew from the top of her head. Her teeth were sharp and the middle of her lip was drawn upward toward her nose, but the most remarkable thing of all was that, while her right arm was ivory-skinned and delicately shaped, her left arm was covered with black fur and ended in a large padded paw. And so she was called Catspaw. In the mouth of her adopted mother, it was her name, but on the tongues of the villagers, it was a cruel taunt.

One day in her seventh year, Catspaw was returning to the old woman's house with some berries she had picked for their supper. A group of village children saw her, and they called out to her. "Familiar!" they called. "Hellcat! Go back to where you came from." Catspaw turned around and hissed at them, baring her claws. This cowed the children into silence, but one of the more fearless boys picked up a stone and hurled it at her. A few more children followed his example and began throwing sticks and rocks at her. "Catspaw, Catspaw," they called. "Go chase your tail."

At that moment, the king of the realm was passing through the village with his advisor and his twelve-year-old son. When he saw the children and the strange cat-child, he ordered the carriage to a stop. His advisor remarked that such a creature would perhaps make an excellent addition to the palace's trophy room. The king replied that he did not think much of that idea, then he nodded at the carriage-driver to continue through the village.

Or . . .

His advisor remarked that such a creature would perhaps make an excellent addition to the palace's trophy room, but, for reasons which the advisor could not possibly fathom, the king's heart went out to the sad-eyed cat child. He stepped down from the coach and, his ermine cloak fluttering behind him, chased away the village children, coming upon them like a great angry bear. When they had all fled, he turned to Catspaw and said, "Do not cry, child. Fortune, and your king, smile upon you this day. You shall come with me and live in my castle, to be my son's playmate." To this, Catspaw replied, quite boldly, that she would love to do so, but that she could not leave her old mother, who lived at the cottage on the edge of the woods. The king smiled down at her. "So be it," he said, and sent for the old woman.

The king was true to his word. Catspaw and the old woman lived in the castle, and Catspaw was the king's son's playmate. Catspaw, along with the prince, had full run of the castle, its battlements and great rooms. The king had but one rule: no one, under penalty of death, was to enter the chamber at the top of the south tower. At first, the prince professed to dislike the younger tag-along, but he was glad for the company and soon the two became fast friends. They grew up as brother and sister, and treated the castle as their own, but Catspaw was always mindful of the king's one rule, and she never broke it. And so Catspaw and the old woman and the prince and the king lived happily ever after.

Or . . .

Catspaw had lived with the king for nearly seven years. One day she and the prince were playing a game of hide and seek. Their games had grown less frequent, for the prince was becoming a man. Still, when they did play, they played with more vigor and abandon than they ever had before. Catspaw was supposed to be hiding from the prince, and she was sure that he was close behind her, so, without realizing where she was going, she crept up the stairs to the south tower. When she reached the top, she thought she heard footsteps coming toward her, so she opened the door to the chamber and closed it softly behind her.

As soon as she walked inside, she realized that she had never been in this part of the castle before, but she had no time to think about it, for there, in the center of the high-walled alabaster room, was a great misshapen bird. It was a falcon, nearly the size of a man, with dark brown wings and a white breast. But the wings had fingertips protruding from the feathers, and the creature perched unsteadily on distended stumps, which were human feet half-grown into talons. The eyes, which were fully human, stared out at her piteously.

Just then, the king entered the chamber. He was carrying a gold platter piled high with raw meat.

When the king saw that Catspaw was in the room, he dropped the platter to the ground and rushed toward her, tears of rage streaming down his face. "I had but one rule, just one rule," he bellowed and, pushing her against the wall, he put his fingers to her throat and choked her to death.

Or . . .

THE KING RAISED HIS hand, as if to strike her, but then he put both hands to his face and began to weep into them.

"Oh, Catspaw," he cried. "Would that you had not broken my one rule. Now you have discovered my secret."

"Why are you keeping this creature captive?" Catspaw demanded, in spite of her fear.

The king raised his tear-stained face to hers. "She is not my prisoner," he said, "but my wife." Then the king began to tell her, how, not long after the prince was born, a sorcerer, with oily-black hair and a strange purple-red birthmark on his right hand, came and tried to woo the queen. When she refused, and when the king moved to have him killed, the sorcerer had cast a spell on his wife and escaped. The kingdom believed their queen dead, and the king alone knew his wife's true fate.

The king shook his head sadly. "No one must know of this. Catspaw, you must leave the kingdom."

Catspaw felt deeply the king's sorrow, and she thought on all that he had done for her. "My king," she said. "Surely, there must be a way to find this sorcerer. Let me search for him. Perhaps killing him will break the spell."

The king smiled at her. "No, Catspaw, I would not have you killed for finding my secret, nor could I send you off on a journey which would certainly be your end."

"My king," Catspaw replied, "I would rather die than leave your castle forever. So, if I must leave, please let me try to find this magician. Then, if I am successful, I will be able to return to the place I have come to call home."

The king looked at Catspaw with wonder. "Your love for me and my son must be great," he said. Then he wiped the tears from his eyes and, walking across the room to one of the shelves, he took down a metal instrument. It was about the size of a melon and made up of four brass rings, which looped to form a caged sphere. In the middle was a crude arrow, which held a tiny glass vial at its point. The king went over to the she-bird, and, stroking her feathers to calm her, he used a knife to make a small prick in the bird's breast. He held the vial up to the small trickle of blood that seeped from the wound. When it was filled, he walked back to Catspaw.

"This," he said as he handed her the brass sphere, "is a magic compass. The blood of my wife will lead you to the creature that has ensorcelled her." Catspaw thanked the king, and left the castle that night.

Now, all these years, the merchant's daughter had lived as the sorcerer's wife and thrall. She was still beautiful, although she was but a pale wisp of the creature she once was. The magiks that the sorcerer used to keep her bound to him had taken their toll. Her skin was white as bone, her hair thin as spider-webs, and her eyes were empty grey husks. What was left of her soul had hidden itself so deeply in her body that even she could not find it, and her mind was a vast white room, empty of everything but echoes. When she was not making the sorcerer's meals or seeing to his whims, she wandered the castle, running the silk-thin skin of her hands across the stones, or sat in her chamber, staring out the room's one window into the colorless sky. Her only companions were the birds, which she talked to at times. More often, though, she listened to them. She also had a pet, one her master had given her. A small, bristly-haired creature without legs. Each day she fed it, carefully placing the dead flies into the jar next to her pet's mouth.

A few months after Catspaw had begun her journey, the sorcerer discovered that there was a magic force nearing him, that someone was seeking him, using his magic power as lodestar. So he sent a few members of his guard—small, muscled imps with horns and clawed wings and raw-red skin—to seek out the one who was seeking him. The imps came upon Catspaw, and rushed, shrieking, at her, their teeth and talons flashing. They pulled the compass from her, and smashed it on the rocks. Then they returned their attention to her, taunting her, and scratching at her face, thinking to make sport of her before they killed her. Catspaw, though, instead of cowering from her attackers, used her claws, killing three of them before they realized what was happening. The rest fled back to their master.

Catspaw was broken-hearted. She licked her wounds and continued on in the direction she had been going for a few more days, but, without the compass, she was no longer sure where she was going, nor how she would know if she got there. A fortnight passed, and Catspaw finally gave up. She did not know if forward was the proper direction, and she knew that she could not go back to the king. She lay down to die, but after a while some of her will to survive returned. She made herself a small thatched hut at the edge of a wood, where she slept when she was not hunting for food, and there she lived out the rest of her days, empty and alone.

Or . . .

Now, SOMETHING MUST BE said of the prince. Not long after Catspaw began her journey, the prince finally realized the great love that he had for her. When his father told him that Catspaw had left the kingdom, he felt sure that he could not live without her, and so, without telling the king, he set off after her. He did not know where she was going, though, and so he did not know where to look to find her. For a year he searched, and still he did not give up.

One day, while Catspaw was out hunting, the prince came upon a thatched dwelling on the edge of a wood. Something about the manner of the place kindled in him a memory from his boyhood: the old woman's house, which he had seen only once when the king had Catspaw and the old woman brought to the castle. Finding no one home, the prince looked inside and indeed he recognized some of the possessions in the house as Catspaw's. The prince sat down to wait for his love to return, and after a few hours he closed his eyes and fell asleep. When Catspaw found the prince sleeping in her lowly home, she was so surprised with joy that she let out a cry. Hearing this, the prince awoke. He leapt to his feet, embracing her, and, with tears streaming down his face, confessed his love for her.

"But I cannot be with you," Catspaw said, lowering her eyes. "I can never return to the kingdom."

"Then I shall stay here with you," the prince replied, and he did, and the two of them lived on the edge of the wood happily ever after.

Or . . .

WHEN THE SORCERER'S IMPS had returned to him and described to him the foe they encountered, the sorcerer guessed who his enemy might be. In truth, she represented a possibility that he feared, and he cursed himself for his carelessness so many years ago.

"I must," he thought, "go see this girl for myself, so that I can be sure."

Now, it happened that the day the sorcerer came to the woods to find Catspaw and kill her was the very same day that the prince fell asleep in her house. When the sorcerer came upon the sleeping prince, he was sorely confused. He looked into the prince's heart, and when at last he understood, the sorcerer crept away.

That evening, as Catspaw neared her home, exhausted from hunting, she was met by a hunch-backed old woman. When she greeted the crone, she said something which startled Catspaw.

"You seek an evil sorcerer," she said.

Catspaw could only stare at her in surprise.

"You do seek a sorcerer?" the crone repeated.

"How . . . how do you know that?" Catspaw asked.

"I am a witch," replied the decrepit creature, "It is my business to know such things. But that is not important. What is important is that I have a trade to make you." The crone took a small glass sphere from her cloak. She set it in her left hand, and it rose to levitate above her palm.

"This crystal," she said, "has very special properties. You need only to tell it where you wish to go, and it will lead you there." She moved her level hand back and forth slowly. The sphere followed it. "Such a thing would be useful to you, yes?"

Hope glittered anew in Catspaw like the light of a dawning sun. She would have given anything for this chance. Nonetheless, she remained yet cautious.

"You mentioned a trade," she said. "What would you have me give you? I possess nothing of value."

The crone looked from Catspaw to her small thatched dwelling. "I am an old, tired woman," she said. "I wish only to have a place to live the last few sunsets of my life. Your house," she continued, "is small but well-built. If you were to give me your house, and all that is inside it, I would be most satisfied with the bargain."

It was then that Catspaw noticed something strange about the woman. Her right hand, which lay at her side, was red, a sickly purple-scarlet, as if the blood was trying to escape through her skin. Catspaw trembled inside with fear and anticipation, for she remembered well the king's description of the fiend that had transformed his wife. Catspaw leaned close, as if to get a good look at the glass ball, and as she did, she thrust her dagger into the old hag's throat. The screams of the dying sorcerer awoke the sleeping prince. He rushed from the house and saw Catspaw. As the blood pulsed from the sorcerer's throat, so the appearance of the cat drained from Catspaw's body. The spell was broken. The prince embraced Catspaw, and confessed his love for her. The two returned to the kingdom, where they found the king and the newly transformed queen. Catspaw and the prince were soon married, and they lived happily ever after.

Or . . .

"IF YOU WERE TO give me your house, and all that is inside it," the old crone said, "I would be most satisfied with the bargain."

Catspaw thought. There were a few things inside her hut that were of some value to her, but they were nothing when compared with the chance to complete her quest and return home. She agreed to the witch's terms and, with the crystal in her possession, she hastened off to find the sorcerer.

When Catspaw was gone, the sorcerer changed to his true form and went into her hut. He laughed in triumph, for the prince was now bound by his magik. As for Catspaw, the sorcerer was not worried. A magik bargain could not be made with lies, but it could be made with half-truths. The crystal sphere would lead her into his castle, but it would take her by the most treacherous route. If the beasts that inhabited his realm did not kill her, then his own magical defenses would.

Catspaw traveled northward for many weeks. As she walked, the earth became a cold, dead thing beneath her feet. At times, the sky became angry at her presence and threw tiny shards of ice down on her. Shivering, Catspaw trudged on until finally she reached the sorcerer's realm.

The sorcerer's realm filled Catspaw with fear such as she had never felt in her life. The ice for miles around the sorcerer's castle was as black as pitch, so that even day was a darkness of sorts. When the sun fell, the air became alive with sounds of animals. Often, quite nearby, she would hear the roaring of fighting animals. Though she often felt as if something were following her, she never encountered anything more dangerous than a caribou.

At long last the sorcerer's castle loomed large on the horizon. The crystal was leading her toward a cave that seemed to be an entrance into the castle. But as she started across the obsidian plane that stretched between her and the entrance, the ground began to tremble beneath her feet. Suddenly, three ice wyrms broke through the surface of the ground, their sinuous bronze bodies blocking her path to the cavern. They surrounded her, their great horned heads weaving from side to side, liquid eyes searching for opportunities to strike. Catspaw fought courageously, claws extended, her hunting knife in her right hand, but her slashes could never penetrate deep enough to kill them. The wyrms pulled her beneath the ice and tore her limb from limb.

Or . . .

JUST AS CATSPAW THOUGHT she would surely perish, a roar rose above the hissing of the ice wyrms. A great cat, with yellow topaz eyes and deep sable fur, had come up behind the wyrms. Snarling, it leapt onto the head of one, tearing at its throat with mordant claws. The wyrm jerked its head, throwing the cat to the ice, but it was up on its feet again, hissing and thrashing its tail like a whip. Forgetting their previous prey, the wyrms moved to the cat and fell upon it. Catspaw ran toward the cave as fast as she could, the screams of the dying panther rising in her ears and then falling as distance separated them.

She followed the glass sphere through dark winding tunnels until she emerged into a stone chamber. The chamber was empty but for a large hole in the center of the floor and a tunnel entrance at the opposite side. Catspaw started toward the other side, but she had not gotten far when the floor of the chamber began to shift. The entire room seemed to tilt inward. Catspaw lost her balance and slid toward the great hole in the center of the room. She scrabbled with fingers and claws to keep herself from falling, but the floor was slick and seamless. She tumbled into the deep pit and the world went dark. When Catspaw awoke and realized where she was, she tried to scale the walls of the oubliette that entombed her, but it was no use. Each attempt sapped her strength and hope. Many days later, she finally sat down to wait for Death, and she did not rise again until she had met him.

Or . . .

AS SHE LAY THERE, despairing, seven birds came down the shaft, floating slowly to the bottom like snowflakes. Each of the birds grasped a part of Catspaw's cloak, and they beat their strong wings, trying to pull her from the pit. But alas, she was too heavy for them. After numerous attempts, several of the birds seemed to give up. They began flying toward the top, but one of the birds, a little bigger than the rest, flew after them, squawking and pecking at their wings. Before long, each bird floated down and again alighted on Catspaw, straining at her with more might than they had mustered the previous times. At last they succeeded in lifting her from the floor and, with Catspaw scrambling for the tiny holds on the walls, they pulled her from the hole and carried her safely across the chamber to the passageway on the opposite side of the room. When they had done this, they flew from the cave and returned to the chamber of the merchant's daughter, where they sometimes nested.

Catspaw continued on, feeling her way through the blackened tunnels. Soon the rocky passage gave way to a carved staircase, lined with torches and thorny vines. Catspaw reached to take a torch from the wall, and as she did, a vine twisted from its place and coiled around her wrist. As she tried to pull free, more vines curled out to entwine her, pressing their cruel thorns into her body. Catspaw could not move, and she could not reach her knife. Hours passed, and when Catspaw heard the beating of wings, she rejoiced that her mysterious helpers had returned. But the flying creatures that had discovered her were the imps that served as the sorcerer's guard. They flew about her, laughing and spitting on her. Then they went to their master to tell him what they had found.

When the sorcerer heard what had become of Catspaw, he laughed to himself, and then told the imps that she was theirs. When they returned to the stairway, the vines fell away from Catspaw, curling back to the walls. There were dozens of imps. Catspaw turned to run, but the imps threw themselves on her, knocking her to the ground and pulling the flesh from her body.

Or . . .

WHEN THE SORCERER HEARD what had become of Catspaw, he laughed and told the imps to fetch her to his chamber. They bound her hand and claw behind her, and brought her before the sorcerer.

She stood there, weak and hungry, her body bloodied from the hundreds of thorns that had pierced her, not even raising her head so that she could look around. But when the sorcerer began to laugh, Catspaw's pride seared her, and she looked up in defiance. It was then that she saw the prince, crouching at the sorcerer's feet like a faithful hound, his face expressionless, his eyes blank muddy pools. Catspaw sobbed and fell to the ground, mewling. At that moment, she had been thinking that the one and only beautiful thing in the world was her childhood friend, the prince. When she saw him there, kneeling passively at the side of the creature who had become her mortal enemy, the last remnants of her will and hope drained from her body. She wept bitterly, her vision so clouded by tears that she did not see the sorcerer's satisfied sneer.

During this time, the merchant's daughter had been in her chamber, preparing a soup for the sorcerer, for it was near that time when he was accustomed to take his dinner. She had paused in her preparations, and was placing a fly into the jar of her pet, when the sound of Catspaw's soul-wilting cries reached her. Somewhere in the used husk of her heart, something began to stir. She did not know why, nor did she even think to ask herself the reason, but she began to cry. A few drops began to fall into the spider's jar. One of the white birds, the one that had scolded the rest, lifted its head to look at her. The merchant's daughter wept, and as she did, she began to shed tears of blood. The scarlet droplets coursed down her face. They spattering the table and began filling the spider's jar. The pool at the bottom of the jar became so deep that it drowned the piteous creature inside.

Just then, some of the magik inside the merchant's daughter beckoned her. It was time for her master's dinner. She got up, wiped the blood from her face, and went to the cupboard to get a serving tray and a bowl. As she was doing this, the white bird went over to the table, wrapped a talon around the spider's jar, and dumped its contents into the boiling soup. By the time the merchant's daughter returned to the kettle, the white bird had already returned to her perch. The merchant's daughter ladled some of the soup into a golden bowl and walked to the sorcerer's chamber.

Catspaw became immediately quiet when the lovely wraith

carrying the golden tray entered the room. She could not be sure what it was about the woman that pulled at her, but it was something elusive and powerful, like a half-remembered dream. The pale woman presented the tray to the sorcerer, knelt deeply, and then stood to his right, opposite the crouching prince. The sorcerer smiled at Catspaw, deeply pleased with himself, and began to eat the soup, all the time holding her gaze, as if he held a wonderful secret. Just then, the sorcerer's self-satisfied smile twitched, and then contorted into an agonized grimace. The tray clattered to the floor as the sorcerer tried to rise from his seat before slumping back. When he looked down, he saw that blood was seeping from his red right hand. It welled up from his skin, running in rivulets to the floor. Unable to do anything else, the sorcerer sat, watching his gushing hand with disbelief, until the last of his blood trickled from his fingers.

The spell was broken. Catspaw became, for the first time in her memory, fully human. The chains that had bound her mother's soul for so long fell to dust. The prince's eyes cleared, and he ran to Catspaw to put his arms around her. The white birds that had kept constant watch on the merchant's daughter for so many years, were transformed back into her mother and six brothers, and they came flitting into the room, surrounding Catspaw and the merchant's daughter, touching them and crying for joy. Finally, the old bird woman pulled Catspaw close to her mother, and put Catspaw's hand in hers.

After their reunion, they traveled back to the kingdom, and when they returned, the king himself came out to greet them.

"I have been expecting you," he said. He gathered his son into his arms. Then he looked at Catspaw and began to cry. "Thank you," he said. "Thank you, Catspaw, I owe you more than I can possibly repay." He then led the retinue back to the castle, where the queen, freed from the spell that had so long tormented her, was waiting. When the king discovered that Catspaw and the prince intended to marry, he was overjoyed. The wedding was marked by great mirth and celebration in the kingdom, and Catspaw and the prince lived happily ever after.

JOSEF KOUDELKA'S UNICYCLE
Ariana Quiñónez

In the spirit of perseverance
a man rides his unicycle
down the street
to work
or away from a funeral
but the latter is more likely
as he wears black
and carries no briefcase.

And it reminds me of the human spirit
these hopes I impress upon a man
who may not exist
except lodged between
artistic visions
and slipped amidst
idealist dreams
but it made me think
is there no beauty in life
without the struggle
or is it the grief
that allows sight for beauty?

And don't we all go
through life holding an
umbrella and juggling
our own skin
looking ahead but
glancing behind
And shouldn't we feel
safe amongst planes,

trains and in the
arms of our mothers,
lovers.
And in a moment of quiet
I thought to myself:

I hope I die
gazing out the window
on a sunny day.

HANS MY HEDGEHOG
Samuel Valentino

IN HOMAGE TO THOSE
WHO CAME BEFORE

THE PEA DEFENDS HIS POSITION
Colleen Michaels

There are spiders who get
to flush the sweet cheeks
of hungry and idle girls
trussed by pink ribbons.

They are easy prey, palate
content with beige crocks,
weighting down tuffets
until frightened away.

I don't want to work with
hooded girls who haplessly fall
for the axe or fang in drag.
I am no big bad lady killer.

Don't stifle my small power
on fools who cross bridges,
on rubes who start to doze
after a few candied apples,

grabbers of beanstalk, vine
bower, tower length hair.
Consider the smoke and mirrors
to throw one midnight ball.

As applicant to irritate
an insomniac's light slumber,
I worked on the commission
of pleasure. She hired me.

They'll say she was the one to bruise
and I was her green starter for a prince.
Those are just lies, thick mattresses.
She remembers my tender skin like spring.

THE WOLFMAN'S NEW GIG
Mona Awad

So far, it's been a typical Friday night shift at Screamer's for the Wolfman. Ten o'clock and already he's come howling out of the meat locker a thousand times. He's poked a few squealing teenage girls in the butt with an axe that wouldn't cut cucumber. He's chased prepubescent punks through his *Forest of Doom!* and made them go giggling off into the synthetic dark. He's had the run-in with the one fat kid who proved immune to his axe-wielding antics, his hoarse howls.

"*Wolfman?* Aren't you from like the fifties?"

"Fuck you, kid."

Hunched in his meat locker between stints, the acrid tang from the fog machine burning in his plastic snout, the rash from his latex mask getting angrier, the Wolfman plays electric guitar in his mind. When the buzzer sounds, he braces himself for another squall of sixteen-year-olds who will have already spent their screams in the *Slasher Hall of Fame* with only a yelp left for him. He's surprised, to say the least, when into his fog-thick lair saunters a lone girl in a red dress. White limbs all aquiver. Feverish eyes wide between honey-coloured curls. Trailing a perfume he can smell even through the fog of fake rancid meat.

Normally by this hour, when he's deep into the flask of Jack he keeps tucked in his hairy thigh and his suit's starting to itch like a motherfucker, the Wolfman would do his shtick half-assed at best. If he did it at all. Likely he'd stay in his meat locker, dreaming of his orthopedic donut cushion, thinking *Scare yourself.* But there's something about how she teeters through the smoky strobe-lit dark, glances furtively over her thin white shoulder, locks bug-wide eyes with him through the locker slats, that makes a growl bloom in his whiskey-parched throat. And when he comes roaring out—red eyes ablaze, fangs bared, brandishing his bloody axe—she screams a scream that will ring in his ears even when he's back at home sitting on his cushion, nursing a Natty Light.

She drops her glittery swan-shaped purse and runs; he goes bounding after her. Though her breath is ragged with fear and she's broken a heel and snagged her dress twice on the cobwebby branches in her effort to get away, still he chases her far beyond his lair, past even the *Psycho Circus Tent* full of knife-happy clowns. When she trips and falls by the belching *Black Lagoon!*, he crouches over her, gnashing his plastic fangs an inch from her white neck. It's only then he notices the thin trickle of blood on her brow, the darker blossoms of blood on each of her knees, and that she's out cold. Oops.

They make a strange pair entering the ER, this slip of a girl and the sheepish Wolfman, both drenched in blood. Sure it happens to patrons all the time at Screamers but usually it's an Orc or a Psycho Slasher with a circular saw that's responsible. This is a first for the Wolfman.

"This is a first for me," is what he keeps telling everyone in the ER, the paramedics, nurses, the bloody girl on the gurney, but no one appears to listen.

"Wait for me," she tells him, eyes fluttering open, clutching his hairy arm tight as she is led away through the double-doors by disapproving nurses.

He smiles apologetically at the old, the broken and the bleeding in the waiting room. He tries to take his mask off, but it's no use. Ever since that one time his snout fell off mid-shift, Martha in make-up's always going too damn far with the glue.

After hiding behind three dog-eared copies of *People*, he sees her emerge, her arm in a sling, bandages on her brow and both knees, grey eyes cloudy with drugs.

He hands her two free passes to Screamers, standard compensation for injured patrons.

"Thanks," she says.

They stand there staring at each other, the ER automatic doors opening and closing beside them. It's awkward. His fur under her fingernails. Her blood on his suit.

"Guess I got a little carried away back there," he says, realizing how lame it is only after he's said it.

"It's your job," she shrugs. "You *are* a Wolfman, after all."

"I guess so," says the Wolfman, unconvinced. "Well, if there's anything else I can do . . ." He's about to head home and call Amber who's been making "She's My Cherry Pie" come shrieking out of his cell every ten minutes for the past hour. But she raises her slinged arm pitifully and says, "I don't think I'll be able to manage driving. Do you think you could give me a ride, Wolfman?"

Small cherry lips. Straight little white teeth.

The Wolfman smiles despite himself. He guesses he could do that.

After he's cleared away the Del Taco and the lukewarm Big Gulp from the passenger seat, lowered the Slayer that blasts the moment he starts his engine, they head west along the highway in Barbarella, his '86 tangerine Thunderbird. Out of the corner of his red eye, he watches her take swigs from his flask, light a cigarette with his boob lighter, blowing smoke rings into his bug-streaked windshield.

"Hell of a long ways to drive just to get to a haunted house," he says, to make conversation.

"Is it?"

At last she tells him to get off the highway. They're in a town that makes him feel like he should be wearing a tuxedo and using his indoor voice even out of doors. Big white mansions. Shady trees. Dollhouse streets. She has him pull up to a house that could eat his father-in-law's split-level bungalow for lunch. Super impressive with gates and turrets and pillars but not exactly his scene. Whenever the Wolfman reclines on his mother-in-law's liver coloured couch and fantasizes about being a millionaire rock star, he imagines a giant glass cube in the Hollywood hills full of red leather couches and lesbians in pearl thongs and how from every room he can see the sun set over the ocean. Still, it's a trip to see the don't-fuck-with-me gates open for Barbarella.

"You *live* here?"

"Would you like to come in?"

The Wolfman has a flash of Amber in her Hellraiser rollers, the eyes in her imp tattoo spitting fire. "Probably better not. Getting late."

He follows her up the steps, past the rose garden, the gazebo, the pondful of swans gliding across black water, what looks like a dead duck gleaming wetly on the lawn.

Inside it's all arty furniture, paintings of nature scenes in gilt frames. A huge fireplace full of leaping flames. The Wolfman sits perched on the edge of a red velvet sofa in the hairy shadow of a mounted moose head, between a grand piano and a glass statue of a wolf—its head tilted back, jaws frozen open as if howling at the chandelier dripping crystal from the ceiling. He cups his Jack and Coke awkwardly between his paws, while she sits on the couch beside him pointedly eating the cherries in her Zombie one by one, tugging the stems with her teeth.

"Pretty badass place," he says and immediately feels like the grubby window washer in a porno he saw once. A bad one from the eighties that never made it to VHS let alone DVD. He wonders what sort of chick would want to hang out with the dude who sent her to the ER? Or, for that matter, what sort of chick would travel forty-five miles to go to Screamers? What is she, twisted?

He wants to ask her, Are you twisted? Instead he asks, "Live alone?" his voice echoing through the house.

"With my grandmother," she replies, rolling her straw around with little flicks of her red tongue. "But she's not home."

"Oh."

"So tell me," she says, eyes going wider, "how long have you been a Wolfman?"

The Wolfman takes a sip of Jack. He'd really prefer not to discuss his career, but she's looking at him with such—what is it?—expectation?

"Six weeks. Used to work construction but I injured my back

on the job." It was his groin but he's not going to tell her that. "I'm also in a band." Defunct. "We're called *Hunting Accident*," he adds, puffing out his chest a little. "Heard of it?"

She shakes her honey-coloured ringlets.

"We played all over the intermountain area. I was lead singer," he adds, even though it was only two local clubs, both owned by his buddy's wife's uncle, and he played bass.

"Well, you must love what you do," she coos. "Being the Wolfman and all. I mean," she shivers, "you're so good at it."

"Think so?"

"Definitely," she says stroking her slinged arm with shaky fingers, then the silk neckline of her dress.

He has a flash of ripping off the dress and bending that taut little bod of hers over. He gulps his drink. "Probably should head back."

She leads him down a long corridor hairy with shadows of mounted elk heads, stags, more moose. As he enters her bedroom, a tentacle of fear unfurls from his pointed ears to his hairy, horn-nailed toes and his zombie glass goes crashing to the floor. They're everywhere. On the shelves, desk, end tables: wolf stuffed animals, wolf statues, figurines and posters. On the wall, a wolf calendar. Above her four poster bed, a framed print of a Grey Wolf prowling tundra. On the bed itself, wolf-patterned sheets. She sits on the bed's edge staring at him, patting the spot beside her, her eyes large and alert over the rim of her glass. The Wolfman stays huddled near the door.

"Nice room," he hears himself say. A cold sweat pools in his crotch. "Probably should be heading—"

"You know, Wolfman," she says, walking toward him now, "when you came out of that meat locker all hairy with your big teeth? You scared me more than I've ever been scared in my life."

He inadvertently takes steps backward so he's flat against her Wolverine poster.

"I feel bad about that though," he croaks. "I do."

"Don't," she growls, coming in close. "It's your brutish, beastly nature. You're a *Wolfman*."

"Actually, my name's Fl—"

"You're thinking of attacking me right now aren't you, Wolfman?" she says, her eyes big and wild and bent upon the Wolfman, the growl growing in her voice.

"Me? No I was—"

"Don't lie, Wolfman! You are. I know you are! You're dreaming of wrestling me to the floor right now and tearing off my clothes. Oh god, you beast, I only hope I can get away!" And she suddenly seizes his hairy hand, presses it against the silk top of her little red dress and screams.

"Jesus Christ!" he cries, trying to wriggle out of her grasp.

But she keeps him rammed against the wall, pressing his claws into her, screaming her head off.

"Shhh!" hisses the Wolfman. "Shhh for Christ's sake!" But it's only when he puts his free paw over her mouth, pins her down, a growl of frustration escaping his lips, that her scream turns into a moan and she shudders and melts into his clawed hands.

After, they lie in her wolf sheets, her dress slashed every which way and her hair a ratty tangle. The Wolfman, half out of his hairy suit, feels like he's been hit by a truck. His paws are splayed open on either side of him like Christ. He watches her blow smoke rings into her Teen Wolf postered ceiling, her large eyes lazy at last.

"Look, I hope you don't think I . . . you know . . . assaulted you. Or something."

"You're a Wolfman," she says simply. "It's your brutish, beastly nature." She picks fake fur from her torn dress in a way that makes him want to ask her if she's done this before, but it's then he hears the creaking of stairs, footsteps in the corridor. He rises from the tangle of wolf sheets, panicked.

"Grandma must be home from bridge," she says.

He squeezes out of her frilly window, tumbles onto the wet lawn, runs across her yard tripping on dead birds and muttering *fuck me*, and drives off like the devil. It's only when he reaches the interstate that he takes a breath, then a glug of Jack and opens the folded note she pressed into his hands. Five hundred dollars in cash tumbles into his hairy lap. On the Timber Wolf-themed stationary, in loopy red pen is *Call me, Wolfman* surrounded by exclamation marks and arrow pierced hearts.

He prays Amber'll be asleep by the time he gets home, but she's awake in the living room, frowning into her paralegal textbook. After eight hours of ripping the sideburns off exotic dancers and painting their nails pussy pink, she's never in the best of moods, but with her freshly dyed blood red hair and her electric blue lined eyes glaring at him like this, she looks like a psychotic Rainbow Brite.

"Where the hell've you been?"

"Accident," he mumbles, and rushes into the kitchen to avoid further questions, but she's right behind him, acrylic nails tapping on the counter, blue eyes blazing a weary fury.

"What sort of 'accident,' Floyd? Did you get fired again?"

"Just scared this guy pretty good," he says, keeping his head in the fridge. "Had to go to the hospital. Fuck, no Natties?"

"You scared someone?" His wife looks at him for a moment, narrows her eyes.

He's terrified that she'll smell perfume or see where the fur's been torn out of his suit by tiny red nailed hands. Instead, she just shakes her head. "I'm going to bed. Some of us," she adds, stomping up the stairs, "have real jobs."

He falls asleep on the couch, dreams of trembling white limbs swathed in blood red silk, wakes with an erection which dissolves upon hearing his wife trudge into the den in her esthetician's uniform. He pretends to be asleep while she stands over him calling his name, smiles when she gives up, curses and slams the door behind her.

He waits until he hears her Honda screech out of the driveway before he fires up his first Camel Light. On the coffee table, she's left a note that says check messages. She's also left today's classified section, a few prospects circled. Telemarketer. Dishwasher at the Red Iguana. Graveyard stockboy at 7/11.

Fuck that, he thinks.

He pours himself coffee with some Jack to kill the hangover, checks his messages. There's only one, from his boss at Screamer's. He's fired. They want the Wolfman costume back too. Fuck 'em. He pulls the wolf-note from his pocket. Grins at the sight of the loopy penmanship. He is about to pick up the phone when it rings, startling him.

"Hello? Is this the wolfman?" He knows it's her. He can hear in her voice—so little and sweet now—how her eyes go wide and shifty.

"Maybe," he says, thinking she'll like this sly reply. But it frustrates her.

"Well, is it or isn't it?"

"No, no! It is, it is. How did you get this num—"

"I had a dream about you last night, Wolfman. You tore at my dress and devoured me mercilessly. How frightful if this nightmare of mine were to become a reality."

He can hear her twirling the phone cord with white slender fingers.

"Real bummer, " he grins.

"If say, I were to go to the opera tonight. *Marriage of Figaro*, for instance. And I took a little walk during intermission. Around ten. It would be terrible if some brutish, hairy beast were waiting to ravish me in the rose garden."

"Terrible," agrees the Wolfman, snatching a bic from the coffee table sticky with last night's nachos. Over the Classifieds, covered with his wife's circles, he scrawls *Marr of Fig. 10. R garden.*

"And it would be supremely horrible if he tore at my dress a little harder than last time."

"Gotcha. But hey listen. Should I come up from behind you or?" But she's already hung up the phone.

Ah well, he'll figure it out, he's the Wolfman isn't he?

"I am the Wolfman," he tells the ceiling. And for the first time it's a fact that pleases him.

He spends the afternoon getting the blood out of his suit and doing his own wolf make-up, using all the squares of shimmery colour in his wife's eyeshadow kit for good measure. After spraying himself with Stetson, downing two shots of Hot Damn, he leaves a note that says *Got on a new gig* on the coffee table and goes whistling out of the house.

Through his cracked windshield, he sees the glass opera house shimmering in the dark. When all the glittery people have gone in through the grand doors, he tiptoes his way to the garden, leaping from shadow to shadow like a naked man in a nightmare.

As he hunches in a bed of Baronne de Rothschilds, just off the winding asphalt path she will soon walk, his heart thumps dangerously in his chest, sweat making him slippery inside his suit. What if she doesn't scream? What if I trip when I'm chasing her? Such performance anxieties boomerang through his liquor-addled brain. But when he sees her approach, her red silk swathed-silhouette licked by the low yellow moon, the growl is in his throat and he springs up behind her with a force that tears the scream from her lungs like silk from a magician's mouth.

After he's chased her, wrestled her down to the thorny floor, torn her dress with his fake claws, gnashed his teeth within an inch of her throat, she pulls a wad of bills from her swan purse, asks if he's free Wednesday.

The next time is at a cocktail party. Then an art gallery opening. Then another opera. All events she attends with an old red-haired woman draped in oyster coloured silk and fox fur. He assumes this is Grandma. Weird how Grandma doesn't seem to see anything amiss with how her young charge keeps disappearing during intermissions only to return with her thousand dollar dress torn and grass in her ringlets.

"Isn't your grandmother suspicious?" He asks her one night between acts of *Falstaff*, pulling a twig from her curls.

She swats his hand away like a fly. "Just do your job, Wolfman."

He claws at shuddering white flesh in the stone fountain beside the theatre. He tears the pearls from her stretched-forth throat and wrestles her to the earth in the dark woods behind her house. He drives home whistling, Five hundred dollars tucked in the heel of his suit, covered in little finger scratches, her screams ringing in his ears. "Oh Wolfman! Don't get me, Wolfman!" But the Wolfman gets her. For in these moments, he is no longer a man of flesh but a wolf—dangerous, hungry and handsomely paid.

He buys himself a bitchin' black leather suit and a magenta bass. He doesn't practice but he thinks about it as he lies on his in-laws' couch, dreaming up music videos starring a Wolfman and a hot chick in red running scared.

I am the Wolfman, he tells the flamingoes in the yard, the Royal Doulton figurines in his mother-in-law's hutch, his reflection in the bathroom mirror as he gets drunk in the middle of the afternoon on dirty mothers.

"Who the hell are you talking to, Floyd?" asks his wife, catching him.

"Nothing. No one," he mumbles.

"Wolfman," he repeats quietly after she's gone muttering out of the room.

He stops using the donut pillow because The Wolfman needs no pillow. Besides he'll probably never have to go back to construction with the money he's making.

Sure he's a bit worried about the fact that his employer, of late, has become increasingly hard to please.

"Bite me, Wolfman! Devour me!" she cries as they wrestle in the woods around her house. Frankly, it embarrasses him. "I'm trying," he says.

"Harder, Wolfman. Harder!"

He bites harder with his plastic fangs, painfully aware that only a few yards away in the gazebo, Grandma sits wrapped in chinchilla, playing solitaire bridge, polishing her rifles.

"But your grandmother's right—"

"Never mind her!" roars his red-faced employer.

Then there are her screams. She screams so frickin' loudly, the Wolfman worries someone—her grandmother, a policeman—will hear. And the Wolfman can't afford that. Not with his DUIs, his unpaid parking tickets. "Shhh," he pleads. "For God's sake, shhh."

She pouts, picking burrs off her dress. "You're no fun, Wolf-man."

Sometimes, for kicks, she bites him. He pretends like it doesn't hurt but it fucking does. Those pearly whites of hers are little needles.

He comes home, hoarse from howling, covered in little teeth marks, to find his wife isn't speaking to him. Even though he always changes in his car, covers his cuts with concealer, tells her his late nights, well, it's just this new gig, he knows she knows. He buys her a dozen roses, costume jewelry from Sears, the designer perfume she's always ripping samples of from magazines. Still, she folds her arms over her shrimp feast and slaps her palm over the top of her glass to stop him from pouring her more moderately-priced champagne.

"What?" he says, squirming under her eyes. "Can't a man buy his wife dinner at a nice restaurant?"

"A *man* can," she snorts, stabbing shrimp. "You're a whole other story."

"Look, I'm doing something I'm good at for once. *And* I'm making money. I don't see why you have to ride my ass."

Tears cloud her eyes. "I just want to know I can trust you."

"That's all I'm asking for," the Wolfman says easily, "A little trust. Look, if we're not sunning ourselves in Maui in six months you can shoot me with your dad's rifle. You've got my blessing. Alright?"

"Alright," she says, lifting her hand from her glass and letting him fill her up. "But I don't need your blessing."

* * *

FIRST SHE SAYS, "watch the dress" and "could you not put your paw on my heel?" Then she claims his growl isn't getting her going anymore. "Maybe you could growl a little more . . . I don't know . . . *wolfishly?*"

"Well you're not screaming like you were either," sulks the Wolfman.

"You can't expect me to fake it. I mean, isn't that what I'm paying *you* for?"

One night, when he's supposed to scare her in the park on her way home from an experimental one-man play, it happens: instead of his mighty wail, a hoarse growl; instead of her ear-splitting shriek, a mild yelp. There's a going-through-the-motions chase followed by a half-assed wrestle where they both collapse lamely to the woodlot floor.

"You faked it didn't you," he mopes, staring at the stars.

She picks a leaf from her dress, yawns. "Look, it isn't you, it's me."

But the Wolfman knows it's him. "What if I got another suit? Something hairier? That help?"

"I don't think so."

"Bigger teeth? They have these jumbo fangs at RiteAid. Or I

could get redder contacts."

"Mm," she says, frowning at her nails.

"Maybe you just need to be surprised again? We're always planning how I attack you. Maybe if you don't expect it . . ."

"Maybe," she yawns, opening her purse. "At least let me pay you for your . . . trouble."

He refuses. Even a Wolfman has his pride.

"Go on," she smiles, waving the wad around.

He takes it, hating himself, watches sadly as she melts like a fucked up dream, the Wolfman's dream, into the dark.

A long drive home, in which no screams reverberate in his ears. Only the rain pelting on his cracked windshield, tires slashing street puddles.

He comes home to find his wife standing in the front yard among the plastic flamingoes, holding the illicit wolf note in one set of fire-engine red nails and gripping her dad's shot gun with the other. Electric blue tears stream from her eyes.

"You sick twisted fuck."

There's no point reasoning with her. "Can I at least get my bass?"

Shots fire and the Wolfman runs screaming back into his car.

After getting drunk in Barbarella on the cash tucked in his hairy heel, the Wolfman staggers into RiteAid. In the seasonal department, he finds a pair of jumbo fangs, red eye contacts and Freddy Krueger nails. Ouch, fuck, he cries in the car putting it all on. The contacts burn. The fangs cut into his gums. The nails hang heavy. The Wolfman looks into the rearview mirror and screams at his reflection.

He forms his plan as he zigzags Barbarella through the dark, following the broken yellow line of highway. It's the kind of night they try to simulate at Screamer's before any big scare: still and dark and gleaming like a jet monster's pelt. He takes it as a sign.

He expected to have to jump the gates but they open as he pulls up. As he sways in the spiked shadow of her house, debating which window to break, the front door opens. For me, thinks the Wolfman, not noticing how in an upstairs window a light goes on then off.

He gets lost in the corridor of animal heads. "Where's her room anyway?" he asks an elk. "Thirteenth door on the left? Fourteenth?" The elk doesn't know. Fuck 'em. Fourteenth then. Jackpot! Wolves everywhere here. More even, or so it seems, than last time. Wait. Was there a wolf pelt on the bed? All these wolf heads on the walls? He's not sure the glass hutch full of rifles was there last time either. He jumps upon seeing a life-sized stuffed gray wolf baring its teeth to his right. Definitely *that's* new. Jesus. He rubs his hairy forehead with his cheap slasher claws, thinking maybe he should bag it. Then he hears steps in the hall.

As he crouches in the dust-bunny'd dark of the closet, readying himself to be the Wolfman, to give her the scare of her life, his best ever performance, he notices he's surrounded not by red silky dresses but orange hunting vests and lacy beige frocks heavy with old woman sweat and tea rose. Wait a minute.

The bedroom door creaks opens. "Wait," he whispers and sees, through the slats, the silver nose of a shotgun being gripped by a gnarled hand.

He bursts from the doors. "Wait! Wait!"

Her first shot would have blown his head off if he hadn't ducked. The Wolfman, screaming, runs into the corridor. As he dashes past antlers and black eyes big with warning, he hears the old woman reloading the shotgun behind him, the shells clicking in place, the barrel snapping shut. Fuck.

He reaches the end of the corridor when the second shot hits him in the leg; he goes down howling. The pain is blinding. As it overcomes him to unconsciousness, the last thing he sees is shotgun smoke and eyes the colour of skim milk wild with triumph.

When he wakes to see these same eyes bent over him, he screams.

The eye corners crinkle pleasantly. "We're awake," she says, baring a huge white mouthful of false teeth at the Wolfman.

"You. You tried to killed me."

Over the top of her tea cup, her old woman mouth twists into a you-naughty-boy smile.

"Not that you didn't deserve your little lesson. Poking about in my room. Sneaking into my closet. Bad," she scolds, shaking her finger at the Wolfman, eyes dark behind their spectacles.

He looks wildly around and sees he's strapped to a frilly beige bed, surrounded by urine yellow walls patterned with brown flowers.

"No," he protests weakly. "It was a mistake. I got lost, I—"

"Bad!" insists Grandma. "Wasn't he, dear?" and the Wolfman sees his former employer sitting in a corner chair, watching two wolves chase a jackrabbit on the Discovery channel. He tries desperately to make eye contact, but she just grunts at him as if she's never seen him before in her life and goes back to watching the TV screen.

"But alas," continues Grandma, stroking his thigh bandages more roughly. "Wolves will be wolves won't they?" She bares blinding dentures at the Wolfman. "We can none of us control our nature, can we Wolfthing?"

"No," he croaks.

"Which is why I won't be pressing any charges. And look! I've even cleaned your little wolf ensemble. Adorable!"

"No, no—" but his voice is a broken door swinging from a rusty hinge.

"No need to thank me, Wolfthing," she says, patting his cheek. "Besides, I could use a wolfthing about the house. A little light dusting. Someone to skim the scum off the pool. Tell me, do you play bridge, Wolfthing?"

The Wolfman tries to wrestle himself from the restraints, but the pain in his leg flares up, making him whimper. Grandma makes a disapproving cluck with her dentures, takes a world-weary sip of tea. "Well, I suppose I'll have to teach you, won't I? Won't I have to teach him, dear?" she says turning to her granddaughter, who is too mesmerized by the wolves tearing into the jackrabbit to reply, her eyes wide and shining, lips parted in excitement.

Fear flowers in the heart of the Wolfman. He wants to say *Please. Please, if you'll just let me go, you'll see that I'm no Wolfman, that I was never a Wolfman.* He wants to say *My name is Floyd Ackerman.* He opens his mouth but what comes out is a cracked squeak. It's useless. He's useless. As he sinks lamely back into the bed, making the beige frilly sheets crackle, the old woman smiles, triumphant. And with her bright eyes and big teeth hungrily fixed upon the Wolfman, she draws a deck of cards from her alligator purse, and lays them one by one on his hairy chest with hard little thwacks.

PERSUASION
Maude Larke

Aiglantine was hesitant. There was something implausible about it. But there was also something implausible about a talking frog.

"And I cannot tell you what anguish it is, that look that all the princesses give me when I talk to them. The shock first, then afterwards, with luck, haughtiness." He paused. "Without it, disgust."

He seemed to hang his head, but Aiglantine could not tell for sure.

"But you do see . . . it seems awfully untoward to us," she answered.

The black beads stared fixedly at her.

"But, honestly, what would you lose? And think of this; if I'm lying, I'll still be just a frog. A helpless little frog. You could fling me into the pond, you could dash me to the ground and grind your heel into me. So you can see what I have to lose."

"You *do* present the claim well."

"Could we simply dine together, at your castle? Only an hour or two of talk while you're eating. You cannot imagine how lonely it is here with no one to talk to. I will sit quite still, on one corner of the table. If you do not look at me, you might even forget . . ." His resonant, caressing voice drifted off.

She invited him.

And *in fine*, the dinner was pleasant. He was knowledgeable, he had seen the world (somehow, at some point), and he was fascinated with the arts. Aiglantine found herself laughing gaily. She found herself thinking how lonely it was in the castle with no one to talk to.

His mild suggestion, in his mild voice, that he accompany her to bed lulled. Perched on her shoulder like an agile kitten, he complimented her taste in tapestries as they mounted.

And there, as he waxed from suave to stimulating, the gay laughter became abandoned laughter, riotous laughter, free and powerful laughter.

"I do love the way your stomach muscles leap as you laugh! May I sit there a moment?"

And it was delicious to Aiglantine to open her limbs, and luxuriate on her back as she dandled the frog, and he went into ecstasies.

"Ah! Ah! What life! What energy! What flesh!"

Aiglantine felt a thrust against the thrust of her midriff and suddenly the frog landed on her alabaster throat and pressed his lips to hers.

And before she could thrust him away, she saw the black beads acquire deep green irises as the black repeated itself in lustrous locks of hair.

Aiglantine gasped to see him so handsome. So tall. So powerfully, beautifully naked.

She gasped again as he thrust himself between her legs and she felt a sharp pain.

She gasped no more as he closed his fingers around her neck as he thrust. She could not turn away from those deep, green, smiling eyes.

She was found in the morning by her maid, eyes staring, blood crusting the sheets, a strange slime on her belly.

HENRY'S TALE
John Kiste

We have always lived in the cabin near the mouth of the great forest, and we have always been warned not to play too deep within the woods. I don't always listen and I get mixed up occasionally, but I generally get home in time for a good whopping. My sister Gerta always obeys. She's such a sweet little lady. I think that I'm supposed to resent her, but I can't. She takes care of me. She calms our father when he gets angry with me, and she often moves between our step-mother Natasha and me when I am about to get strapped. Gerta is so tiny, but she is fearless.

Anyway, as I mentioned, we are not supposed to go deep into the woods, so I was surprised when Natasha saw my father off on a hunting trip, packed Gerta off to school, and then told me we did not have to worry about my home studies today, since we were going hiking. Boy, did we go hiking. Everything looked the same to me after about an hour, but we kept walking. Natasha didn't say much; she kept her cloak bundled tight against her and I mentioned how cold it was. She just nodded and pushed me forward. After a long time, she gave me a water bottle, and I sat down to drink. While I was drinking, I looked at the tall trees with their colored leaves, and watched a woodpecker pound his brains out against a trunk.

When I looked for Natasha a little later, she was gone. Had I moved? I didn't remember moving, but I do things often without thinking. She was going to be mad. She had lost me in the forest. I knew this was a bad thing. I had hidden a chocolate bar in my suspenders, and thought this would be a good time to eat it and think about my problem. I was going to be in so much trouble—if I even found my way back.

What if I never did? Oh boy. I decided I better start walking in some direction. I moved without much thought to where the sun was, or where the wind came from, or anything else. I just wandered. When the chocolate was gone I started to get really scared. I was just a little boy—older than Gerta, yes—but still a schoolboy. If they had let me in school. I could not seem to pass their stupid tests. I better pass *this* test of getting home, though.

As the day passed to afternoon, I came upon a clearing and saw to my delight an old building in its center. The first floor looked like it had been a tool shop of some kind, long disused, but there were enclosed steps going to the second floor, and an old woman was sweeping the stoop. I ran up and said hi. She stopped her sweeping and looked me over. Then in a cackling sort of voice she asked me my name.

"I'm Henry," I told her.

She tucked a gray curl back beneath her bonnet. "What are you doing this deep in the forest, young Henry?"

I shuffled my feet and admitted I was lost. She chuckled, but in a kind way, and told me to come inside for "refreshment." I followed her up the dim and musty stairs. Her rooms above the shop were small and worn. We entered into a sitting room that held only a bureau, a huge rocker, and an oval throw rug. There was a second-floor window in the back wall, and a huge cold-air register grate beside it. I was more interested in the kitchen to the right. There the floor was bare wood, but it was stocked as no kitchen I had ever seen. There was a sink and a small wooden icebox, a huge gas stove, a giant deep fryer, and an entire wall of spices and utensils.

The old lady pulled a bottle of soda from the icebox. It was cherry. I was so delighted that I began to gulp it as soon as she handed it to me. "This is swell," I managed between swigs. "I bet Gerta would love this, Mrs. . . ." I realized I had not asked her name.

Suddenly she pulled the bottle from my fist. "Don't chug this so," she said. "You will get a headache. I'm Mrs. Morley. I've lived in these parts forever. Did you say 'Gerta,' Henry? Is that your sister?"

"Yes." I answered, eying the half-empty drink. "My little sister. She never has any adventures. But she never gets in trouble, either."

"Well, you're not in trouble, my fine fellow. Where do you live?"

I shook my head a little. Specks swam before my eyes. I was even a little dizzy. "Why, we live in St. Peter's; our cabin is just at the forest entrance."

Mrs. Morley walked me to the rocker and sat me down in it. "Do you suppose your sister would like soda and candy?"

"Candy?" I cooed.

Suddenly she was filling my hands with chocolate drops and jellies and mint smoothies. I stuffed my pockets and she filled my hands again. "Why don't you bring Gerta to visit as well—perhaps tomorrow?"

I nodded drowsily. "She would play hooky to see all this. Yes, I am sure she will come. But I don't know how to get home—and I could never find my way back. Some say I am a dim wick."

Mrs. Morley led me to the door and carefully helped me down the steep set of steps. On the stoop she pointed between two huge oak trees. "Go straight between those trees, Henry, and don't veer in either direction. That will take you right into St. Peter's village square. And take these dozens of wrapped caramels. They are not for eating—drop one every few paces and you can use this marked trail to come back tomorrow with Gerta. How is that?"

My head was clearing a bit. "Wonderful!" I shook her withered hand and started home. I was still a little woozy for some unknown reason, but I kept on straight enough, dropping wrapped caramels as I went, and found home within two hours. Natasha seemed surprised but not overly angry that I had been misplaced. Still, Gerta watched our stepmother with narrow eyes throughout dinner and said very little. As we retired to bed, I told my sister of the wonder house. She thought things over and said she would meet me at the spring the next morning, after she pretended to leave for school.

The next day was sunny and cold. Natasha slept late and I dressed and met Gerta along the path. We had some little trouble finding my trail, but once upon it, the way was easy. No creatures had opened the treats and all were still in place. Before midday we saw the quiet building. I marched right to the door leading to the steps, but Gerta pulled me back. "It's okay," I said, and then it had to be, for Mrs. Morley opened the door and welcomed us.

"I trust this is Gerta," and she rubbed her palms together in an odd way. "Come up, dear. Come up, Henry. We'll have a fine day!"

I darted around her up the dark stairs, with Gerta trying to reach me. At the top all was the same as the day before. Mrs. Morley handed me a cherry soda and ushered Gerta into the kitchen. I stood by the window slowly drinking it and watched through the doorway as Gerta received a grape soda from the icebox. All was right with the world. Mrs. Morley turned and smiled a toothy grin at me, but I looked beyond her and saw Gerta pour half her bottle into the sink. I frowned, but when Mrs. Morley turned to my sister, she seemed happy that the bottle was half gone. I took another drink, Mrs. Morley looked at me again, and Gerta dumped the rest of the soda. My head spun a little. I was dizzy, and that's why I didn't think it odd when the old woman walked in front of me and shot the bolt on the door. I stumbled slightly.

"It's drugged!" hissed Gerta from the kitchen.

Mrs. Morley perched herself on the huge rocker, watching me.

"What is?" I stammered.

"The drink, Henry!" Gerta was yelling now. "Stop drinking!"

The old woman turned to chide Gerta but only got out "Young lady—" before the soda bottle hit her full in the face, stunning her. I eyed all this with fascination and began to take another drink when Gerta dashed to my side and knocked my bottle to the floor.

"Hey!" I moaned.

Gerta grabbed my bottle and smashed the window with it. She surveyed the ground, twenty feet below. "I'm going down the rainspout, Henry. You're too tipsy, you would fall. The bolt on the door is too high to reach." Gerta looked to Mrs. Morley who was beginning to rise. "Get into the furnace duct," she threw the register cover open. "Go! I'll get help. Go!"

I was really confused, and starting to realize there would be no candy today. Out of the corner of my eye, I saw the woman advancing. Then Gerta pushed me and the old lady's bony fingers brushed by me as I slid into the vent. I dropped down a space and heard Gerta holler as she leapt from the smashed window to the rainspout. I found myself covered with dust—and worse, the dripping red spilled soda. I was cramped and dizzy—and slipping. I dropped down quite a ways and landed hard at a ductwork junction. I thought I had better crawl along it horizontally, and in an instant I was sliding down another pipe. Before I could right myself, half of my body was in the furnace itself. I had slid all the way to the basement.

I decided this was probably a good thing because I could see some light, so there must be a vent opening. I found it, and it was big enough to allow me through, but it was hooked on the outside of the furnace. Through its slats I surveyed the basement. Dingy, damp and moldy, it held an unpleasant smell. I saw a workbench with many sharp tools like hatchets and saws and sickles hanging above it. As my eyes dropped to the surface of the bench, I felt my head swim even more, my breath catch, and my heart pound hard. The workbench was littered with skulls and gnawed bones, all the size of children. This was clearly a bad thing.

Suddenly there was a huge shaft of light and a loud bang as the furnace gas jet cover came off. Mrs. Morley's grinning face peered in at me, and her fingers began that long reach to where I crouched. "Going without a goodbye?" she cackled. This was clearly a *really* bad thing.

Just then the register cover popped off and Gerta offered me her hand. She had come through a basement window while the old woman had clambered down the steps. I thrust myself into the opening and dropped onto my head beside the furnace just as Mrs. Morley leaned completely in to grab me. From the floor I watched Gerta crank on the gas jets and strike a match to the pilot. The interior of the furnace burst forth with an orange glow as Mrs. Morley shrieked in disappointment and, an instant later, in pain. Then in agony. The scent of roasted flesh filled the dank room, covering the other smells there.

We sat awhile on the cold floor. Finally, Gerta climbed onto the workbench and took down one of the sharper-looking sickles. "All right, Henry," she said firmly. "Let's go have a little talk with Natasha, shall we?"

THE STORYTELLER'S JIG
Simon P. Clark

He sat beneath the old stone bridge, among the dirt and the shining stones, all wet from the rain, all wet from the slime that drip-drip-dripped from the tracks above. It was a closed up world, waiting for him—the track and the paths, the bridge, the mess, all abandoned long ago. He shuffled in from another town, a different place where the stories dried up, and here it was, empty and waiting, his.

The children came to him, gathering round, the younger ones scared and hiding behind coats, their pale faces staring, open-mouthed, doubting. Some held stones. Some held back. A boy, Robbie, clutched a stick. The sky rolled above them, a grey, crinkled sheet.

"Ain't true," said a voice. Others murmured. A little one sniffed.

"Is, though!" said Robbie, stepping forward. He faced them and then turned back again, pointing with the stick to the pile of clothes.

"Right there," he said, and he nodded, firm and steady.

"Robbie . . ." said a girl. He glared at her and looked around. "Give us a can," he said. "A can, a can! Come on, guys."

Someone handed him a bottle with a shrug, shuffling away again, muttering something. Robbie grinned a wolfish smile, and he glared around, daring the others.

"Watch, okay?" he said.

The bottle flew through the air and it spun, a blur, a dancing baton, as it went. They watched. The water dripped and the red dust bricks shone in the gloom and the cold. Robbie smiled, proud and triumphant, and pushed out his chest with a huff.

"Look," he said, pointing. A hand, black with dirt, rough and old and covered with grime, shot out from the trash and long fingers grasped the bottle.

Screams, laughter, shrieks and gasps. Robbie beamed.

"Hah! See? I told you. He's here."

The pile shook and the man stood up, coughing and muttering, and he slumped against the bricks. The wall above him shuddered. The children backed off, staring, silent, looking at Robbie and back to the man. Some ran.

"Flippin' kids," said the man. He coughed and smiled. "Robert," he said. He groaned.

"I told 'em," said Robbie. "I said, 'storyteller's come, he's under the bridge,' just like you said. I told 'em."

"And they came."

"Aye, here's the lot," said Robbie.

The others watched, still silent. The man stood up. He wore a trench coat, black with oil, stained brown with dust, torn and shredded and old. His hair was dirty grey, hidden under a wide brimmed hat, itself old and dark green and just as dirty as his face. White stubble brushed his chin and circled his mouth, which was frozen for a moment in a strange half-smile. His eyes shone out, blue as starling eggs, white as salt, black as night. He bowed.

"Greetings, kidlings!" he called. "Allow an old tramp to make your acquaintance. Ahem. Jack's the name—Jack the Teller, and I'm here to dazzle and bamboozle and shock and amaze you mighty fine folks! With the ancient profession—the noble profession!—of the scop, the bard!, the storyteller!"

He bowed again, his thin smile building, his eyes never leaving their faces. Robbie chuckled.

"I told you, eh?" he said. "Storyteller's here, just moved to the town. He's gonna stay here and make us stuff. Make magic and myth and history."

"Aye," said Jack. "Magic. Myth. History."

"He's here for us," said Robbie.

"Poetry," said Jack. "Legends. Angels and demons. Blood and honour. Tales and fables and stories."

He raised up the coat tails and shifted his feet, a strange, halting jig. The children watched. They laughed.

"Where'd you find 'im, Rob?" asked a girl.

Robbie frowned. His eyes shifted down. He bit his lip. "Dunno," he said, shrugging. "Dunno. In me dreams I saw him. In the moon in the night, in the diamond stars. In the chalky moon and the velvet sky."

"Eh?" they laughed. "You what? You what, Rob?"

Water dripped from the ancient rails.

"Dreams," said Robbie. "Thoughts. Calls from birds. Screeches of cats. Screams of foxes. Dunno. I knew."

"Oh, yes," said Jack. "One in every village. One in every town. To call the lucky to hear the truths I know how to whisper."

He winked and danced and fell against the shining brick. He coughed and fell to a slump. "Knackered!" he whispered. "Gotta find grub."

"What you eat?" asked a boy.

"You like chips?"

"You want crisps?"

"What you want?" they asked. They pushed forward, moved nearer, crowding round to see.

"Haha!" he laughed. "Haha! What you got? Nuts and bolts and bottles and glass?"

"He ain't us," said Robbie. "He's not a kid. He don't want that."

Jack the Teller reached to the ground, feeling around the wet earth, the old bags, the dust and the grime and the trash. He grinned. "Got ya!" he said, opening his hand. The children gasped and laughed at him. A broken light bulb, burned metal, scorched glass. He grinned and looked around him. "Good for the heart, good for the teeth!"

He popped it in, crunching down, scraping and chewing, rolling his eyes, "Yum," he said. "That's the ticket."

"You're mad!" they screamed. "You can't! How'd you do that?

What's the trick?"

"No trick!" he beamed. He showed them his mouth, his dark, rough tongue, his sharp, yellow teeth, his cheeks. "All gone," he said, "for now."

Robbie stepped forward and raised his hands. "Quiet, you lot. Don't crowd him, neither. We're gonna get a story. A story from a Teller. You don't even get how lucky that is."

"Thank you, young Robert," said Jack the Teller, nodding his head and crossing his legs. "Come forward, young sprogs! Come forward, little spittles. It's your turn. This town. This night. Your turn, with the Teller."

The light was fading, turning shade into shadows, and the sky, a charcoal grey, was flecked with early stars. The children gathered closer. The youngest trembled and held to others' hands. Jack raised an eyebrow. He sniffed the air.

"Cold?" he asked. "Cold and shivery? Tremblin' and quiverin' and queasy in the shadow looms?" He spat on the ground and sprang up with a clap, rubbing his hands and clicking his tongue. "Fire!" he cried. "Good for the bones. Good for the chills. And good, bleed me, for the stories. And what comes from eating all light bulbs and sparks? What comes of that, eh? Eh? Hm? Hm?"

He turned this way and that, thick eyebrows raised high, searching their faces, stroking his chin. "Eh? Hm? Eh?"

"Dunno," they muttered. They kicked at the dirt, hid hands in their pockets.

"Ha!" he laughed. "You wouldn't, eh? Wouldn't know. Watch close."

He moved back, stretched his limbs, winked, showed his teeth. He lurched forward and huffed, a huge, hollow sound, and with a rush of wind and a bitter, odd smell, blew fire into the mouldy leaves, the shoe laces and rotting bags, the trash that lay beneath the bridge, the things lost and forgotten, and they burned beneath the bridge. The flames roared for a moment, all hot air and hunger, and then settled a warm yellow of butter and sunlight, a deep, dark red of bricks and blood, and sparks, green, white and copper brown, spat and danced in the air. The children laughed and applauded.

"Roll up!" cried Jack. "Roll up, one and all, and listen, close and crowded, to the story I will tell you . . ."

They huddled down, crouched in the dark, shadows from the fire making ghouls of their faces, making claws of their hands. Robbie sat and watched them, proud as a teacher, as a mother, as a priest, to see the story begin, to see the one's he'd chosen hearing it.

Jack the Teller grinned and coughed and put his face low to the flames, to the smoke that bubbled, to the dirt and the lost and forgotten things, and began to tell the story.

"Once," he said, "upon a time. Oh, once upon a time . . ."

He spun webs in the air, drew them in with his words, cast out nets to their minds, laid out bait for their hearts. The children listened, the fire burned. The sky, black now, was filled with stars that shone above the broken bridge. Late in the night, Jack the Teller strode on, spreading rumour and magic and tales that he knew. He grinned and winked and danced and bowed, stroking his chin, feeling the bristle, wiping the grime from his cheeks with his thumbs. The children sat and watched and listened. Jack the Teller danced on.

FOUR GRIMM TALES, REVISITED
Erin Virgil

I

Crouched down with the littlest birds
I watch them pick lentils from ashes:
the good ones for the pot
the bad ones for your crop
I say it over and over, a prayer.
Their tiny heads bob up and down
little black beaks peck the hearth stones, click and drag.
Why do they care
if I go to the ball tonight
and curtsy for the king?
Maybe they're just hungry.

II

My favorite blue ball
has rolled into the cage
where they keep the wild man.
His disheveled head is a nest for sparrows,
his beard, a mass of black wires.
He squeezes my ball with a hand as long as my arm
and stares at me through the iron bars.
His eyes are the color of a dead fish's belly
and never let go of mine.

III

When I pushed her into the oven
I thought she'd smell like melting sugar,
like the dripping walls of her house.
No. A sickly foreign smell:
burning flesh, soiled cloth, mud, grease, hair.
We hear her toothless screams for a while.
From his cage, my brother licks his lips.

IV

He says, "If you chop off her hands,
I won't take you with me."
Imagine a scale,
on one side hang my daughter's small white hands
on the other, a poor man's soul.
I fetch my axe.

All are takes on fairy tales of the Brothers Grimm: "Cinderella," "The Wild Man," "Hansel and Gretel," and "The Maiden Without Hands."

THEY SAY ONCE THE TREES BEGIN TO
TREMBLE IT IS TOO LATE
Steven Ehret

TROUBLE BOUGHT
AND BORROWED

BOTTLE
Danielle Fontaine

I lived in a closet
of ripped paper
dolls, crumpled
clothing, and stray
mice. I kept them
as pets, and named
the dead I found floating
in our fly bottle. We kept
the small glass sculpture
on the kitchen table.
It was so pretty
empty, but my father,
too practical for art,
filled the bottle with milk
and arsenic.

THROUGH THE DIAMOND BLUES
Kimberly Duede

That stupid Tabby Cat was waiting for Jamie again. It was the first thing she saw when school was over and she passed underneath its seat on the high marble pillar beside the doors. As she felt its enormous, amber eyes burrowing into the back of her skull, she tightened her fingers around the spray bottle hidden in her pocket.

She slung her backpack further up on her shoulder as she saw the Cat crouch down. Just as she passed the pillar, she felt one clawed paw bat at an unruly, brunette curl on top of her head. The second she felt it, she whipped around, brandishing her spray bottle, and pulled the handle, sending a jet of perfume at its face.

The Cat recoiled and hissed. It leaped off the pillar and dashed off through the bushes on the other side of the sidewalk. Despite the disapproving glances she was receiving from a group of girls nearby, Jamie smirked. In her mind, spraying the Cat was payback for the time she had been having lunch on the front lawn of the school and the Cat had snuck up behind her and started nibbling on her tuna sandwich while her head was turned. Or the time when the Cat had followed her back home and had left a brown, slimy hair ball on her window shelf. Or the time when . . . well, the list went on and on.

The Cat never seemed to run off anywhere specific after their encounters and it didn't have a collar, so Jamie figured it was a stray. Still, she couldn't figure out why the Cat had chosen to stalk *her* for the past two months, but as long as it wanted to bother her, she would go right on bothering it back. Feeling smug, she packed the spray bottle safely into her pants pocket and took her usual route home, enjoying the way the sun shone on the large patch of blue delphiniums in front of the entrance to the park, in which the city had cultivated a public garden. She had never spent nearly as much time in the gardens as she wanted to, but when she did, she always remembered to pick some of the Diamond Blues (a nickname for those startlingly beautiful delphiniums). Through the gate, she could see the cascading branches of willow trees brush against patches of irises and geraniums.

She breathed in the sweet scents, pausing to bend down and pick a batch of delphiniums, but the moment her fingers wrapped around the flowers, she heard an ominous growl from underneath the flower bed. She barely had enough time to move back before the Cat sprang out, making a mad lunge for her jacket sleeve.

She fumbled for the spray bottle again and batted the Cat away. The Cat whipped between her legs and then crouched, ready to attack her socks. Jamie aimed the nozzle at the Cat's nose.

"Just try it, buddy," she said.

It was just then that she heard a giggle, as light as the tinkling of wind chimes, behind her. She gasped and peered around at the flowers.

"That's quite enough of that," someone said, but Jamie couldn't tell which direction it came from.

"Who's there?" Jamie demanded. Her target on the Cat faltered as she ducked down to look through the delphiniums. Beside her, the Cat was still crouched, its ears laid back against its head while its tail flicked deftly back and forth.

Jamie reached down to part the flowers and look for the source of the voice, and a burst of pale blue light dazzled her. She covered her eyes with her free hand and felt a rush of wind zip past her, as though a bird had just taken flight inches from her head. When she recovered and looked up again, she found herself staring at a flower that was even stranger than the pictures of Amazonian flowers in her school's biology books. It was like a turquoise pinwheel with long vines wrapped around its stem. Jamie rubbed her eyes and looked again, just to make sure they weren't playing tricks on her. When she dropped her hands, she found that the flower was actually a purse that hung by a strap off of a small girl only half Jamie's size. The girl had flowing blond locks and piercing blue eyes. Her dress was patterned with the same flower as her purse.

Jamie shook her head as if to clear her thoughts. The girl must have snuck up behind her and hidden in the flower bed. There was no way she could have just appeared from thin air.

"The two of you jesters love to play tricks. I do as well," the girl said.

"What are you talking about?" Jamie asked.

The girl pointed a slender finger towards the Cat. "This creature has been teasing you and you have teased him. I know. I have been watching you for weeks," she said.

"You've been watching us?" Jamie said in disbelief.

The girl tilted her head. "You barely hide your shenanigans. I can hear you screaming at him all over the city."

"He started it," Jamie mumbled.

The girl smiled. "Sometimes it doesn't matter who takes the first turn in a game, so long as the players keep moving."

Jamie raised an eyebrow and said, "All right. Whatever you say. What's your name and why were you watching us?"

"You may call me Celeste. You make me laugh and I love watching things that make me laugh," she said, winding a thick strand of hair around her index finger.

"That's a pretty name," Jamie said. "I haven't seen you around here before. Where do you live?"

"I go wherever I please," Celeste said.

Jamie waited for Celeste to say something else, but the girl remained silent. It certainly didn't seem like she was going to reveal the directions to her house, so Jamie said, "Well, it's nice to meet you, Celeste. My name is—"

"Jamie. I know," Celeste said.

"How did you find that out?" Jamie said, a chill running down her neck.

Celeste continued talking, ignoring Jamie's question. "I want to play a game. The both of you like games, right? That's why you always pursue and torment each other."

Jamie frowned in confusion before she realized that the Cat was the other player Celeste was referring to. The Cat was watching Celeste very closely, with its back arched. The fur on his spine bristled. However, Jamie knew that if the Cat felt truly threatened, he would have run off into hiding.

"I've made my own special game for you," Celeste said.

Before Jamie could say that she wasn't interested in playing any games, Celeste approached her and beckoned her closer. Without thinking, Jamie obeyed, leaning down. When her face was close enough, Celeste pressed the space between her eyes with the pads of her index and middle finder and there was another brilliant flash of light.

Jamie gave a startled yelp and staggered backwards, grasping her eyes. The skin Celeste had touched tingled as though ice had been pressed over it. The tingling grew and spread across her face. With her heart pounding, Jamie rubbed her cheeks, trying to warm them. She watched the odd girl then turn towards the Cat, who squirmed away. Jamie would have thought the Cat would be able to outrun the girl, but her hand shot out and pressed against the messy 'M' on the tabby's forehead. This time, the Cat rushed away, disappearing into the bundle of delphiniums.

* * *

BEFORE JAMIE HAD A chance to worry over the Cat, she stared at her hands, which were growing tiny, dark hairs out of the pores, the same color as the hair on her head. The tingling spread throughout her arms and legs until it reached the tips of her fingers and toes. She dropped her backpack and wrapped her arms around her belly, but she couldn't stop her insides from feeling as though they were being squished through a wine press. The houses across the street and the flowers of the garden distorted and lengthened as though they were being inflated like balloons.

She gasped and fell to her knees on the sidewalk. The world kept growing and the hairs on Jamie's skin grew long and thick.

The next time she inspected her hands, she didn't have hands at all, but two paws. The tingling receded and she tried to stand, but her legs wouldn't obey in the way she wanted. The world had lost its color; it was now a monochrome gray, except for the faint blue of the delphiniums.

Oh my god, she thought as she crawled out from the baggy pants of her school uniform. She took a look at her new, long, sleek body, with a tail swishing frantically behind her. *I'm a cat.*

She glared at Celeste as best she could, which caused the girl to give a devilish laugh.

"You look much nicer, little miss. Are you ready to play our game?" she said.

Jamie opened her mouth to protest and found out that a cat's lips were not made to form human words. She gave a long yowl instead.

"Don't worry, I'll change you back, so long as you win my game," Celeste said. "I propose a race, between you and your old rival."

Jamie cocked her head, baffled at the mention of a rival. She followed Celeste's gaze towards the delphinium patch, where something large was stirring. The very lean, very naked body of a man with short, dusty hair and amber eyes slowly sat up from the patch of flowers. If Jamie could have blushed in her new, unusual form, she would have. The man was clutching loosely at his head and glancing around him as though disoriented. He focused on Celeste and growled, but it sounded strange, more like a hiss. Jamie realized with a start that the man was the Cat, only human. Whatever spell Celeste had cast on her, she had cast on the Cat as well, only in reverse.

"Now that the players are ready, I will tell you the rules," Celeste said. From seemingly out of nowhere, she lifted a mahogany box, carved with floral designs. On the front of the lid were three keyholes. "This is my treasure. Inside is something that will grant a wish, which I will offer to you, provided you win our game. Around these gardens are the keys to the lid. To whomever finds the keys and brings them to me, the wish will be given."

Jamie's tiny heart leaped. If she found the keys, she could wish to be turned back into a human! She just had to ensure that she found them before the Cat. The Cat himself looked as though he wanted to protest, but he could only speak in a series of small grunts. Of course, he wouldn't know how to speak in his new body just as Jamie didn't know how, given hers.

Celeste sat on the short flight of stairs leading to the garden, setting the chest down on her lap and caressing the top of it. "I will be waiting here for your return. Don't be long!"

Amongst the flowers, the Cat tried to stand, as he had probably seen many humans do before, but his legs were long and limber and he stumbled. He glanced from the garden to Jamie, and frowned. Jamie would have a much easier time getting used to her much shorter legs. Deciding not to waste a moment of her bought time, she set off through the flowers towards the gate to the gardens. It didn't take her long to realize that she couldn't see through all of the stems and trunks of the growth around her. Her sensitive ears picked up every cricket chirp and tweeting bird while her nose smelled every floral aroma mixed with the stench of earthy decay. Despite the flood of sensations, however, she stayed focused. She needed to find the keys!

In the middle of the gardens, there were life-sized statues of hooded figures, kneeling as though they were plotting. She decided to search there first. She picked her way through the towering plants, ignoring the scents of other cats and dogs who had marked this territory as their own. Eventually, she came across the cement walkway that led through the rest of the gardens. She immediately had to maneuver around the legs of the humans passing by. She glanced up at their dizzying heights, trying to make out their faces. She had never realized just how large people must seem to a cat. When a stern woman with pursed lips shooed Jamie away, she retreated to the brush again.

Somehow, miraculously, she found her way to the three statues, which were seated inside a ring of stones, facing each other with their heads bowed. With a quick glance to see if anyone was watching, Jamie made her way over to the statues and carefully circled each one. The granite of each was faded and cracked, but she found no openings for any keys. She paced to the center of the circle, looked up and paused. From the folded hands of one of the statues dangled a silver chain. She scrambled into position and tried to leap at the chain, but the movements of her hind legs were awkward. She crouched even lower and leaped again, extending her claws at the top of her jump, only to miss the end of the chain by inches. It took two more tries before her right paw grazed the statue's hand with a claw and snagged on the chain. The key came sliding out on her way back down.

With her heart swelling with pride and victory, she inspected the key. It was a silvery-gray, iron key with a simple design in its handle, reminiscent of the flowers on Celeste's box. She picked it up in her mouth and carried it with her as she headed off back to the undergrowth. She racked her brain to remember what other monuments were in the gardens. It only took her a moment to remember the fountain further down the path. She hurried along, avoiding an excitable greyhound that pulled on its owner's leash, straining to chase after her as she flitted away. Its barks rang in her ears, making her pause and threatening to give her a headache.

She could make out the head of the statue that topped the fountain over the rose bushes. She picked her way through them, wincing as she felt tiny thorns penetrating her fur coat and graze her skin. She crawled, low to the ground on her belly until she reached the other side and stretched in relief. The world was so different from this angle. The centerpiece to the fountain itself was a large chameleon with water spouting from its mouth.

Mindful of the couple sitting on a bench nearby, Jamie neared the stone steps leading up to the edge of the pool and stared into the water. Several points of glittering, copper light glinted back at her in the sunlight. She tested her toes in the water and immediately withdrew them. Beads of moisture clung to her fur and claws.

Out of the corner of her newly extended line of vision, Jamie saw the couple on the bench pointing and having a fit about seeing a cat in the pristine water. She would have to search quickly. She stepped each paw into the pool, one after the other. The surface of the water came up to her head, which she kept raised with the iron key clutched between her teeth.

She waded out to the center of the pool until she was underneath the chameleon's head and climbed atop the statue's pedestal.

Her fur felt slick and plastered against her skin, so she shook it out. There were fewer wishing coins resting at the bottom of the pool nearer the statue. She scanned the area, looking for the key. At long last, she caught a glimpse of dark gray against the creamy white bottom of the pool. Jamie laid her key on the pedestal of the chameleon and re-entered the frigid water. Determined, she kept wading until she felt a thin, hard shape under her paw.

Just as she was trying to figure out the best way to hold her breath without lips, she heard sloshing steps behind her. She carefully turned and saw that the same man from the delphinium patch —*the Cat*, she reminded herself—had stepped into the fountain and was coming towards her.

He had figured out how to use his legs more quickly than she had expected. *And* he was wearing her pants. He had figured out human modesty quickly, too, unless he was just trying to save the other humans in the garden the grief of seeing his naked body. The couple on the bench were still raising a stink about the pair of them in the fountain. They were the ones who must have alerted the Cat to Jamie's location.

The Cat reached Jamie and grinned. With a flourish, he reached past her and withdrew the iron key from the water. Jamie hissed at him and tried to scratch his leg. He splashed water on her face and swatted her away.

"Don't . . . try it . . . buddy," he said.

Jamie's eyes grew as wide as dinner plates. How could the Cat have learned to speak?!

As though he could sense the question, the Cat said, "I've been . . . listening to you humans . . . for a while. I'm going to find the keys first."

He strode out of the fountain, past the gawking couple, dropping the iron key into his pocket as he went. Jamie made her way back to the statue and grabbed her own key. The Cat might have the second key, but Jamie could still get the third. But where should she look now? Time was running out.

She left the fountain and disappeared down the path before the couple tried to capture her. She was picking her way through the undergrowth that ran along the garden's stone wall when she heard a set of rough, baritone voices before her. She ducked into a hole in a nearby tree and waited for them to pass. The rancid odor of rotten eggs and stale mud hit her before the owners of the voices came into view.

Jamie couldn't believe her eyes. Three hunchbacks—all with olive-colored leathery skin, bulbous noses, and large, watery eyes—were hobbling in the direction Jamie had just come from. Draped loosely around their heads and shoulders were horribly familiar cloaks, the same ones that the kneeling statues had been wearing. She blinked and then blinked again, just to be sure her eyes weren't fooling her. Then, she realized that she could understand perfectly the words that they were muttering to each other.

* * *

"Mistress will be pleased, she will," the first goblin said.

"Oh yes, all she needs is the two keys left and then she won't need to wear that hideous disguise no more. She can wish us all pretty. I wonder how long it will take those two dumb cats to find out Mistress has the third key in her bag . . ." the second goblin said, causing the third to whack him upside the head with a massive hand that was half-buried in thick bandages.

"Not so loud! Who knows what could be listening!" The third goblin said. "Oh, scab it, you made me hurt my hand."

"That cat got you good when she plucked that key from you, you ugly brute!"

"It's what you get for clubbin' me!" the second goblin said, rubbing the bump on his scalp.

"She musta had somma that smelly water on her feet. Some says it smells like flowers, but it stinks to me! Her scratches stung, they did," the third muttered.

The goblins continued bickering, but Jamie had stopped listening. She needed to find the Cat! After flitting around in the garden for a few minutes, she picked up on the Cat's scent. She bolted after the trail, which lead her away from the fountain and back towards the entrance to the garden. Her little heart pounded inside her furry chest. She had to get to him before he went to Celeste and she tricked him into believing more of her lies!

Just as the garden gate came into her view, she felt a muscled, oily fist tighten around her tail and hoist her up into the air. She yowled, opening her mouth wide and dropping her key. All four clawed paws swept the air, trying and failing to dig into the hand that held her. She found herself looking upside down at the cackling faces of two more hunchbacked goblins.

"Mistress will like the fur offa our prize!" one said, poking at Jamie's soft belly. Its companion guffawed and reached for Jamie's neck. She howled again, but this time, her call was followed by the sound of a large body crashing through the flowers and weeds. Suddenly, the Cat appeared behind the goblin holding Jamie suspended in the air. He shoved the goblin with all of his weight, causing it to drop Jamie and topple into the other goblin. As soon as Jamie landed on her four feet, she scrambled to collect her fallen key, not a second before the Cat picked her up and carried her towards the gate. The pair of goblins were left in a struggling heap on the ground.

"Children . . . did that all the time to me," the Cat told Jamie. "They always held my tail and tossed me. I know how it hurts."

At first, Jamie was grateful for the chance to rest in the Cat's arms, but then she twisted and looked up at him, silently pleading to be put down. The Cat held her by her armpits, hesitating for a moment, and then gently set her on the ground. She came closer and reared up on her hind legs, patting the pocket of the Cat's pants that held the spray bottle.

He took it out and peered down at her, puzzled, but Jamie had already started off through the garden gate. As she had promised, Celeste was waiting for them on the entrance steps. Jamie wasted no time leaping in front of her and presenting the iron key in her mouth. The Cat held his key out as well. Celeste giggled when she saw him in Jamie's pants.

"They suit you," she said, covering her mouth. Jamie tried not to snarl. Celeste was very talented if she could mask her goblin stench along with her appearance. Jamie was still furious that she and the Cat had been fooled.

"I told you to collect three keys. Where is the third?" Celeste said.

Puzzled, the Cat met Jamie's eyes, who then stood, went over to Celeste, and proceeded to tear at the center of her floral purse. Celeste shrieked and tried to throw Jamie off, but then the third iron key fell from the bag and onto the bare skin of Celeste's legs. As soon as it made contact, the skin began to sizzle and blister. The girl sprang up, dropping the chest onto the ground and cursing at Jamie, who ran behind the Cat. They watched as Celeste's burnt skin began to change, turning green and leathery. Jamie pointed a paw towards the spray bottle and the Cat took the hint, aiming it towards Celeste's injury and pulling the handle.

The searing ache was enough to break whatever focus Celeste had over her disguising spell. The little fairy grew twisted and warped, growing large, watery eyes and a balloon-like nose. Her long, golden hair turned thin and crackly like straw. She staggered backwards, panting. The Cat held the spray bottle pointed at her face while Jamie rushed forward to collect the third and final key.

"You figured it out, did you?" Celeste said in a voice quite un-like her former lyrical tone. "The others must have blabbed about everything, the idiots!"

"We will take our wish now," the Cat said, retrieving the key from Jamie and kneeling in front of the chest. He jammed the keys into the keyholes and turned them. The chest opened to reveal one long stem of small, purplish-blue buds—a delphinium stalk before the flowers had bloomed.

"These flowers can grant wishes, you know. You have to bite the buds before they've opened and released the wish. If they bloom, you've lost your chance. This particular flower was picked under-neath the blue moon, and as such, its powers are more potent. However, you must first speak your wish to the flower," Celeste said, smirking at Jamie. She looked towards the Cat. "While you both bested me, as I can recall, only you can speak," she said, indi-cating the Cat. "So I will give the flower—and the wish—to you, Cat."

Jamie looked away, forlorn, because she knew the cat would only wish to stay human while she stayed a cat. Why wouldn't he want to take revenge on Jamie for her poor treatment of him by forcing her to remain as a cat? But when the Cat spoke next, he surprised her.

"I wish I had my body back and I wish for this cat to be human again. This body is . . . clumsy. Humans are strange," he said. He peered sideways at Jamie. "But this human here is the clumsiest and strangest of them all."

Jamie glared at him while he took the flower out of the chest and carefully bit off one of the buds. Jamie felt her entire body tingle and change. The flowers and trees around her shrank and the fur on her arms retreated into her skin. When Jamie was a human and the Cat was a cat, Jamie grabbed her jacket off the ground to cover herself up, took her spray bottle, and chased the grotesque form of Celeste into the garden. Before she could run off in search of her ghastly entourage, Celeste yelled, "We will meet again, girl! You and that beast will remember me!"

"And we'll be ready to wish you down!" Jamie cried out after the goblin. She picked up the wishing flower in one hand and the Cat in the other before she set off to go home. She was going to make tuna for her and her new best friend. This time, there would be no tricks.

BRING IT, BERNADETTE
Angela Buck

was out one Sunday afternoon shopping for cake toppers when I ran into my friend Bernadette. It was my husband's birthday and I wanted to get him something really special. "Why not put me on the cake?" Bernadette said.

I hadn't thought of that. Although in the end it made a lot of sense because Bernadette was two inches tall and made out of sugar.

"You're sweet," I said. I took her by the hand and led her into my purse.

When we got home, my husband was asleep in the den. I quietly unpacked the groceries, took a mixing bowl out of the cupboard and began making the cake.

While it was baking, Bernadette and I chatted over coffee. I had to fetch a thimble from my sewing kit so that she could drink hers, but even the thimble was too big for her. She had to lean over and take sips from the edge like a grown person drinking out of a soup pot.

"Coffee's delicious," she said and gave me a wink. Bernadette was, on the whole, an agreeable little woman. I didn't know why we didn't spend more time together.

Soon enough the cake was done. I let it cool for a bit on the counter, topped it with icing and then put Bernadette in the center.

"What should I do?" she said.

"I don't know," I said. I hadn't thought that far ahead.

"Maybe this?" she said.

"No, that's not quite right."

"This?"

"Do like this," I said and showed her.

"Oh, that's good," she said.

I counted out the candles and arranged them in a circle around Bernadette. Then I dimmed the lights and very ceremoniously carried the cake into the living room where my husband was still sleeping.

To tell you the truth, I have no husband. It was not his birthday. It was no one's birthday. I just like cakes and wanted an excuse to bring Bernadette home.

"Can I open my eyes now?" she said.

Poor Bernadette. She was so small and fragile and the world was so big and full of violence.

THE LIBRARY
Paul Crenshaw

One day in early March, a few months before school let out for the summer, things started happening at the library. If the library were a car, you would say it was making a noise. Or it wouldn't turn over. Or one of the tires was flat. The library needed oil, or new spark plugs, or a new head gasket. Something. No one knew what was wrong with the library—they just all knew it needed something. One day smoke was coming from the library. Everyone thought the books were burning so they rushed to help. But the books weren't burning.

AT FIRST, IT WAS small things. The air-conditioning blew hot air. The water in the water fountain turned green on Wednesdays. The windows that look out over the town became translucent, then opaque. Some of the words disappeared from some of the books, and all of the words disappeared from some of the other books. Some books wouldn't open. Others wouldn't close. Kelly got lost on the fourth floor. When they asked her how she got lost on the fourth floor, she said it wasn't the fourth floor anymore.

WHEN THE LIBRARY MOVED itself for the first time, they decided to call in experts. They brought in architects, astrologists, astronomers, psychiatrists, psychologists, mechanics, engineers, other librarians, tech support, social workers, a dentist, a doctor, a few politicians, an exorcist and a snake-charmer. The exorcist and the snake-charmer came on the same day, which was unfortunate. They tried to fix each other instead of the library.

No one could find anything wrong, though they all agreed something wasn't quite right. They decided to start a Save the Library fund. They put jars at grocery stores and Walmart and NASCAR races, but the jars stayed empty, so the librarians started an art campaign to save the library. Kids come in and draw pictures and the librarians hang the pictures all over town to remind people what a library is. When parents pick up their kids at school they see the pictures. Many of them don't know something is wrong with the library but by the time they get home they have forgotten about it.

The best pictures are displayed at the post office and the bank, right above the plastic jars that collect no money. One kid drew a picture of the library on fire. The librarians brought in a fire marshal, but he said the library wasn't on fire. The librarians said they knew that, but they had to check anyway.

THE LIBRARIANS ARE: CAROLINE, Kelly, Switch, and Quail. They are not old. They are young and have perky breasts and degrees from East Coast universities. They wear summer dresses and cowboy boots. They braid their hair in pigtails. They paint famous scenes from books on their fingernails. They go on weekend trips to Intercourse, PA (just to say they were there) or vacation trips to small villages in Honduras (to help). They don't have to show up at the library since it stopped working, but they do anyway.

Switch is tall and slim—she reminds the others of a willow tree. Her eyes are gray, like rain on early mornings in October when the season is just turning cold. Quail is small and dark, with eyes that are almost too big. Her hair is the color of peat moss and dry sand. Kelly is blond. She calls it iridium-blond. Her eyes are the same color as her hair, which is almost, but not quite, platinum. Caroline has blue eyes. Her hair is somewhere between blond and brown. She wears it in braids most of the time. She wears loose white shirts and no bra.

The librarians all smell like lavender. They smell like lapis lazuli. Switch and Quail work nights. Caroline and Kelly work days.

They all work the in-between times, dusk and dawn. Quail calls dusk the magic hour. She says the world is in-between not only day and night, but also in-between light and darkness. She says there is a difference.

THE LIBRARIANS SLEEP ON the third floor. They have little rooms like dorm rooms from when they were in college on the East Coast. The librarians miss the ocean. They miss reading on the beach. Sometimes the fourth floor sounds like the ocean, but they don't go there because the fourth floor is where all the wrongness is concentrated and the sounds of the ocean could just be a way to lure them up there. There are things on the fourth floor they won't talk about. They can feel them lurking above their heads. The lions from Ray Bradbury's story "The Veldt" are up there. They live in the walls and only come out when one of the librarians has been lured by the sound of the ocean. When they come out, it smells like meat.

Besides the lions, there is something on the fourth floor that scares the librarians. They don't know what it is, but they don't like it one bit. Caroline imagines it to be something made of shadow, with red eyes. Kelly thinks it is something that looks entirely normal until you get close to it. Switch says it is all the bad things in the world put together, and Quail says it is worse than the way you feel on rainy days in November when no one calls on your birthday. They all agree it is scarier than being the last person on Earth, then hearing someone knock on your door.

Now THE PHONE HAS started ringing late at night. At first Switch and Quail thought it was perhaps an old boyfriend drunk-dialing them. It was very late and the lions were prowling on the fourth floor above them. Kelly and Caroline were asleep. Switch and Quail had dressed up in zoot suits they got from the sixth floor and were drinking scotch and waters and smoking long thin cigarettes.

When the phone rang they looked at the clock. They were on the second floor, which is normally a well-behaved floor—only rows of computers and a few reference books here, nothing to make any trouble. The library was empty, the way it always is late at night. The phone kept ringing. Finally Quail put down her glass of scotch and answered it. Switch leaned in close, put her ear to the phone, too.

Quail said, "Hello?"

When the phone kept ringing Switch and Quail let the answering machine get it. The messages were always long silences, with just the thinnest hint of breathing. In the morning they play the messages for Kelly and Caroline. Kelly's iridium hair is loose, falling past the small of her back. Caroline hits the button to stop the machine. The red light keeps blinking. They walk away from it.

Caroline tells them there are other problems, too. She thinks the days have more hours now, at least twenty-five or twenty-six. Switch and Quail tell her the nights are the same length but they have felt like they were sleeping longer.

SOMETIMES THE THING ON the fourth floor howls and howls, like wind rattling leaves through an empty street. Sometimes the lights slowly dim so that before they know it they are reading in the dark and straining their eyes. Other times the book they are reading disappears when they put it down and they can't find it again. Kelly started writing down where she left her books, but then the notepad she wrote it down on started disappearing too.

ONE NIGHT, CAROLINE WAKES from a dream. She doesn't remember the dream, and wouldn't tell anyone if she did. When she goes to get a drink she remembers it is Wednesday and the water is green. Kelly is asleep on the bunk bed above her. The room is dark. There are books lying everywhere. She takes off her t-shirt and wipes the sweat off her chest. Kelly talks in her sleep. When Caroline gets back in bed the sheets stick to her skin. She is almost asleep when she thinks she hears the door open. Then a hand touches her forehead, but she is too asleep to know if it is real or not.

THE NEXT MORNING, CAROLINE leaves the library. It is early June, she has not been outside in months, and the air sticks to her skin. A thunderstorm is coming from the west. The other librarians stand looking out the door (they can't see out the windows). They see Caroline shading her eyes from the sun. They see her turn and look back.

"What's she doing?" Quail asks, but none of them know.

CAROLINE HAS BEEN DRIVING for an hour and she can still see the library in her rearview mirror. From far away it looks like a spaceship, a cloud, a pump jack. She doesn't know where she is going, but she knows she needs to get away. She can't see the forest for the trees, can't fix the library while in it. She tried turning on the radio but all she could get were Latin channels, like monks reading old manuscripts. Which reminded her of the word aspergillum.

It takes the better part of the day, but finally the library disappears behind her. Still, she keeps looking in all three mirrors, even the extra one her father added onto the driver's side mirror, a mirror attached to a mirror. She isn't sure what the extra mirror is supposed to do, but her father thought it would be safer. Blind spot, maybe, she might remember him saying.

She drives through small towns already wilting even though it is still early summer and the big heat hasn't come yet. She passes old barns faded of color, old barns tilting groundward. She passes cows standing belly high in orange ponds and old tractors baling hay and long rows of corn and alfalfa and cotton and tobacco turned parallel to the road and she drives looking at the rows switching past and thinks of Switch, which makes her think of the library, so she looks again in her extra mirror but there are only silos shaped like vibrators behind her.

When the fields end she enters the suburbs, houses all in a row, curled like the sleeping tails of strange beasts. If this were winter there would be sleds and snowmen and perhaps a few curls of smoke from houses that still have chimneys, but it is summer and the streets are almost empty except for a few bicycles, until she passes the pool, and the pool is so thick with children they cannot move. It reminds her of "Where's Waldo" or that Post-Impressionist painting by Seurat. Something about a lake. Or an island.

Past the suburbs she goes through the shadows of buildings and under overpasses and the green interstate signs go overhead like rolling hills. The sun is setting behind her in the west and she passes all the skyscrapers, all the advertisements for luxury condos and the chain restaurants and strip malls. And then she is in the suburbs again, and then there are more orange ponds and tractors.

Near dark she stops at an all-night diner sitting alone at the edge of a small town. The "E" is missing in "Diner" on the sign, and she likes this, she likes it a lot. She orders pie and coffee because she's read a hundred novels where people order pie and coffee at a diner with the "E" missing. She can see her reflection in the glass. The inside of the diner is bright and clean and white and the woman who brings her pie and coffee smokes too much and has bad arches from standing all day. Caroline eats her pie and watches cars go by on the road outside and wonders what in the hell is wrong with the library. In the light from a passing car she sees the extra mirror attached to the driver's side mirror and she smiles, suddenly remembering her father leaning over her at night, reading *Goodnight Moon* or *Where the Wild Things Are* or *King Lear*. He has his glasses on, and attached to his glasses is a small mirror so he can see behind him. She knows now this was for when he rode his bicycle to work, through the busy streets, but in the memory she asks what it is for and her father tells her it is so Caroline's mother can't sneak up on him and then she knows where she is going. She tries to call the library from the payphone but the line is busy.

THE LINE IS BUSY because the librarians have taken the phone off the hook for the evening. Earlier, when they were eating Chinese food atop one of the library tables, the phone rang. When Switch answered it a voice said, "Have you checked the books on the fourth floor lately?" and she screamed and dropped the phone. Later, she said the voice sounded like snakes through an empty tomb or the sound candles make when you blow them out.

THE LIBRARIANS THINK, BESIDES the Stranger, which they have begun calling the thing that lives on the fourth floor, that there may also be dinosaurs up there. Quail thinks aliens may be there, malevolent aliens. Switch thinks there are dragons up there, and possibly trolls. Kelly thinks there is only darkness, and one distant white light that you will never reach. Caroline (driving east) thinks there are shadowy characters up there, like Jack the Ripper, or Sauron. All of them fear there may be weapons of mass destruction up there, on the fourth floor.

The LIBRARIANS WRITE NOTES in hieroglyphics and cuneiform and leave them for each other. The librarians make their own papyrus and clay tablets. They each have a reed stylus. They have developed hieroglyphics for their own names. Caroline's is shaped slightly like North Carolina. Quail's is a small bird. Switch's is a bundle of long thin sticks. Kelly's is a smiley face.

Before the things started happening in the library the notes only said "Is there any Chinese food left?" or "Do you have any tampons?"

Then for a long time the notes said "How many floors were there yesterday?" They said "The fifth floor is bigger than Dallas. It is larger than life."

Now the notes mostly say "It called again last night" and "Have you heard from Caroline? Do you know when she is coming back?"

When SHE REACHES THE coast, she turns north, drives along through the palm trees and resort towns, the smell of saltwater filling the car. She drives through the fort towns, the shipyards, along the bays and waterways and beltways, through the heavy traffic of metropolitan areas, gray cities in the rain now, dark clouds, windshield-wipers, trains running in the distance, airplanes overhead coming through the envelope ahead of her until finally she is turning and turning onto increasingly smaller roads, past small churches of old brick with enclosed cemeteries and old gravestones and through small towns with old names and into the driveway of her parents' house, where she sits with the car running and the windshield wipers off, the rain running in rivulets down the windshield. The door opens and she sees her mother look out and she doesn't know she is crying, then her mother is there and she is telling her mother about the library and she isn't making any sense but her mother leads her inside and up the stairs to her room, which is exactly the same as she left it. And then she is being tucked into bed and the rain is still raining out the window of the room where she grew up.

When Caroline wakes up, the room is dark. She has a fever. Her lungs hurt. Something else hurts too, deeper than her lungs, but it is not physical pain. Outside, faint streetlight comes in the window. Her room is in shadows. She might be a child again. She might be a child with a cold waking up in the middle of the night, wondering how far away morning is, how long until someone comes in and checks on her, places a warm hand on her forehead and tells her she is burning up.

When the Stranger calls now they pick it up and listen. They say "Who is this?" and "Why don't you just come down here and we will figure this out." They have been instructed to keep the Stranger on the line long enough for the trace to work so Quail says "We can be friends if you come down here," and Switch adds "There's no need for all this," but the Stranger hangs up. They decide he is wily, and they will have to come up with a better plan.

In the afternoon Caroline's mother brings her chicken soup. She sits on the edge of the bed and watches her eat. She asks the questions she is supposed to ask and Caroline answers with the answers she is supposed to give, but they both know something is lurking beneath the surface. Caroline jumps when the phone rings and her mother puts a hand on her arm. She says, "What is it?" and Caroline knows how crazy it will sound so she says she is just really tired and goes back to sleep.

She wakes when her father comes home from work. If she sits up in bed she can see him getting out of the car. He looks tired and much older, and the continual passage of time comes to her all at once. She looks around at the room, the posters she had as a teenager, the bookshelves with her old books still there, stuffed animals. On one wall is a sheet of paper she had done in elementary school, the kind with a blank space at the top to draw a picture, and below that carefully measured lines to write about the picture. She had drawn her house—square body, triangle roof, two rectangles for windows. Her cursive was tight, controlled. It reminds her of something.

When her father checks in on her she is working her way through her books. He stands in the door and looks down at her. His lips are dry when he leans forward to kiss her. She reads until her father and mother come back in together and her father takes the book from her—*The Lorax*—and clears his throat and begins reading. She knows he will read all night so when he finishes *The Lorax* she pretends a yawn, leans forward to accept kisses from both of them, and fakes sleep. When they go out she can hear them whispering in the hallway about why she is here, what's wrong, what they can do to help. Caroline smiles, waiting for their voices to wander off down the hall. Then she gets her flashlight and reads under the covers. There is something she is almost remembering, something she needs to know.

WHEN THE STRANGER CALLS the next time, they are ready. Kelly has stayed awake this night, and the three of them are dressed in garter hose and lace from the "Prostitutes Through the Ages" clothing exhibition on the sixth floor. Quail wears patent leather. Kelly is all in white, and Switch is blood red. They swirl red wine in their glasses, pretending not to watch the clock.

When the phone rings they all stare at it. They have written notes in hieroglyphics, a transcript of what to say. But they just stare at the phone. Switch says, "I wish Caroline were here," and Kelly rolls her eyes and picks up the phone.

"Hello?" she says. First there is just breathing. Then a low moan. "Have you checked the books on the fourth floor lately?" the Stranger asks.

"We have," Kelly says. Her voice is butterscotch and lace. "We find them . . . erotic." The breathing stops suddenly. All they can hear is silence. Switch talks from the back of her throat, husky and slow. "Maybe you could come read to us," she says, and Quail says "We're all alone down here."

They hold their hands over the phone, looking at each other wide-eyed. The Stranger seems even more dangerous now that they have spoken to him. They all look at the stairwell, wondering if they hear a door opening, if they hear footsteps creeping down toward them. They can't even hear the Stranger breathing.

"You there?" Kelly says, and then the phone gently clicks. They wait. Kelly finishes her wine and pours again. Her lipstick stains the edge of the glass. In a minute the phone rings. It is the police.

"The calls are coming from inside the library," the cop says, "you need to get out right now," but the librarians tell him they already knew that.

When the police arrive the librarians are still wearing garters and hose and lace but they have trench coats on now. The police, two of them, knock on the glass doors and Switch lets them in. She walks back slowly and stands at the counter and takes a drink of wine. The cops look at them like they have never seen librarians before.

Quail says, "Fourth floor," and tosses back her wine.

It is not long before the cops come down again. They walk straight for the door, not looking in either direction. Both of them are pale. Their knuckles on their nightsticks are white, shaking slightly. All these things the librarians notice. When the cops are almost at the door Quail says, "Well?"

The cops don't look back. One of them unscrews a flask and takes a long drink and hands it to the other one. "There's nothing up there," the first cop says in a shaky, scared voice. "Not a thing in the world."

They start to tell the police they are wrong, but the police leave before they can say anything else.

CAROLINE KNOWS SOMETHING IS wrong, but she can't figure out what it is. So she just reads. She sits up with a pillow at her back and reads in her parents' house. It is late at night. Her parents are asleep. She can hear the house settling and ticking around her.

She has worked her way through the young children's books and now she is reading young adult. Her bookshelves are categorized like the library, not like that Dewey crap but the way it would be if Dewey hadn't been the way he was. When she finishes all the YA books she will move on to whatever is next. And then, she hopes, she will remember what it is she needs to know, something she has forgotten, that all of them have forgotten.

IT IS RAINING NOW outside the library and the rainwater runs down the windows in streams like the one on the fifth floor. The willow trees in front of the library switch and sway in the wind and lightning flickers the lights each time it hits and the quick clap of thunder makes them all jump. They sit with their backs together holding candles for when the power goes out, which they know it will. They try not to look at the door to the stairwell, where something from the fourth floor might or might not be sneaking toward them in the flashes of darkness.

When the power does go out Kelly says, "Shitfuck."

"Better to light a candle than to curse the darkness," Quail says, lighting a candle while Kelly curses the darkness. She cups the flame. "And God said 'Let there be light'."

And Switch says, "Deliver us from things that go bump in the night."

And above them, something goes bump.

IN THE DARKNESS, THE librarians huddle together. They can hear the slow steps coming down the stairwell. The candles flicker in the air. Their faces are red. They sit waiting, watching the door to the stairwell. The thing is big. It drags its feet. It is coming for them, and they can only wait. The sound is like carrion beetles crawling over corpses. Like flesh rotting. It is like the darkness before dawn or the calm before the storm. Kelly is whimpering and Quail is shaking and Switch's nails are digging into her palms deep enough to draw blood. They listen as the thing goes down to the third floor, where it pauses at the landing, then continues on. Switch imagines it stopping for a moment, head cocked to listen. She imagines it smiling to itself. Her image of the smile is not comforting. Its mouth is like an open wound. Or a ringworm. Or a piranha. She can't see its face, but she imagines she does not want to see it.

It drags its way down to the second floor landing. It stops again. Kelly is whispering now. "Hail Mary, full of grace, don't let the Stranger reach our place."

It stops for a long time on the landing. Kelly is holding her mace on her key chain. Quail has a chair. Switch threads her keys through her knuckles, holds a fist with spikes flailing out. When the Stranger starts down again they pull closer together. They count the steps in their heads. The footsteps stop outside the door. The emergency light above the door says EXIT in red letters and they can hear the Stranger breathing. When the door starts creaking open Kelly screams, and then the lights come on and they hear the Stranger scurrying back up the stairs. At the fourth floor the door opens and closes and the Stranger is gone. The lights flicker once more and then they are hugging each other. Later, Quail will say it was like cancer and tuberculosis and emphysema all rolled into one.

They leave the candles lit.

THE LIBRARIANS CUT UP newspapers and rearrange the words. Switch makes obituaries into birth announcements. Quail puts new captions under the comic strips. Charlie Brown tells Lucy he's going to karate chop her in the neck if she moves the effing football one more time. He tells the little red-headed girl he loves her, and she loves him back. They get married and have long baroque dinners and intimate conversations about why their children don't visit. On a state visit President Obama tells Putin that he's all out of love, he's so lost without him. Karl Rove is arrested for vagrancy and sentenced to fifty lashes with a wet noodle.

After the power went out they rearranged an article about the upcoming butterfly festival and made it say that a man known as the Stranger had been apprehended and was awaiting trial for being "creepy." But as the day pushed on toward nightfall, they knew that the Stranger was still with them.

WHILE THE SUN IS going down over the library and the librarians are sitting watching the door to the stairwell and wondering what the night will bring, Caroline is driving toward the sunset. She has left the smell of the ocean behind. She has left behind the smaller and smaller roads and the stone churches with enclosed cemeteries. She left her parents' house with her parents standing on the doorstep waving and a slow feeling of warmth crept up through her stomach, and she turned the car west and set her mouth in a grim line and scowled at the approaching horizon. She has not slept in thirty-six hours. She left her room strewn with books. She worked her way through all her children's books, and then the young adult books where young girls changed the fate of the world. They rode on wolves and tricked fairy queens and bargained with dragons, and after she had finished them all, she read the Brontes and Joyce and all the stuff people tell you you are supposed to read, through poetry and Gertrude Stein and the ex-pats, who were running from things scarier than the Stranger. Or maybe not.

So now she is driving back through the suburbs, where children play in the streets in the last hour before dark, chasing fireflies or running through the small tracts of forests behind their houses, their voices echoing off the walls of the places where they live. She is driving past all the old barns and silos and rusted tractors and cows in brown grass. She is driving through the bad parts of this story. She is chasing the sun. She is driving back in time.

It is just dark when she reaches the library. Inside, the Stranger has started his slow descent, and the librarians huddle together, knowing tonight will be the night. They cannot see the sweep of headlights as Caroline pulls in the parking lot, and she cannot see them huddled inside, as she stands outside the library. It looks normal now, but looks deceive. She takes a deep breath and squares her shoulders.

When she opens the door the librarians swivel their heads to look at her. The Stranger is just outside the stairwell door, pausing before rushing in. The librarians are angels, fearing to tread. Caroline takes in the library, follows Quail's eyes to the door to the stairwell, feels the Stranger lurking there.

"I know what's wrong with the library," she says. "I know what's waiting behind the door." She takes a deep breath and tells them what they are going to do, and then they all turn toward the door, waiting for the Stranger to come through.

MISERY AND BLUE
Joyce Winters Henderson

At first we tried to call him Midnight. But he were way blacker'n the time between sunset and moonrise. He were blue-black. So we took to just calling him plain old Blue. Tall. He were six hundred, sixty-six feet straight up in the air. And child you talk about smooth. He could talk the green off a leaf or outta your wallet, either one.

Now Blue had himself a brother. Big, wild guy by the name of Wind. Nine hundred and ninety-nine feet tall. A singer. Wind would sound so pretty on a soft Spring day that old Orpheus would just lay down his fiddle in shame.

Now back in those days I had me a little sister by the name of Misery. She didn't have no better sense than to go liking after Blue. Me and Mama counseled her against it, but love got a deaf ear. Wasn't long before she was ironing old Blue's shirts and giving him all of her hard-earned money.

Wouldn't've been so bad but Blue called himself liking another woman. Wind's woman. Fat sassy old thing by the name of Trouble.

They say that one of Wind's good friends tried to clue him in on what was going on between his brother and his woman. But. Love got a deaf ear. Wind got so mad just at the idea of somebody telling him something like that, he sang up a storm, finally let the poor fellow down in some place called El Paso. So after that we all just hoped that Wind wouldn't ever find out for sure about what was what.

Well one day Wind coming home after a long day of trying to sing some dark clouds on over into the next county. Here he come heading home looking forward to some rest and dinner. He get to the door and he don't hear one woman's voice in there, but two. Misery in there trying to talk to Trouble.

Misery say:

"You got yourself one man
Why can't you leave mine to me?"

And Trouble laugh a little bit and say:

"Just cause I got the one man
Why should I let his brother be?"

Whoa, now! Wind let out a holler that shook the whole quarter. Folk come running from every which a way to see what was up. And Blue didn't have no better sense than to come running with the rest of us.

Well, in a minute was Blue was up. Wind picked up his brother and threw him straight up into the air. Then he grabbed up that old Trouble and took off. I don't know what he wanted with that girl, all things considered, but I hear they riding together yet.

Wind had flung old Blue so hard, he hung up there in the air for three whole days. When he finally came down he hit the ground so hard, all of those big, pretty words got knocked right on out of him. He just lay there on the ground moaning with nothing at all left to say.

Wouldn't you know, Misery would be the one to finally have mercy on him. She went on over to him and dropped these words into his mouth. Say:

"Fell in love with Trouble,
Trouble let me down."

And Blue moan right back at her:

"Fell in love with Trouble,
That no good let me down."

Then they both end up together:

"When you love somebody who don't love you
Trouble's all you found."

Well folks kind of liked that little tune and we took to singing it amongst ourselves. At first we called it Misery and Blue's song, but after awhile it got shortened to just plain old Blues.

My sister, Misery, she always did get the short end of the stick.

POST-RIDINGHOOD RED
Danielle Bellone

My mother will not let me catch fireflies;
I am not allowed outside past dusk.
My days have turned relentlessly predictable.
Which is not to say that I am not grateful
To the Woodsman. But what happens now?
I learned to skirt peril by sticking to the path
And not talking to strangers. I traded in the
Crushed cherry velvet cloak for burlap.
Grandmother died, but she was bound that way.
And I didn't die, despite the efforts of
Crashing teeth and stomach acid. I kicked and squirmed,
And did not die, but for what?
For a chance to die by something other than a predator?
My, what high hopes you have.
Let me tell you this: wolves are everywhere.
Behind the door of every cottage and
In all flowers there are wolves.
In the winsome smiles of chatty
Neighbors are rows of moving teeth,
The better to eat you with.

ABOUT THE AUTHORS & ARTISTS

MONA AWAD (**Providence, RI**) won the Summer Literary Seminars/*Matrix Magazine* Editor's Choice Award for Fiction in 2009. Her fiction has appeared in *McSweeney's* and *Matrix Magazine*, and is forthcoming in *The Walrus* and *St. Petersburg Review.* She holds an master's degree in English from the University of Edinburgh and is currently pursuing an MFA at Brown University.

CATEE BAUGH (**Alexandria, VA**) recently won the Mark Carver Poetry Award and received an honorable mention for the Virginia Downs Poetry Award. Her work has been published in *ArLiJo*. She received her bachelor's degree in creative writing and literature from Eckerd College, and is in her final semester of the MFA program in creative writing at George Mason University.

TIM BELDEN (**Canton, OH**) has a bachelor's degree from Bowling Green State University and an MFA from Cornell University. He currently runs the Joseph Saxton Gallery of Photography and Tuscora Realty in the downtown Canton arts district.

DANIELLE BELLONE (Austin, TX) is a storyteller, fabulist and word-shaker from the Gulf South. She holds a bachelor's degree from Louisiana State University, and is finishing an MA in storytelling from East Tennessee State University. Her debut storytelling album, *Moon-Eyed Sister,* was released in October 2012. Her poetry and stories have won slams in Asheville, NC, and Johnson City, TN. She has been called "a hurricane of joyful absurdity," as well as "lexidrunk," which is to say, completely inebriated on sheer love of language. She currently resides in the strange hills of Austin, TX, with her equally strange ewok-dog, Sufjan.

AMANDA BLOCK (Edinburgh, United Kingdom) is a writer, ghostwriter and literary consultant. In 2008, she completed her master's degree in creative writing at the University of Edinburgh, for which she was awarded a distinction. She now divides her time between her freelance work and her own creative writing. Block has been shortlisted for the Bridport Prize, the Waterstone's Bookseller's Bursary Award and the Chapter One Promotions Short Story Competition. She is currently working on a collection of fairy tale-inspired short stories and is thinking about getting back to her half-finished novel.

ANGELA BUCK (Denver, CO) is currently a Ph.D. candidate in creative writing at the University of Denver. Her stories have appeared in *Western Humanities Review* and *Mid-American Review.*

Originally from England, **SIMON P. CLARK (Old Bridge, NJ)** graduated with a bachelor's degree with honors in English literature from Bristol University before moving to Japan to teach for three years. From there he moved to New Jersey, where he works as a writer and children's author. His children's novels are represented in the United States and United Kingdom by The Bent Agency.

Michael Harris Cohen (Blagoevgrad, Bulgaria) is the recipient of the *Modern Grimmoire* literary prize. He is a graduate of the MFA in creative writing program at Brown University. His writing has appeared in *The Virgin Fiction* anthology, *Conjunctions* (online), *The Land Grant College Review,* and several other fine journals. He is the winner of Mixer Publishing's "Sex, Violence and Satire" contest (2012), and his debut collection, *The Eyes—A Novella and other stories,* is due out in 2013 from Mixer. He is the recipient of a Fulbright research grant to translate Bulgarian folk and fairy tales, as well as residencies at the Djerassi Foundation, Jentel Artist Residency, and The Blue Mountain Center. He teaches creative writing and literature at the American University in Bulgaria.

Paul Crenshaw (Greensboro, NC) teaches writing and literature at Elon University. His stories and essays have appeared or are forthcoming in Best American Essays 2005 and 2011, anthologies by W.W. Norton and Houghton Mifflin, and numerous literary journals, including *Weird Tales*, *Shenandoah*, *North American Review* and *Southern Humanities Review*.

Kimberly Duede (Chicago, IL) graduated from Southern Illinois University Edwardsville with a major in English and minors in creative writing and Asian studies. "Through the Diamond Blues"

is her first published work. She plans on publishing original novels—fantasy, mystery, science fiction, and horror—on the Amazon Kindle.

Finding inspiration at dusk, STEVEN EHRET (**Massillon, OH**) paints panels filled with phantasmal creatures and landscapes. His obscure scenes and psyches bob between terror and hilarity, influenced by abstract realms of experiences. His uninhibited characters roam old vacant buildings and decaying structures reminiscent of his hometown, exposing pleasures and misfortunes in the twilight. Starting to paint only several years ago, Ehret has quickly built his credentials within the art community by exhibiting his work in Cleveland, Akron, San Francisco, and at both the Canton Museum of Art and Massillon Art Museum.

DANIELLE FONTAINE (**Jarrell, TX**) has recently received an MFA from the University of Massachusetts Boston. Her poems have earned honorable mentions in writing competitions for both *Writer's Digest* and The Academy of American Poets. Her work has also appeared on *NPR's* "Here and Now" website as well as in *Prick of the Spindle*, *Front Range*, *Juked Poetry*, and others.

J. M. R. HARRISON (**Harpers Ferry, WV**) trained and worked in a scientific field for thirteen years, but then returned to her first love and avocation: poetry. She has studied at the Writer's Center in Bethesda, MD, and through the brief residency program of Spalding University. She is currently the guest poetry host for the "Winners and Losers" radio show on *89.7 WSHC*. Her poems have been published in *Antietam Review*, *Sow's Ear Poetry Review*, the *Anthology of Appalachian Writers Vol. II*, *Wild Sweet Notes II* and others.

JOYCE WINTERS HENDERSON (Memphis, TN) presently teaches English at Lemoyne Owen College. Her stories have appeared in various journals, including *Magnolia: A Journal of Women's Socially Engaged Fiction*, *Calyx*, and *Folio*. She's published *Ayo is For Endurance*, a book of poetry funded through a grant from the Fulton County Arts Commission, and has been nominated for the AWP Intro Journal Award. Currently, she's working on two novel manuscripts, *Seedtime* and *The Original Norris Family Kwanzaa*.

JOHN KISTE (New Philadelphia, OH) is the executive director of the Canton/Stark County Convention & Visitors' Bureau. He is a graduate of Malone University and Kent State University, and also attended Yale and the University of Akron. Kiste has taught business, mathematics and purchasing courses at Kent State. He serves as president of the Ohio Association of Convention & Visitors' Bureaus. For the past five years, he has portrayed Edgar Allan Poe in a one-man show at the Warehouse of Usher in Canal Fulton, Ohio.

DAVID KOLINSKI-SCHULTZ (Canton, OH) has a diverse background, including work in music, theatre, technology, and martial arts. His first literary endeavors were in theatre. In 2009, Kolinski-Schultz wrote *Broadway & the Tonys©*, a tribute to Tony Award-winning shows. "The Music Box" is his first venture into short fiction, but other fantasy and science fiction stories are underway. He has degrees from Stark State College and Excelsior College, holds twenty-seven patents, is a certified martial arts instructor, a member of Phi Theta Kappa Honor Society, and a member of the American Federation of Musicians, Local 111.

MAUDE LARKE (Dijon, France) has come back to her own writing after working in the American, English and French university systems, analyzing others' texts and films. She has also returned to the classical music world as an ardent amateur after fifteen years of piano and voice in her youth. Winner of the 2011 PhatSalmon Poetry Prize and the 2012 Swale Life Poetry Competition, she has been published in *Oberon, Naugatuck River Review, Cyclamens and Swords, riverbabble, Doorknobs and BodyPaint, Mslexia, Cliterature,* and *Short, Fast, and Deadly*, among others.

CLAYTON LISTER (Hexham, Northumberland, England) has a master's degree in creative writing from the University of East Anglia. "The Black Widow" is from the collection *The Cracked Objective Lens*. Other stories from the collection appear online at *The Squawk Back* and *5 Minute Fiction*. In physical form, they have been published in the Thames River Press anthology *Pangea*, Park Publications's *Scribble* magazine, and *Countryside Tales* magazine.

CARLOS F. MASON WEHBY (South Hadley, MA) studies creative writing through the MFA program at Goddard College. His writing has been influenced by the works of Ursula K. Le Guin, Herman Hesse, and Michael Ende. While his early writing explores poetry, songwriting and theater, Mason Wehby has come to embrace prose as the means for grounding the transformative power of narrative. His works have been published in *Calico Tiger* and *Porch* magazines. He has shared his music through the Sarasota Folk Festival and the *Animal Tracks!* children's album.

COLLEEN MICHAELS (Beverly, MA) directs the Writing Studio at Montserrat College of Art in Beverly, MA, where she hosts The Improbable Places Poetry Tour. Her poetry has appeared in *The Paterson Literary Review, Blue Collar Review, The Mom Egg, Stoneboat, Constellations, Paper Nautilus,* and the anthology *Here Come the Brides: Reflections on Love and Lesbian Marriage.* She was a 2010 finalist for the Split This Rock Poetry Competition and the recipient of an honorable mention in the 2011 Allen Ginsberg Poetry Prize.

ERIN T. MULLIGAN (Canton, OH) is a fine oil painter. She learned her skill from many different people, including her Mom, Grandma, and oil painting master Frank Dale. Her work is inspired by a fascination with living things: plants, animals, and human life; physically and philosophically. Mulligan was recently awarded best in show at The Great Lakes Art Fair in Novi, MI, and at the Mill Valley Fall Art Festival in Mill Valley, CA. She was awarded second place at the Plein Air Paint Out in 2011, and best in show in 2012. Her oil painting, *Hatching,* took the second place award at a Show of Heads in Hudson, NY, in October 2011. She has previously been recognized as a signature member of the Akron Society of Artists.

Once upon a time, **JASON DANIEL MYERS (Bath, OH)** left home to seek his fortune, and instead found his happily ever after. Her name is Alexandra. He did not promise his first-born to a witch or a strange nameless gnome. Though he might wish to destroy all the spindles in the world for his daughter Jadzia, he realizes that to do so would be foolish. Aside from Jadzia, his greatest accomplishments include making clothing for members of the royal family, killing seven with a single blow, and learning how to shudder. He currently resides under your bed, collecting the dreams that fall from your mind like breadcrumbs.

Joann Oh (Colorado Springs, CO) has lived in Indonesia and the United States with a brief stint in Australia. She studied visual art and TESOL at Biola University, and now lives in Malaysia as an assistant English teacher with Fulbright U.S. Student Programs. This is her first publication.

Elodie Olson-Coons (Rodemack, France) studied English literature at Magdalene College Cambridge, and creative writing at the University of Edinburgh. She is variously attached to the U.S., France, and Britain—by blood, soil and strong Earl Grey, respectively. Her words have appeared in *The Literateur, McSweeney's, The Hill, filling Station, The Dial,* and *Work in Prowess,* and will soon appear in *Paper Darts.*

Julia Patt (Chestertown, MD) is a graduate of Sweet Briar College and the MFA program at the University of North Carolina Greensboro, where she was a fiction editor for *The Greensboro Review.* Her young adult novels—*i was a fourth grade zombie slayer* and *Through Waterless Places*—were both shortlisted for Mslexia's

2012 Children's Novel Competition, and her short fiction has appeared in publications such as *Surreal South '11, Stymie,* and *PANK.* She currently lives on Maryland's Eastern Shore, works in Annapolis, and attends the Graduate Institute at St. John's College.

MANDY ALTIMUS POND (Massillon, OH) is the recipient of the *Modern Grimmoire* **artistic prize.** She graduated from Kent State University with a bachelor's degree in history, summa cum laude with honors. Her photographs have been seen across Ohio and Michigan. Her photograph, "Waiting," was the first place commercial winner in the 2011 Joseph Saxton Gallery's Luminaries Competition, in Canton, Ohio. She is currently working on *A Long Time Ago,* a photographic series featuring the fairy tales of "Snow White," "Cinderella" and "Sleeping Beauty." Pond works as the archivist for the Massillon Museum. In her spare time, she enjoys performing with the improv comedy troupe Scared Scriptless, and the choral organization Voices of Canton.

ARIANA QUIÑÓNEZ (Bakersfield, CA) graduated from Loyola Marymount University in Los Angeles, CA, with a bachelor's in English. While at LMU, she traveled to six different continents and studied abroad in Madrid and London, where she was an intern at the Writer's Guild of Great Britain. She has been published in the journals *Attic Salt, LA Miscellany,* and *La Voz,* and won the Denise L. Scott Memorial Poetry Contest in 2010. In her spare time, she enjoys playing mariachi music, reading *Game of Thrones,* watching telenovelas with her grandma and kung fu fighting.

Tay Sanchez (**Cary, NC**) received an MFA in creative writing from North Carolina State University. Her fiction and poetry have appeared in *Expression, Carolina Woman,* and *The Acentos Review.* She lives in North Carolina with her husband and children.

Sarah Elizabeth Schantz (**Boulder, CO**) has a bachelor's degree in writing and literature, and an MFA in writing and poetics. In 2011, she won a fiction contest hosted by Third Coast; in 2012 she was the recipient of the Fall Orlando Prize in Short Fiction hosted by the A Room of Her Own Foundation. She is a Pushcart nominee and has a story forthcoming in the next anthology of *New Stories from the Midwest.* She just finished her first novel, *The Calendar of Ordeals*, which uses fairy tales to express a world undone by mental illness, and is now working on her second, *Roadside Altars*. Schantz's work has appeared (or will appear) in *The Adirondack Review, Alligator Juniper, Bombay Gin, Midwestern Gothic, Los Angeles Review* and *Hunger Mountain*. Her favorite fairy tale is "Little Red Riding Hood" because it's not marriage-centric. She never understood why Snow White wanted to leave the little cottage in the enchanted forest.

Alex Stein (**Boulder, CO**) received his Ph.D. in creative writing from the University of Denver in 2007. His recent book are: *The Artist As Mystic: Conversations with Yahia Lababidi* (Onesuch Press); *Made Up Interviews With Imaginary Artists* (Ugly Duckling Presse); and *Weird Emptiness: Essays and Aphorisms* (Wings Press).

Michael Wasteneys Stephens (**Athens, GA**) is an undergraduate student at the Maryland College of Art and Design in Baltimore, MD. He has been in a few exhibitions in the Baltimore area, including a MICA undergraduate exit show, showcasing the top work of all undergraduate students. This is his first publication.

CHERYL STILES (**Marietta, GA**) has published numerous poems, essays, and reviews in journals such as *Poet Lore, The Atlanta Review, Storysouth, SLANT, Plainsongs, Red River Review,* and *POEM.* Her work has also been included in several anthologies including *Sincerely Elvis,* a collection of original poems about Elvis Presley. She was recently nominated for a Pushcart Prize. Stiles works as a university librarian in the Atlanta area and hopes to complete her Ph.D. at Georgia State University this year.

Once upon a time, illustrator **SAMUEL VALENTINO** (**Westwood, MA**) was asked for all manner of work: digital, animation, books, character design, even storyboards. And yet, despite the absence of evil stepsisters or wicked queens as a counterfoil, he loved his work. Or so Valentino's story would read as a fairy tale, a genre he equally loves. Upcoming artwork includes a young adult fantasy and a book on Tolkien. And, to conclude in true fairy tale style, he did indeed marry his one true love, and is living happily ever after.

ERIN VIRGIL (**Golden, CO**) is a poet and visual artist living in an RV in northern Colorado. She holds an MFA in poetry from Naropa University in Boulder, CO, and a bachelor's degree from Barnard College in New York. Her poems have been published by *Wolverine Farm Press, Open to Interpretation, Fast Forward Press,*

Poets for Living Waters (online), *Delirious Hem* (online) and in *Colorado Life Magazine*. She has written one little volume of poems and a comic book, both available through Amazon.com.

JENNIFER WHITAKER (**Greensboro, NC**) earned her MFA from the University of North Carolina Greensboro, and her poems have appeared in journals, including *Beloit Poetry Journal*, *New Orleans Review*, *Mid-American Review*, *New England Review* and *Cave Wall*. She teaches and is assistant director of the University Writing Center at UNCG.

SARAH WILSON (**Anchorage, AK**) lives an often chilly life in Alaska. She is the author of four previously published short fictions, which are available for reading at the *Every Day Fiction*, *Penduline Press* and *Liquid Imagination* ezines. In her free time, she writes eclectically, reads more than is probably healthy, and attempts to dodge the moose.

ACKNOWLEDGMENTS

We will begin by thanking **YOU, THE READER**, for keeping us in business (and what a business it is!), followed quickly by our gratitude to the **THIRTY-SIX AUTHORS AND ARTISTS** bound within these pages, along with the others who submitted their works for consideration.

Thank you to anthology judges **DR. JOHN ESTES** and **DR. JOHN KANDL** for your arduous work in pouring over the texts to select the finest writing to represent our anthology, and in helping to select our two prizewinners—as anthology judges go, we know no better Johns. Thanks also to Dr. Kandl and **DR. CYNTHIA WISE STAUDT** for carefully reading the final collection to make sure all the T's were dotted and the I's crossed, er, scratch that . . . reverse it.

Thank you to the Indigo Ink Press Board of Trustees, including board president **DAVID KAMINSKI**, and members **TIM BELDEN**, **SUE GRABOWSKI**, **ELIZABETH JACOB** and **CINDY STAUDT**, for your support from day one, and to **MIKE NASVADI** and **KELLI J. SCOTT**, the two new kids on the Indigo Ink Press board, welcome and thanks in advance!

Thank you to **Tim Belden** for always saying yes, even when no is the more appropriate answer, all things considered. To **Len "The Voice" Grabowski** for use of The Voice. To **Marci Lynn Saling Lesho** for the world's first Poison Apple Ball and all that entails. And to **Doug Bennett** for, well, everything.

Thank you to **Gail Martino**, **Jennifer Hickman** and **Courtney Eason** for bringing our education program to life, and **Sarah Lutz** for bringing it to the page.

To **ArtsinStark**, our amazing arts council: You are one of our community's greatest treasures, and your vision for the arts is what keeps so many of us going. Also, a special thanks to **Robb Hankins**, for finding a loophole.

The world would be short a few fairy tales if it were not for the generosity of our donors. Big thank you to all who donated to us for this project, but special recognition to **our major donors**, as listed on the next page.

This book is set in Adobe Garamond Pro. Other beautiful fonts used in the design of the book were created by Lauren Thompson (Champagne & Limousines), Georg Herold-Wildfellner and Marcus Sterz for FaceType (Ivory), and Nick Curtis (Madison Square).

OUR DONORS

JOHN & GEORGIA ANDREAE

TIM & KAY BELDEN

ROMAN & JOANNE BENNETT

LEONARD & SUE GRABOWSKI

ERIC R. SMER

CYNTHIA WISE STAUDT

***

DAVID & ANNE KAMINSKI

CHRIS & MARCI SALING LESHO

SARAH LUTZ, KETAN & SUNITA BHATIA

JOE & GAIL MARTINO

SU NIMON & JOURNEY ART GALLERY

ALYSSA PAPADOPULOS

KAREN & JAY VRABEC

***

BARBARA ABBOTT

DYLAN & HOLLY "BUFFY" ATKINSON

DAVE BILLINGTON

JOHN, CHELI & CONNOR CURRAN

BETSY ENGELS

RYAN FITZPATRICK & BRANDY OGLESBY

TIMOTHY T. NGUYEN

DAVID & ANNETTE ROSENBERGER

JEN SISSON AND JOHN BELT

TODD AND VICKY STERLING

BARBARA WEIKART-KUDER